Laura Martin writes historical romances with an adventurous undercurrent. When not writing she spends her time working as a doctor in Cambridgeshire, where she lives with her husband. In her spare moments Laura loves to lose herself in a book, and has been known to read from cover to cover in a single day when the story is particularly gripping. She also loves to travel—especially to visit historical sites and far-flung shores.

Also by Laura Martin

A Ring for the Pregnant Debutante
An Unlikely Debutante
An Earl to Save Her Reputation
The Viscount's Runaway Wife
The Brooding Earl's Proposition

The Eastway Cousins miniseries

An Earl in Want of a Wife
Heiress on the Run

Scandalous Australian Bachelors miniseries

Courting the Forbidden Debutante
Reunited with His Long-Lost Cinderella
Her Rags-to-Riches Christmas

Discover more at millsandboon.co.uk.

HER BEST FRIEND, THE DUKE

Laura Martin

MILLS & BOON

First published in Great Britain 2020
by Mills & Boon, an imprint of HarperCollins*Publishers*
1 London Bridge Street, London, SE1 9GF

Large Print edition 2020

ISBN: 978-0-263-08651-5

This book is produced from independently certified FSC™ paper to ensure responsible forest management. For more information visit www.harpercollins.co.uk/green.

Printed and bound in Great Britain
by CPI Group (UK) Ltd, Croydon, CR0 4YY

To Luke, for fourteen years
of love and friendship.

And for everyone who married
their best friend.

Chapter One

Walking quickly, Caroline ducked behind a group of middle-aged women, straining her ears to hear the conversation between the two young debutantes just to her left.

'It's not that she's ugly,' Rebecca Preston said with an air of authority. Caroline could imagine the quizzical tilt of the girl's pretty head as she searched for the right way to describe her.

'No,' Sophie Saltwell agreed, 'not ugly as such.'

Caroline grimaced. At least she wasn't out-and-out ugly.

'Just a little *angular*. And old.'

'Far too old.'

That she couldn't argue with. At twenty-four years old she was well past her prime in the eyes of potential suitors.

'If it were me, I would bow out gracefully,'

Miss Preston said and Caroline had to smother a laugh. Miss Preston was considered the diamond of the Season and, with her thick golden hair and brilliant blue eyes, it didn't seem to matter to the eligible gentlemen that she was cruel and shallow. She would be inundated with proposals by Christmas and no doubt be married to someone titled and wealthy by spring. The idea of her bowing out of the search for a husband was absurd.

'Isn't she connected to the Duke of Heydon somehow?' Even above the din of the ball Caroline could hear the wistful sigh at the mention of James.

'Not romantically.'

Normally Caroline would step out at this point, fix the gossiping girls with a hard stare and make some acerbic comment to throw them off balance, but their words had been a bit too close to the uncomfortable truth and instead she found herself just wanting to slip away.

Quietly she turned, not wanting to hear what they were about to say regarding her relationship with James. Her very firmly platonic relationship. A wonderful friendship, but definitely nothing more.

With her head down she hurried from the ballroom, avoiding eye contact with the people she had grown to know so well these past few years. The same few attended each ball, each evening at the opera, each dinner party. It was suffocating rather than comforting and she had an intense desire to keep walking out of the front door and never look back.

She stilled that impulse, reaching instead for one of the doors that led off the grand hallway and slipping into the semi-darkness.

The ball was an annual event held by Lord and Lady Strand a week before the proper start of the Season in London. Caroline had been attending for seven years and knew the house well by now. She had escaped to the library which led to a small terrace at the back of the house. The terrace wasn't accessible from the rest of the garden so unless anyone else came in through the library she knew she would get a few minutes alone.

Caroline shivered as she stepped out into the cool air, wishing she had something to put round her shoulders. It was only October, and a mild October at that, but this evening felt cold and crisp and seemed to signify the end of summer.

There were no chairs on the terrace, just a low

stone balustrade running around the edge that Caroline pulled herself up on to, lying back so she could look up at the stars. The sky was clear and even here in London it was easy to pick out the constellations.

'You're a fool,' she muttered to herself, as she replayed Miss Preston's words. They had been unkind, but not untruthful. She *was* too old to be searching for a first husband. Most of her friends were married and producing their second or third child by now. A couple had even been widowed and were approaching the Season with the hope of finding husband number two.

'Not a fool,' a low voice said from behind her. Caroline jolted upright, forgetting for a moment she was lying on the narrow balustrade and nearly flying into the garden below.

Strong hands gripped her and pulled her to safety, only letting go when she was steady on her feet. In her chest her heart was pounding and she felt the familiar rush of desire and hopelessness and comfort all at the same time.

'James.' She regarded him for a moment, watching as he opened his arms before moving in to embrace him. She had to suppress a sigh as he wrapped his arms around her body, giving her a little squeeze before releasing her. 'I didn't know you were back.' Quickly she stepped away. She wasn't worried about anyone seeing them, more about her reaction to being so close to him.

'I wanted to surprise you.'

'You did. I nearly ended up in the flowerbeds.'

'That would have given the gossips something to talk about.'

Caroline grimaced—they didn't need any more fodder.

'I'm so glad you're back,' she said, feeling the warmth swell inside her as she always did when James was close.

He stepped to the stone balustrade, swinging a leg over and sitting on the edge, his feet dangling in the void below. 'Come sit with me, we have a few minutes until you're missed.'

'I think they'll miss you before me,' Caroline said grimly. She was a mere Miss, a spinster, inconsequential to most people in the ballroom. James was a duke, an *unmarried* duke, and as such was always trailed by a horde of hopeful young women and their mothers, besieged everywhere he went.

'I was rather stealthy,' James said with a grin.

'I'd only just arrived when I saw you escaping out here. Hardly anyone could have seen me.'

'It only takes one…'

He laughed, the sound cutting through to Caroline's core and piercing her heart. She steeled her mind, reminding herself it was always like this when James first came back. She just needed some time to adjust, some time to get used to him being close again. In a few weeks she wouldn't feel as though her heart were about to rip apart every time she saw him smile, knowing he would never look at her with anything more than a friendly regard.

'Where have you been?' she asked.

He'd written, but he was a poor correspondent. She'd received one letter eight months ago telling her about his time in Rome and another two months later detailing his travels to Naples. Then nothing, a whole six months with no word from him.

'Italy. Venice, Rome, Naples, Sicily. It was wonderful, Cara. The people, the culture, the food. It's divine. You should go, you would love it.'

'I think the only way my family would allow

me to travel to Italy would be if I announced I was joining a convent.'

'A legitimate life choice.'

'I don't look good in black.'

'Perhaps your abbess could give you special dispensation to wear blue.'

'Clothing aside, I'm not sure I have the right disposition to become a nun.'

He regarded her, a mock-serious expression on his face, 'No,' he said slowly, 'Too mischievous. That wouldn't do.'

She sighed. Perhaps she would find a husband who liked to travel. A man who could show her the canals of Venice and the Colosseum in Rome.

'You weren't enjoying the ball?' He leaned in a little closer so Caroline caught a hint of his scent, a blend of lavender and citrus—the cologne she had presented him with two years ago at Christmas.

'I wasn't.'

'It's the first of the Season, a novelty still surely after the long summer in Hampshire.'

'Can you imagine doing the same thing over and over again, year after year?' Caroline asked quietly. 'I go to the same balls, see the same people, dance with the same gentlemen. There's no variety, there's no freedom.' She eyed him, watching as a smile tugged at the corners of his lips.

'You should have been born a man.'

She closed her eyes, imagining having the endless options afforded men of her class.

'I'm too old,' she said quietly. It wasn't something she'd admitted to anyone else, not even her mother, who grew increasingly desperate each Season as it came and went without a single marriage proposal. At first Caroline had purposely scared any potential suitors away. She hadn't wanted to be tied to some old goat of a man, losing what little power she had over her own life. Then she'd gained a reputation for being a little too forthright, a little too free with her opinions.

And now...well, now she was wondering if she hadn't been too quick to decide she didn't want the same life all her friends had settled into.

'Too old? You're twenty-four, Cara, not sixty. Too old for what?'

'For this.' She looked at him in the moonlight, her expression grave. 'Most of those girls in there are seventeen or eighteen. They're young, they're nubile, they're impressionable. Who would choose me over someone like Miss Preston or Miss Saltwell?'

'Anyone with half a brain.'

Caroline shivered as a breeze caught the material of her skirt, rippling it against her legs. James shrugged off his evening jacket and draped it around her shoulders, his hands brushing against her bare skin and sending sparks of heat through her body.

'Where has all this come from?' James turned to face her. 'I thought you didn't want to marry.'

She grimaced. It had been what she'd said for so many years. For so long she'd been convinced having no one was better than settling for second-best. The man she loved would never think of her in the same way, so she'd decided she would grow old a spinster.

'I didn't. I don't...' She paused, knowing she should guard her feelings, keep her secrets, but as always James's eyes found hers and the words started to spill out. 'I'm twenty-four. Most women in my family live well into their sixties. That's forty years of solitude. Of returning home each night to a quiet house, to seeing all my friends dote on their children and one day their grandchildren. I don't want a husband, but I do want to be married.'

James sat there looking at her, blinking rapidly as if he thought a bandit had stolen the woman he knew and replaced her with an impostor.

'Any man would be lucky to have you,' he said eventually. 'More than lucky.'

Caroline scoffed. 'If you could just remind the eligible gentlemen of that fact, I'd greatly appreciate it.'

James opened his mouth as if he were about to say more when they both stiffened. The door to the library was opening, letting in a swell of music from the ballroom for a couple of seconds before dying away. She squinted into the darkness, trying to make out who was walking silently through the library.

They couldn't be caught together, not like this. The members of the *ton* were aware of Caroline and James's unique relationship. An unlikely friendship she'd heard it touted by some of the more polite gossips. Still, she was an unmarried woman and he a single gentleman. They had to be cautious and being found together with no chaperon on a private terrace would cause a grand scandal.

Caroline closed her eyes for a second, imagining the pain and humiliation that would follow if James was forced to marry her. He would, of course, he was a gentleman and, more than that, he cared for her, just not in the way she wanted. Still, it would be painful, knowing he'd been forced into the one thing she wished for every day.

'Arrivederci,' James whispered, then launched himself off the wall into the flowerbeds below. Caroline slipped off his jacket and dropped it down to him, then he was gone, blending into the darkness as he disappeared into the bushes.

'Miss Yaxley.' It was Rebecca Preston, her face a picture of suspicious confusion as she stepped on to the terrace.

'Miss Preston.'

'Are you out here alone?'

'Of course,' Caroline said sweetly. 'The ballroom was a little too hot for my liking. I thought some fresh air would be pleasant.' She swung her legs back over the balustrade and stood to face Miss Preston.

'I thought...' Miss Preston began, stepping up to the balustrade and peering over suspiciously. 'Have you seen the Duke of Heydon?'

'No, not for some months. I believe he's still in Italy. Why do you ask?'

'No matter.' She waved a dismissive hand, then turned slyly to Caroline. 'You two are friends, aren't you?'

'We are.'

'Perhaps you could introduce me to the Duke. I would love to make his acquaintance.'

Caroline looked at her, blinking in amazement at the request. A wave of nausea roiled through her as she imagined pretty Miss Preston fluttering her eyelashes at James, before she quickly reminded herself that one of his strengths was an ability to see past an attractive façade to the person underneath.

'I'd be delighted to introduce you,' she said, knowing she should stop there, but unable to help herself. 'He is quite a particular man, though, and can be a little abrupt if you stray from the topics of conversation he is interested in.'

'Oh?' Miss Preston leaned forward as if eager to snatch the knowledge from Caroline.

'He *loves* to talk about the weather, he's quite an expert, and he is very interested in fashion and clothing, both men's and women's.'

'Really? How extraordinary.'

'He's an extraordinary man.'

'Thank you, Miss Yaxley, I shall await the introduction with anticipation.' Miss Preston paused, her lips forming into a rosy pout that Caroline would wager the young woman practised in the mirror to make sure she got it just right. 'Of course, if you need any introductions from me then it would be my pleasure. It may be my first Season, but I seem to be *inundated* with invitations already.'

'You're too kind, Miss Preston.'

She inclined her head and then turned, heading back out through the library and to the ballroom. Caroline knew she should follow her—by now her mother would have noticed her absence and would be growing frantic—but before she moved she took a moment to peer wistfully into the darkness of the garden below. It was too much to hope that James had waited, hiding himself in the bushes somewhere. He was a duke, not accustomed to having to creep around in the shadows, and no doubt he was striding through the ballroom leaving a trail of hopeful young debutantes behind him.

'Enough,' she said firmly. This dreaming would have to stop. She'd decided to find a husband this Season and spending her time obsessing about James wasn't going to help her achieve that aim. From this moment on he would occupy her thoughts only when he was in the direct vicinity.

Turning, she walked back through the library, hearing the music that signalled a waltz as she opened the door to the hall and slipped back into the crowd.

Chapter Two

'Have you met my daughter?' Mrs Wilson said, gripping a petrified-looking girl who didn't look as though she should be out of the schoolroom. James inclined his head, murmuring all the right words as his eyes searched subtly for a way to escape. He would swear the debutantes were getting younger and grimaced at the recognition it was most likely just him growing older in comparison.

Artfully he slipped away. He'd spent a lifetime being accosted by hopeful mothers and shy daughters and knew how to take his leave without causing any offence. He was used to being the most eligible bachelor present and over the years had honed the skills that meant he could enjoy a social occasion without it being all about the women who wished to marry him despite not knowing him at all.

His eyes were on the slim figure on the other side of the ballroom and he walked briskly to try to avoid anyone else interrupting his passage.

'Miss Yaxley,' he said as he came up behind her. She was with her mother and another middle-aged woman, her eyes darting around the ballroom in her customary fashion as if looking for a means of escape.

She turned to him, the smile on her face full of pure happiness for a second before she remembered her surroundings and set her lips into a more demure half-smile.

It was always like this when he came home. Caroline was his closest friend, despite the outward observation that they had little in common. They'd become unlikely friends when he had proposed to her friend Lady Georgina several years ago. After Lady Georgina had left him on their wedding day to run off to Australia with an ex-convict, he and Caroline had drifted closer and he'd found her wry humour uplifting ever since.

In public, though, they had to remain cordially distant. He would bow and she would curtsy. He would ask for a dance, at most two. They might spend a couple of minutes conversing in plain view of all the other guests, but certainly no more. Anything more than that would invite gossip, even scandal, and they had been careful to avoid any hint of that throughout their friendship.

Not that there was anything inappropriate about their relationship. They might embrace on meeting in private, but there wasn't ever anything more than that. They were blessed with that strikingly rare thing—a friendship between a man and a woman that was strictly platonic, with no desire for anything more on either of their parts. It was one of the things James was most grateful for in his life.

'Lady Yaxley, Lady Whittaker.' He inclined his head to each of the older women.

Lady Yaxley smiled at him, the warmth radiating from her. Over the years he'd been a regular guest at Rosling Manor in Hampshire and James suspected Lady Yaxley viewed him as the son she'd never had.

'Might I request the pleasure of a dance with your daughter?'

'Of course, Your Grace, it is wonderful to have you back in the country.'

'You must meet my daughter, Your Grace,' Lady Whittaker said as he took Caroline by the arm. He smiled non-committally and whisked Caroline off before he had to supply an answer.

'Smoothly done, Your Grace,' Caroline said, laughing at his haughty expression.

'You may have been playing this game for seven years, Cara, but I've been attending balls for almost two decades.' It was a sobering thought.

'Two decades,' Caroline mused. 'You'd have thought you'd have perfected a simple waltz by now…'

'Cheeky minx. I'll have you know I'm the most sought-after dance partner in the northern hemisphere.'

'I've always said the women of Europe are fools.'

He slipped his hand around her waist, maintaining exactly the correct distance from her slender body. She looked elegant tonight in a light blue gown made of silk, embroidered with silver flowers and with a dark blue sash around her waist. As usual her blonde hair was swept back, revealing the delicate skin of her neck. She was tall and slim, but not in the gangly way some tall women seemed to be. Her height suited her and she glided gracefully around the ballroom as if she were floating a few inches from the ground.

'No one saw you in the garden?' Caroline's eyes flicked up to meet his.

'I was as stealthy as a mouse.'

'Mice aren't very stealthy. We had a bit of an infestation one summer when I was seven or eight at Rosling Manor and they were surprisingly bold and quite loud for their little size. I even saw one climbing the curtains and doing a rather impressive jump from one curtain pole to the next.'

'Acrobatic mice?' he asked incredulously. 'I'm not sure I believe you. Surely they would have been collected and placed into a tiny mouse circus if they were that impressive.'

She rolled her eyes at him as he swept her into a turn and he found himself grinning. England had lost some of its appeal these last few years and he found himself spending more and more time abroad, but one thing he did miss whenever he went away was Caroline. He didn't have any close family and almost everyone else was dazzled by his title and wealth. They were polite, sometimes gratingly so, but it meant meaningful connections were hard to make.

Caroline treated him as though he were an unruly friend or a brother, with healthy doses of sarcasm, and never seemed to feel the need to agree with him just because he was a duke.

'What do you deem stealthy, then?'

She chewed on her bottom lip as she always did when she was thinking. 'A lioness.'

'A lioness rather than a lion?'

'The females do all the work to bring in the food,' she said with a certainty that told him it was something she'd read about extensively in the huge library at Rosling Manor.

'Do they now?'

'I'd have thought with your *years* of education you would at least know a little about the animal kingdom.'

'It was a subject sadly lacking at Eton.'

He spun her again, exerting just a little extra pressure to bring her in closer as they changed direction. They must have danced together a hundred times, perhaps more, and he could anticipate her every step.

Suddenly Caroline's body stiffened in his arms and he felt her miss a step. It was unusual—she was an excellent dancer—and he found himself turning slightly to see what had caused her to stumble.

'What's wrong?'

'Nothing,' Caroline said, her voice with too cheery a lilt to it. It sounded false and he turned again to try to catch what she was looking at. 'Stop it,' she whispered furiously.

'Tell me what you're looking at, then I can be more discreet.'

'I'm not looking at anything.'

He made to turn again and saw her teeth clench together, the minuscule movement of her jaw giving away the inner tension.

'Fine. Just stop it and dance normally.'

He obliged, sweeping her across the dance floor as he waited for her to speak.

'It was Lord Mottringham,' she said eventually, not meeting his eye.

'Lord Mottringham?' From what James could remember the man was well into his sixties and had been balding for quite some years. Not the sort of man who would normally make a young woman swoon.

'Yes.'

'Cara, you're going to have to tell me more

than that. Do you have a *tendre* for Lord Mottringham?'

She pulled a face, scrunching up her nose.

'What then?'

'It doesn't matter,' she said.

'Of course it does.'

'Father said he has expressed interest in marrying me previously,' Caroline said, not meeting his eye.

'Then you'll laugh off the idea, remind your father you're twenty-four, not sixty, and forget about Lord Mottringham and his shiny pate.'

Glancing down, he saw her cheeks were flushing. Caroline did not blush, even when she'd fallen through the ice two winters ago skating on the Serpentine and had to be hauled out by three young men who got more than a passing glance at her undergarments. Or when an elderly acquaintance had assumed he and Caroline were married when they were out walking together and had congratulated them loudly and enthusiastically. *Nothing* made her blush, which made the pink hue of her cheeks all the more fascinating.

'You're blushing.'

She glared at him, missing her step again and

stamping on his toe—this time most certainly on purpose.

'Before I lose a limb will you just tell me what is going on?'

Caroline inhaled deeply, then looked up at him. 'I'm going to get married.'

'You said so on the terrace, but surely not to Mottringham?' His voice was louder than it should be when he spoke, so Caroline shot him a warning glance and pressed him to continue dancing.

'Yes. No. Maybe.'

He blinked. 'You must know.'

'If he offers. If anyone vaguely suitable offers. The person doesn't much matter,' she informed him.

'Your husband doesn't much matter?'

She shrugged. 'I wish to get married. I doubt I will find someone who makes my heart flutter and my head swoon. As long as he is kind enough then, no, I don't think his actual identity is all that important.'

James stopped, aware of the other couples spinning around them, but unable to take in everything she was saying. It was such a reversal of everything she'd ever expressed before.

'You never wanted to marry. Now you'll accept any old fool?'

'I didn't wish to marry. Now I do, that's all there is to it.'

Insistently she tugged on his hand, trying to get him moving again.

'Dance,' she whispered, 'Everyone is staring at us.'

He raised his arms again and took her back into the hold, letting his body remember the steps so his mind could try to piece together the shocking news Caroline had just delivered.

She'd always been insistent that she didn't want to settle. Time and time again she'd told him of her friends' miserable lives, saddled with husbands they could not stand and no freedom to make their own decisions. Of course there were exceptions. Lady Georgina, the friend who was like a sister to her, had found true love with her Australian and now lived in wedded bliss on the other side of the world, but it wasn't love Caroline was thinking about. It was marriage. A loveless marriage, probably arranged by her father to a man she had only ever made polite conversation with.

It was one of the things that bound her and

James together. Both of them were growing older, unattached when the world thought they should be married. It had always been for different reasons—in James's case he'd always been holding out for love, that lightning strike of a moment his parents had always talked about. For Caroline it was a desire to maintain her freedom, her ability to have some control over her life. It might have been for different reasons, but as the years had passed and one after another all their friends had married, it'd been something they had shared.

The last notes of the waltz swelled, then faded and Caroline was quick to pull him from the dance floor before the couples could take their places for the next dance.

'Close your mouth,' she muttered as she led him to the edge of the ballroom. 'I don't know why you're so shocked, it's not as if I've just announced I'm running away to do missionary work in Africa.'

James rallied. She was right. In anyone else he would think it the most normal of suggestions.

'Cara—' he began, but was interrupted by a pretty young woman positioning herself in between him and Caroline. There was a momentary flash of irritation on Caroline's face before she recovered her normal composure.

'Miss Yaxley, you were saying earlier you wanted to introduce me to the Duke of Heydon,' the debutante said with a flutter of her eyelashes.

'So I did.' Her voice was flat and from her body language James knew she didn't much like this young woman. 'Your Grace, this is Miss Preston. Miss Preston, it is my pleasure to introduce the Duke of Heydon.'

'Delighted,' James murmured, wishing the young women would move on so he could get back to questioning where Caroline had lost her senses.

'Miss Yaxley is a *dear* friend,' Miss Preston said, clutching hold of Caroline's arm, 'and she's said on more than one occasion she wished we could meet.'

'Mmm.' Often in these situations he found it easiest to use as few words as possible.

'I saw you dancing a moment ago. You dance very well, Your Grace.'

She stood there, looking at him expectantly. Of course she was angling for a dance and it would be supremely rude of him not to offer. Still, he considered staying quiet, not least because it looked as though Caroline could not stand the woman beside her.

In the end manners won out, 'Would you care to dance, Miss Preston?'

A hand went to her chest in a move he would wager she'd practised in front of a mirror. 'I'd be delighted, Your Grace. It would be an honour.'

'Perhaps…' He'd been about to suggest he pencil in his name on her dance card for one of the dances later in the evening just as the music for the next dance began.

Quickly she linked her arm through his and angled herself towards the dance floor. James shot a look back over his shoulder at Caroline, wanting to call out and tell her to wait for him so they could discuss her announcement further, but she was already disappearing into the crowds.

The dance passed in a blur, with Miss Preston doing her best to engage him on the mundane subjects of the weather and men's fashion. He was glad of the quick pace of the dance and used every turn as an opportunity to search the ballroom for a sign of Caroline. With her height and the striking blue ballgown she should be easy to pick out, but despite his best efforts she had disappeared. At the end of the dance he bowed to

Miss Preston, resisted her efforts to take a stroll in the gardens, and searched in earnest for Caroline. After ten minutes it was clear she'd left the ball and he retreated to the gentlemen's sanctuary—the card room—to mull over the evening's events while playing a few hands.

Chapter Three

'Slow down, Bertie,' Caroline called, laughing as the dog pulled harder on the lead in response to her pleas. He was pulling so hard she was almost running and, despite the overcast skies, there were still plenty of people in Hyde Park to see her unladylike conduct. She could imagine her mother's face and almost hear the lecture about the proper way to walk when out in public. It would not include a fast trot.

Bertie had his nose to the ground and was following some invisible scent, pulling Caroline off her normal route and taking her deeper into the park. Not that she minded. Four hours she'd spent that morning at the dressmaker's, being pushed and pulled and prodded as she was fitted for a wardrobe of new gowns.

She closed her eyes as she remembered her mother's face when she had announced last night she had finally decided she wished to marry. Lady Yaxley had crumpled with joy, the tears falling without check. Seven years Caroline had been *out* in society but never before had she suggested she wished to truly start to look for a husband.

Her mother had embraced her, whispering into her ear that she would find Caroline a suitable husband before the year was out.

Caroline had smiled weakly, wondering if she already regretted her decision. This morning her mother had woken her at the crack of dawn, announcing Caroline would need a new wardrobe for the Season, something fitting for a woman looking to attract a husband. Then she'd bustled Caroline off for a whole morning at the dressmaker's, overseeing as the seamstress brought out reel after reel of material.

Bertie barked, a sound of joy, and pulled even more, wrenching the lead out of Caroline's hand. She stiffened on the spot for a moment, unable to believe the brown streak already a hundred feet away was her dog. Hitching her skirts up, she began to run after him, keeping her head bowed in the hope no one would see her on this most unladylike dash through the park.

She followed Bertie down the path and around a bend, past a dense copse of trees, having to follow the bark now he'd disappeared from view. With a curse under her breath she ran faster. Bertie loved to swim and the last thing she wanted was to reach the Serpentine to find him terrorising the ducks.

Caroline had her head bent low and the first thing she saw as she rounded another bend was an expensive pair of boots. Too late she tried to slow herself, instead hurtling into the solid body. She felt arms wrap around her, steadying her for just a second before setting her back on her feet.

Bertie was sitting on the path, wagging his tail in delight, looking as though he were the most well-behaved dog in the world.

'I see you haven't got very far with training Bertie this past year,' James said, reaching down and stroking the bloodhound's silky ears.

'Father says he's untrainable,' Caroline said, looking into the dog's deep brown eyes. 'Either that or there's a problem with his owner.'

James picked up Bertie's lead, then offered her his arm. They hadn't arranged to meet, not directly, but when James was home they often orchestrated a pleasing half an hour together strolling through Hyde Park around this time in the afternoon. After his reaction the night before Caroline had been tempted not to come, but the desire to see him again, to feel her body brush innocuously against his as they walked arm in arm, to hear his deep chuckle and listen to tales of his latest adventures through Europe had proved too much.

'I thought you might not come. Not after you left so abruptly last night.'

'I didn't leave abruptly.'

'If you'd moved any faster, you would have been running.'

'You had the pretty Miss Preston to entertain you.'

'Yes, she is pretty, isn't she…' James mused. 'Shame about her rather terrible conversational skills. For some reason she seemed intent on twittering on about nothing but the weather and fashion.'

Caroline let a little giggle escape.

'I'm guessing that was your handiwork?'

'I might have dropped a few hints about your favourite conversational topics, but she *is* awful. I couldn't help myself.'

Bertie was walking sedately for James, allowing the lead to go slack as he trotted contentedly alongside them, sniffing the path as he went, but not haring off after every scent as he would if Caroline was holding his lead.

'Miss Preston was under the impression you were the closest of friends. She informed me a grand total of nine times how close you were.'

Caroline snorted. 'Yesterday was the first time she's ever spoken *to* me. I've received my fair share of disparaging remarks from her before, but she only struck up a conversation when she knew you were back in the country.'

'So I'm to thank for your blossoming friendship.'

'More like to blame.'

They walked a little way in silence, Caroline's revelation the evening before hanging between them.

'Have you a moment to sit with me, Cara?' James motioned to a bench. He was the only person in the world who called her Cara. To most she was Miss Yaxley, and to those close to her Caroline—even her mother didn't shorten her name—but James knew the truth. One day a few years ago she'd confided that she disliked Caroline and he'd spent half an hour suggesting alternatives until they had settled on one they both liked. So now he called her Cara. She was sure James knew the meaning behind the name—it meant beloved—but he couldn't know how much she wished it were true, that she *was* his beloved.

She nodded, allowing him to lead her across the grass, perching on the cold stone of the bench.

'Your announcement yesterday took me rather by surprise,' he said quietly. His dark eyes were fixed on hers and Caroline found it hard to concentrate on his words. To the world their bent heads and relaxed manner would signify intimacy and inside that was what Caroline really yearned for.

Quickly she pushed away the fantasy, hastily looking up and focusing on a spot in the distance.

'I think I may have reacted poorly. I wanted to apologise.' He tapped her lightly on the hand, as ever oblivious to the effect of his touch.

'There's no need. I can see why you would be surprised.'

'I do understand, Cara, I understand the desire to share your life with someone, the allure of waking up next to a warm body every morning, to have someone you can discuss affairs with over a leisurely breakfast.'

'It's not just that.'

He looked at her and nodded his understanding. 'Children.'

'Yes. Although I suppose I would be lying if I said that was everything I yearn for. I think it's different for women. As a man if you are single you still live in your own house, follow your own rules. As a spinster I'm expected to stay in the care of my parents until they die and then I will probably be saddled with some elderly relative as a companion.'

'I can see how that could feel oppressive, but you've always said you wouldn't want to give up your freedom, not to a husband who will make all your decisions for you.'

'Perhaps I just need to find the right man. Someone mild in manner and not overly interested in what I am doing.'

'Someone who marries you just for your dowry?'

'You make it sound so tawdry,' Caroline said with a flash of heat in her voice. 'That is what most marriages are, James. Hardly anyone marries for love. A few lucky people might find it unexpectedly along the way, but love matches are few and far between.'

'I know. Of course I know that. Look at me, just the wrong side of forty and still holding out for something that occurs in one relationship in a thousand. Perhaps you have the right idea of it.'

'You were tempted to settle once, too,' Caroline reminded him gently.

'Lady Georgina.'

'She would have made you happy.'

'I'm sure, but I would have always had that doubt. Wondering whether the next woman I met would be the one I fell completely and hopelessly in love with, miserable because I couldn't do anything about it.'

Caroline had never met James's parents, but knew they were the ones responsible for his completely absurd notions of love. His father had been a duke, his mother a governess, and they had fallen in love at first sight. From the way James told the story they had been perfect for one another, never arguing, always in complete harmony. Caroline suspected he was remembering with a child's nostalgia, but she couldn't deny their marriage had stayed strong despite society's disapproval. All his life James had been waiting for the same thunderbolt of love to strike him.

'It may be a moot point anyway, I have to find a suitable man willing to marry me. No one has offered yet.' Caroline picked at the embroidery on the hem of her coat. This was one of the issues that had been eating away at her, this fear that she would declare herself finally ready to marry and no one would step forward and offer to take her.

'Don't be absurd, of course they will.' He patted her hand again as if she was an elderly spinster aunt and quickly she withdrew it.

'Seven years I've been out in society, James, and I've not had a single offer.'

'Not one?'

'Not one. Not even from a lecherous old man or a penniless fortune-hunter.'

'Why ever not?' He sounded genuinely astonished.

'Perhaps I'm unmarriageable.'

'I'm being serious, Cara. You're intelligent, funny, can make conversation about more than just the weather, and you've got a decent dowry and good family connections. The gentlemen should be lining up to ask for your hand in marriage.'

'I lack a certain vital ingredient,' she said softly, noticing he hadn't commented on her appearance.

'What?'

'Beauty.'

'Nonsense. You're a fine-looking woman, Cara.'

Fine was not beautiful.

'Besides, beauty doesn't come into it most of the time. As you said yourself, the majority of matches are business transactions.'

She sighed—she knew it was true. The most likely reason she'd not received a single proposal was because she'd so adamantly *not* wanted to be proposed to. Over the years she'd actively discouraged courtship from any man who'd shown an interest in her and no one had been interested enough to fight through that discouragement.

'I don't think I know how to encourage a gentleman's suit,' she said softly.

'You don't know how to flirt?'

She shook her head. 'I think I did once, but years of trying to discourage gentlemen has left me unable to remember how to.'

Caroline thought back to the giddy couple of years after she'd made her debut. She and Georgina had revelled in the attention they'd received, enjoying the dancing and socialising at balls and always having full dance cards. Still, she had always been careful not to encourage anyone too much, to keep everyone at a distance until she had worked out what she wanted. Even from a young age Caroline had been wary of the marriages of the *ton*. Although her parents were happy, you only had to look around to see the number of couples who disliked each other, who avoided one another all evening or even lived most of their lives apart. It had never been what she wanted.

'Go on,' James urged, grinning. 'Flirt with me.'

'I most definitely will not.'

'It's the only way you'll learn.'

'I hardly think this will help.'

'Won't it? You said yourself you used to be able to—perhaps it is all about practice.'

Caroline felt her heart begin to pound in her chest at the idea of looking into the eyes of the man she loved and casually flirting with him.

'No,' she said, standing abruptly.

James caught her by the hand, holding on to it long enough for her to relent and sit back down. He looked at her earnestly, his rich brown eyes burning into hers.

'I want you to be happy, Cara.' He was still holding her hand and Caroline was finding it hard to concentrate as his fingers moved against hers. 'And if this is what you think will make you happy, then I will do whatever I can to help.'

She nodded, not trusting herself to speak.

'But I think you may have a point. For so long you've pushed eligible gentlemen away, instead choosing to dance with the husbands of friends or the men you know have their sights set on someone else. You've shied away from interacting with the men who might view you as a potential wife and as such you've forgotten how to talk to them, how to make them want to bring you flowers and write terrible poetry extolling your beauty.'

Quietly she pressed her lips together. She knew where this was leading and already she wanted to stop him. It would be far too heartbreaking.

'Let me help you. I'll introduce you to all my eligible friends, of course, dance with you at the balls, extol your virtues at dinner parties, but let me do more than that. Let me be your teacher.'

'My teacher?' Caroline repeated weakly.

'Twenty years I've had women flirt with me—some are bold, some are timid, some are downright bizarre—but I've experienced a whole range of tactics and behaviour from women who would like to become my wife. I'm perfectly placed to know what works and what doesn't.'

It made sense. Women threw themselves at James wherever he walked, fluttering their eyelashes or trying to engage him in deep conversations. Even so Caroline wasn't sure her heart could withstand the man she loved tutoring her on how to catch the attention of another.

'I'll make it fun.'

Closing her eyes, Caroline nodded. It was a mistake, of course it was. It would mean weeks spent in James's company, more than she had ever done before.

Your last chance, she reasoned with herself. Whoever she married wouldn't be happy about her spending time with an unmarried man. These next couple of months would be the last time she and James would be able to be together without a disapproving spouse getting in the way.

'Wonderful, I'll draw up a lesson plan to-night,' James said with a little too much glee in his voice. 'We can start tomorrow.'

Weakly Caroline nodded. 'Tomorrow we will start, but for today can we talk of other things?'

James stood, giving her the lopsided grin she loved so much, and offered her his arm once again. She knew this was the side that only a treasured few got to see. In public, when surrounded by others, James was reserved and kept his wicked sense of humour hidden. He was the epitome of a perfect duke, almost regal in his bearing and demeanour. In private he was a different man, a man who spun riveting tales out of the smallest adventure, who laughed and teased and found light in any situation.

'Did I tell you about my dip in the English Channel on my way home?' he queried as they began the stroll back towards the Serpentine.

'You know you haven't.' Caroline was smiling already.

'It was a dark and stormy night…'

Caroline whacked him on the arm lightly.

'Fine, it was a mildly blustery afternoon and I was taking a stroll about the deck. Every time I climb aboard a ship I have this notion that I will learn a little about sailing during the voyage, but in truth all I ever manage to do is get in the way.'

'I'm imagining you in a jaunty seaman's outfit, telescope in hand.'

'You mock, but I've always had a hankering to run away to sea. Although I think they'd take one look at me and tell me I was far too old and far too soft to be of any use.'

Never too soft. James might have been raised to command, but Caroline knew he kept himself in peak physical condition, sparring regularly at his boxing club and riding for at least an hour a day while in England.

'Anyway, I paused to look at the horizon, fancying I could see England. My eyes were fixed on the dark shadow in the distance and I didn't see the coil of rope at my feet.'

'You tripped?'

'I tripped. In quite a spectacular fashion. It was at exactly the same moment the ship crested a wave and I—' He was cut off by an insistent voice from somewhere to their left.

'Your Grace! Your Grace!'

Together they turned, Caroline recognising the voice immediately and finding it hard to fix anything more than a grimace on her face.

'Miss Preston,' James groaned under his breath, 'come to regale me with more snippets from the world of fashion, no doubt.'

'We could run,' Caroline murmured.

James glanced at the wide open space around them and the water of the Serpentine just in front as if actually contemplating the idea.

'Or set Bertie upon her.'

They looked down at the placid dog, thumping his tail happily on the grass.

'He could lick her to death, I suppose.' Caroline took a small step to her left, putting just a little more distance between her and James before Miss Preston could reach them.

'Miss Preston, how delightful to see you again so soon,' James said, no hint of the exasperation from a second ago in his voice.

'It's as though we were fated to be thrown together again,' she twittered prettily.

Caroline snorted, having to turn the sound into a rather unconvincing cough.

'Good afternoon, Miss Yaxley.'

'Good afternoon.'

Only now did Caroline see Sophie Saltwell trailing behind her friend and she marvelled at how fast Miss Preston must have moved to intercept them.

'I did enjoy our dance last night,' Miss Preston said, moving in closer and trying to angle herself so she cut Caroline out of the conversation.

'Indeed,' James murmured.

Caroline was thankful James was a sensible man. She'd long ago resigned herself to the fact he would never think of her romantically, but a small part of her had always worried he would fall in love with someone completely horrible. She *wanted* James to be happy, of course she did, but the thought of him marrying someone like Miss Preston made her shudder. Luckily he was an astute judge of character and was practised at seeing who was only interested in his title and his wealth.

'I hope we will get chance to dance again soon. Will you be attending the Tevershams' ball tomorrow?'

'Perhaps.'

'I do hope so. It would make my evening.' Her voice was sickly sweet and Caroline found herself trying to mimic the coy little half-smile and failing miserably.

Miss Saltwell finally arrived by her friend's

side, her cheeks flushed and her chest heaving. She looked expectantly at Miss Preston, who sighed before deigning to introduce her.

'This is Miss Saltwell, Your Grace.'

'Delighted to meet you, Miss Saltwell.'

Caroline felt Bertie shift on the end of his lead and braced herself. He was a strong dog and when he caught the scent of something he liked there was no stopping him. The last thing she needed was for him to pull her into the Serpentine while Miss Preston looked on, an expression of mock horror on her face.

'Sit, Bertie,' she whispered, trying to instil a forcefulness in her voice in the hope the bloodhound might choose this moment to listen.

Bertie strained forward and she gripped the lead with both hands, willing James to find some way to extricate them from the two eager young ladies.

'Such a pleasant autumn day for a stroll,' Miss Preston was saying. 'A little blustery, but the clouds are so interesting.'

'Sit, Bertie,' Caroline commanded a little louder.

James turned just as Bertie pulled. He lunged for the lead as it was wrenched from Caroline's hands, his fingers grasping the very end, but it wasn't enough. Bertie leaped, his tail wagging as he dashed between Miss Preston and Miss Saltwell, making both totter as he bounded past their skirts.

Caroline gasped as he went at full pelt into the Serpentine, sending a huge splash of water in their direction. It was only luck that saved Miss Preston and Miss Saltwell from being covered in muddy water.

'Scandalous,' Miss Preston muttered, shaking her head as if Caroline had urged her dog to be so unruly.

Next to her she heard James suppress a laugh as Bertie paddled through the water, making his way for the family of ducks swimming serenely a few feet out from the bank.

'That dog is fascinated by ducks,' James said, shaking his head.

It was true, Bertie loved them. He barked madly every time he saw a duck and was forever trying to pull Caroline off to inspect them whenever they passed by water on one of their walks. It wasn't the first time he'd jumped into a body of water to investigate further, but the other times it had been when they were safely private in the grounds of Rosling Manor.

'Bertie, come here,' Caroline shouted, trying to make her voce as authoritative as possible.

He ignored her.

'Bertie,' James called, his voice firm.

Of course the dog turned, then serenely began to paddle back.

'Even my dog prefers you to me,' Caroline murmured, watching as Bertie emerged from the water dripping and muddy.

He paused, legs apart, on the banks of the Serpentine and with a gasp of horror Caroline watched as he began to shake. She ducked behind James, peeking out to see the droplets of muddy water flying through the air, splattering over the rest of their party. Bertie had short hair, but even so he managed to cover them with an impressive amount of water.

For a moment no one moved and no one uttered a sound. Caroline didn't dare look up and instead gripped James's arm fiercely.

'How refreshing,' James said, pulling gently on her hand to bring her back round to his side.

Miss Preston was standing there completely still, the look of horrified shock on her face quickly replaced by a surge of white-hot anger. She looked down at her mud-spattered dress, her eyes wide, her mouth opening with no sound coming out.

'What an unfortunate accident,' James said, sweeping forward and taking both ladies by the elbows, turning them slightly so their focus wouldn't be on Caroline. 'Let me escort you home.'

Miss Preston flashed a look of contempt over her shoulder at Caroline, but allowed herself to be guided away from the water and the still-muddy dog.

As Caroline knelt down beside Bertie, picking up the soggy lead, she saw James look back and give her a wink that made her heart contract.

'Come on, Bertie,' she said softly. 'Time to go home.'

Chapter Four

Relaxing back in his chair, James regarded the smoky room, taking in the three men playing cards at the next table, the few lone gentlemen perusing the pages of the newspapers and the two having a quiet but heated argument in the corner.

'We thought you might be gone for good this time,' Milton said, pulling James back into the conversation.

'I was convinced you'd found yourself some pretty little Italian heiress and settled down in a vineyard somewhere,' West chuckled.

'If only,' James murmured.

Milton, also known as the Earl of Hauxton, and Lord West, a very wealthy baron, had been his friends for almost a decade. They were influential men, with large estates and much sway in the world of politics, but James still saw them as the youths he'd known years earlier. West was the same age as him, they'd been contemporaries at Eton, although only friends long after they'd left school. Milton was about ten years younger, but easily the most serious of their little group. James had known Milton's older brothers before they had both tragically died young, but despite the age difference it was Milton he would turn to if he ever found himself with a practical or moral dilemma to solve.

'How is your wife?'

West groaned, as if wishing to talk about anything but domestic matters.

'She was so beautiful,' he lamented. 'And sweet as an angel.'

'She's still beautiful.' James swirled his brandy around in his glass before taking a sip.

'But she's not sweet. Nothing is right. Nothing I do, nothing I say. You'd think I make her live in squalor.'

West had married the diamond of the Season five years ago, a pretty and accomplished young woman he'd spoken to only on a handful of occasions before declaring she would do for his wife. She'd come with a hefty dowry, but they seemed poorly suited and West had lost some of his spark and humour in the past few years.

'It's probably your fault,' Milton said sagely. He was always abrupt and to the point, but the harsh words were accompanied by a genuinely caring nature.

'How is it my fault?'

'Think of what young ladies are told to expect from a marriage,' Milton said quietly. 'Romance, an attentive husband, pleasant domesticity twinned with the occasional adventure. Then they're saddled with a man who'd rather be out drinking with his friends than conversing with someone he doesn't share any interests with.'

'That's not my fault. It is society's, giving them unrealistic expectations.'

James laughed at the exchange between his friends, but as always felt a little as though he were on the outside looking in. Both men had experiences he did not. Milton was a widower, married for four years to a wonderful woman he'd known since childhood. And West might gripe about his marriage, but he was a husband and a father, unlike James who might never be either of those things.

'Stop moaning or you'll put Heydon off marriage once and for all.'

His two friends eyed him for a moment as they often did when the subject of marriage arose.

'No young ladies have caught your eye?' West reclined back in his chair as he spoke.

'No.'

'I think you should just marry that Miss Yaxley of yours and have done with it.' Milton held his eye, showing James it was not a humorous suggestion.

'She is looking for a husband.' James swirled his drink round in his glass again and considered the idea, not for the first time. She'd make a fine wife. She was good-humoured and down-to-earth and fun to be with. There wouldn't be any wondering if they would sit in uncomfortable silence at the dinner table, or if she would be a well-mannered duchess. He knew her better than he knew anyone else. Often he had wondered if they should just marry one another and be done with it. He knew they'd be happy, but there was always that niggling doubt at the back of his mind. What if he married her and then the next day the woman he was truly meant to be with came along? The one who made his heart sing, the one he was destined to be with?

'She's not bad looking,' West said, staring into the distance as if weighing up Caroline's physical attributes.

'And more importantly you enjoy being with her. The passion, well, that can come later. Learn a lesson from West's marriage—don't marry a stranger you have nothing in common with.'

James shrugged. Perhaps if they were still both unwed in five years' time he'd suggest the match to Caroline. She'd probably laugh him out of the room.

'If you don't marry her, then someone else will,' Milton said, pushing his chair back and brushing down his jacket.

West stood as well, looking at the clock on the mantelpiece, mumbling something about his wife. James bade them farewell, watching the two men as they shrugged on their coats and disappeared out into the night.

James sat for a few minutes longer, enjoying the warmth of the club and the soft burn of the brandy in his throat. He wasn't going to propose to Caroline, but Milton was right, soon their relationship would change irrevocably. Despite her misgivings Caroline would find a husband this Season. She was from a good family, had a decent dowry and was personable and kind. Their friendship was not the norm among the members of the *ton.* In general, women were friends with women and men with men. Theirs crossed this boundary and to guard Caroline's reputation they'd had to be very careful with how they'd conducted themselves, but somehow it worked.

It wouldn't when she had a husband to answer to, a family of her own to put first. They might still talk a little at social occasions, but the walks in the park and the long, easy conversations would end. James was surprised to realise what a hole that would leave in his life. He often left England for months at a time, travelling around Europe, but when he returned Caroline was always there, ready to pick up their friendship where they'd left off.

'Don't be selfish,' he murmured to himself. He *wanted* her to be happy, but at the same time he didn't want to lose her.

'Excuse me, Your Grace,' a man well into his fifties said quietly, as if not sure he wished to interrupt James's thoughts.

James looked up, recognising the face of the

balding man in front of him, but grasping for the name that was just out of reach.

'Lord Whittaker, Your Grace, we met a few years ago.'

'Of course. Forgive me.'

'Nothing to forgive. Forgive me for interrupting.' Lord Whittaker looked uncertainly at the empty chair across from him where Milton had been sitting a few minutes earlier.

'Please, sit.'

'Thank you. I won't take up much of your time.'

James felt his stomach sinking as he realised why Whittaker had sought him out. The mild-mannered man looked as though he didn't really want to be here, but something was driving him on.

'I believe you are acquainted with my daughter,' Lord Whittaker said, flashing what appeared to be an apologetic smile. 'Miss Rebecca Preston.'

'We were introduced last night.'

'Quite. My wife told me all about the ball. I was not in attendance unfortunately.'

Miss Preston was certainly tenacious. It wasn't twenty-four hours since they had been introduced and already she'd engineered a meeting in the park and orchestrated her father furthering her cause.

There was a moment of awkward silence as Lord Whittaker mulled over what to say next. James was a charitable man, but he wasn't about to make this any easier for the Baron.

'My wife and I were hoping you would honour us with your presence at a small dinner party next week. It will be an intimate affair, just family and a few close friends.'

It was an ingenious ploy, no doubt thought up by Miss Preston or her mother, as James didn't think Lord Whittaker had the deviousness to come up with such an idea. Issuing the invitation in person like this made it so much harder to decline—a note was easy to send back with a polite excuse, but face to face it was much harder to say no.

'I know you're a busy man, Your Grace, but it would mean a lot to my wife if you would consider the invitation.'

For a moment James wondered if there was more to the seemingly bumbling Lord Whittaker than met the eye. He almost had James agreeing just out of sympathy.

'I shall have to check my calendar. What date is it?'

'Ah. Well, my wife rather suggested we choose a date based on your diary. She really is very eager to receive you.'

'How kind.'

'Is there a day next week that would work for you?'

James considered. He could refuse outright, state he was too busy, even lie and say he was planning on spending a few days away from the city. He wasn't overly eager to encourage Miss Preston and from what he had experienced so far she was the sort of woman who might even connive to land them in a compromising situation to force his hand. Still, looking at the hopeful face of the man in front of him, he found himself relenting.

'I shall have a footman bring over a note tomorrow with my availability,' he said, regretting it even as the words left his mouth.

'Wonderful. Thank you, Your Grace. My wife will be ever so pleased.'

'Perhaps you could see to it that a mutual friend of Miss Preston's and mine could attend. Miss Yaxley, she is the one who introduced me to your daughter.' It was cruel to inflict a whole evening of Miss Preston on Caroline, but at least her presence would stop it being the intimate family affair he suspected Lady Whittaker was planning. He should have asked for Milton and West to be invited as well.

'Of course, what a splendid suggestion. I'll inform my wife.' Lord Whittaker, stood, gave a deferential little bow and hurried away.

Chapter Five

'Are you sure you will be safe on your own for two hours?'

Henrietta motioned to her maid trailing a few steps behind her. 'I'm not alone, I have Elise. I will be perfectly fine, you have no need to worry about me at all.'

Caroline pursed her lips and hesitated. She knew Henrietta was right, she did have the company of her lady's maid and it was only a short amount of time, but she still couldn't help feeling a little uneasy that Henrietta would be loose around London with just a maid for company because of her.

Henrietta smiled at her reassuringly. 'Trust me, Caroline, I go for strolls by myself all the time. I am quite content.'

'Two hours, we'll meet back here. Try not to be late.' Caroline watched her cousin hurry happily away, pleased to be given the freedom of a morning alone without any older relative chaperoning her and watching her every move. Henrietta was eighteen and wonderfully rebellious, although her parents thought she was saintly in her behaviour.

When Caroline had suggested she might act as her alibi for her trips to James's house, Henrietta had jumped at the chance to be involved in the subterfuge. They had decided Henrietta would call for Caroline and together they would leave the house with their ladies' maids. Once out of sight Caroline would make her way to James's house and Henrietta would occupy herself somehow. After a couple of hours they would meet up again and return home together, as if they had been with one another the whole time.

Caroline smiled at Anna, the young woman who'd been her lady's maid for the past six years. Although strictly speaking she was employed by Caroline's parents, Anna was staunchly loyal and would never betray Caroline and would happily spend the morning sitting in the warm kitchen gossiping with James's servants. Together they walked the couple of streets to Grosvenor Square.

James was waiting for her in his study, a wonderful room that seemed to reflect his personality perfectly. There were bookcases filled with books covering half the walls and, in the gaps in between, huge maps of Europe and the world. Dotted on shelves were treasures from his travels. A beautiful statue of a goddess brought from Rome, a painting of the canals of Venice, an ancient urn from an archaeological site he'd visited in Greece.

Caroline took her favourite seat, a worn leather armchair that was angled perfectly to look out over the terrace and gardens beyond, situated just the right distance from the fire in the depths of winter.

'Good morning,' James greeted her, perching on the edge of his desk. 'Welcome to your first lesson in attracting a husband.'

Caroline laughed, eliciting a theatrical frown from James.

'Sit down properly or I'll be too distracted to concentrate on what you're saying.' She watched as he slipped from the edge of the desk into the armchair opposite hers. He was dressed casually today, in light brown trousers and a shirt with the sleeves rolled up a couple of inches revealing tanned forearms. There was no sign of a cravat or waistcoat or jacket and Caroline realised she had never seen him only half-dressed like this. Quickly she tried to think of something else, anything else, cursing silently as her rebellious eyes roamed over his physique again.

'Today's lesson is going to focus on identifying the men you are going to target.'

'You make it sound like a military campaign.'

'I was awake far too late last night thinking about you,' James said, making Caroline shift in her chair. 'Or more specifically about you and Mottringham. *That* can never happen.'

'Why not?'

'He's too old. And a bumbling fool. You would want to murder him before you'd been married a week. I forbid you to marry him.'

'Forbid?'

'Forbid. You'd be miserable.' He held up his hands in a placating gesture. 'Now I understand you're not looking to find the love of your life, but I think a modicum of happiness isn't too much to ask for. We will strike off any man who drinks too much, is cruel to women, gambles excessively, or is so old you'd question if his heart would make it until the wedding day.'

'Is there anyone left on your list after we eliminate all of those?'

'You must have more faith in the men of England, Cara. One or two remain.'

'When I informed Mother of my plans to finally look for a husband, she thought I should focus my attention on widowers, given my age. She suggested Lord Renley and Mr Waterman.'

James frowned, shaking his head. 'Lord Renley is rich but his first wife was not a happy woman if the rumours are to be believed. And Mr Waterman is sinking in debt.' He paused, looking at her appraisingly. 'You've been in society for seven years, there must be someone you have your eye on. Someone you've considered at least.'

Glad she was not often prone to blushing, Caroline quickly shook her head. Whereas Henrietta would often single out gentlemen she would declare an interest in and then a few days later move her affections to some other young man, Caroline had never felt even the slightest spark for anyone but the man sitting across from her.

'No.'

'No one?'

'No one.'

'Interesting. Well, shall we start with a list of attributes you would like your future husband to have?'

Caroline looked at him blankly. Over the last few months she'd slowly come to the realisation that she did wish to marry, but the idea of a future husband seemed shadowy and unclear to her, as if she couldn't quite bring herself to imagine who he might be.

'There must be something you want?'

'Of course, but nothing so important that the lack of it would rule a man out. I'd like him to be comfortably wealthy, pleasant to look at, kind and respectable.'

'We need to narrow down the possibilities more than that. What is your most important attribute for your future husband?'

Caroline sighed—this was proving even more difficult than she'd imagined. She wanted to shout out that he should look in the mirror, take every aspect of himself and consider that to be perfection in the man she wished to marry.

'Perhaps I could suggest a few gentlemen who have shown a mild interest in the past?'

'Splendid idea.'

'Mr French.'

'Too besotted with his mistress. Next.'

'Lord Huntingdon.'

'Far too old and grouchy.'

'Mr Reston.'

'Terrible at cards and always at the gaming tables.'

'Lord Potteridge.'

'A complete bore.'

She fell silent.

'I think we need tea.' Standing, she walked over to the wall and pulled the bell cord to summon one of the maids.

'How about Lord Hauxton?' she suggested quietly. She knew Milton was one of James's closest friends and Caroline had been close to his wife before she had died in childbirth. Lord Hauxton was seen by many of the *ton* as abrupt and on occasion rude, but Caroline had always found him refreshingly straightforward in a world where no one said what they really thought.

She watched as the emotions flitted across James's face. He might not love her as she wished, but she knew he would find it hard losing her. Theirs was a friendship that they both cherished equally.

'Milton is a good man,' he said after a long minute of consideration.

'But…?'

'There's nothing wrong with him. He's wealthy and titled and a good friend, a good man.'

'But…?'

'He wouldn't be right for you.' James shifted in his chair, frowning as he spoke. 'He's too serious. You need someone to bring joy into your life. To laugh with, to share every moment with.'

'I think he should go on the list. He's the best we've come up with so far.'

James started to murmur something, but was interrupted by the door opening and the maid slipping inside.

'Can we have some tea, please, Mary?'

'Of course, I'll fetch it straight away.'

Caroline returned to her seat, feeling her heart begin to thump a little harder in her chest as James moved closer and took her hand. 'I'm failing you on our very first day.'

'Let's move on to something else. Perhaps you can teach me how to flutter my eyelashes to gain a man's attention.'

James grimaced. 'Please don't. Ever. It annoys me so much and I can't imagine any other man is enamoured with the action. All it does is signal how naive a young woman is. And you, Cara, are not naive.'

Intrigued, Caroline edged forward. 'How about pouting?'

'Makes young ladies look like a surprised fish.'

'Hair flicking?'

'Likens the lady to a horse. And it can be dangerous—I've known many a man almost lose an eye from a vigorous hair flick.'

'Now you exaggerate.'

'Only slightly.'

'How about a coy head tilt?' Caroline moved her head very subtly to one side as she had seen many of the young debutantes do, tilting ever so slightly to give the best angle.

'Probably the safest of the lot, but I can assure you it isn't going to make a jot of difference to the gentleman you're speaking to.'

'So what should I do?'

'Honestly? Smile. You look beautiful when you smile. Look a man straight in his eyes and smile. Not a coy or seductive smile, just your natural, normal smile. Not many men can resist a woman who looks at them, only them, and smiles genuinely.'

Caroline considered. As she thought about it she realised it was good advice. If she noticed the eyelash fluttering and hair flicking and pouting and found it annoying, it was only to be expected that a man would, too. It was unnatural, put on, a show, when really what most people wanted was a glimpse of the woman underneath. The woman they would have to wake up to every morning without the sheen of the ballroom and the alluring rustle of silks.

'Go on,' James prompted her, 'smile at me.'

'Don't be ridiculous.'

He stood, reaching out for her hand and pulling her to her feet. Caroline felt her body brush against his, felt the heat from him despite the layers they were both wearing. She swallowed before she raised her eyes to meet his, feeling her throat turning dry and her tongue sticking to the roof of her mouth.

'Look at me,' he said so quietly it was almost a whisper. As she looked up, meeting his dark eyes with her own, she felt the rest of the world slip away, leaving them in a wonderful intimate seclusion. 'Hold my gaze, then smile at me as if I'm the only man in the world.'

She almost pulled away, but somehow she

stayed where she was, resisting every sensible fibre in her body that told her to run for the door. For a long few seconds she held his gaze, letting her eyes take in every detail of his: the dark brown irises with the lighter ring just around the pupil, the flecks of gold bursting from the centre, the thick lashes that framed his eyes, the smooth skin above and below. Then she smiled, slowly, languidly, directing it completely at him as if he were the one thing that made her happy.

They stayed with their eyes locked on one another for ten more seconds until the door rattled open and Mary slipped inside with a tray of tea. Caroline saw James stiffen in surprise, then the moment between them was gone as he turned and took the tray from the maid.

James was glad of the routine task of preparing the tea to distract him as his pulse slowed to a more regular rate. He poured slowly, watching the liquid splash into the cups before adding just the right amount of milk and a spoon of sugar for Caroline. By the time he looked up and handed over her cup he felt almost back to his normal self.

Careful, he cautioned himself as his hand brushed against hers.

It was only a smile, a smile he'd seen hundreds of times, thousands. Caroline smiled at him multiple times a day. Little secret smiles at jokes they shared, the full, joyful smile when he returned from a trip away, the smile that cracked through when she meant to admonish him, but couldn't quite keep a straight face.

Thousands of smiles, but never before had he reacted in such a visceral, primal way. He'd felt the urge to reach out, to draw her to him, to cover her mouth with his own and claim her.

Risking a look up, he felt himself relax a little. It was just Caroline sitting across from him, no different from usual. And no unsettling urges to reach across the space between them and pull her into his lap.

'How did I do?' Caroline asked as she cradled the cup of tea in her hands, slipping off her shoes and tucking her feet underneath her in the armchair.

'It was perfect. More effective than pouts and hair flicks.'

Much more effective.

Five years, that was how long he'd known Caroline, and not once in those five years had she affected him like she had just now. It was one of the main reasons their friendship worked so well—there was no blurring of the lines between them.

'Smiling is all very well,' Caroline said, taking a sip of her tea, then swirling the liquid round in her cup as she spoke, 'but that assumes a gentleman is taking an interest in me. I can't run around grinning like a mad woman. How do I get the *right* sort of man to engage me, to ask me to dance?'

'It's all in your demeanour,' James said, feeling as if he were heading back towards safer ground. 'Just think. Last Season, if you suspected a gentleman might be interested in you, what would you do if he obtained an introduction from a mutual friend and struck up a conversation?'

Caroline considered for a moment, her head to one side. He could tell she was running through a catalogue of such meetings in her mind and he couldn't help but smile when she grimaced.

'Perhaps I haven't always been the most welcoming.'

'Talk me through how you would react, what you would say. No...' he placed his teacup back in the saucer and stood '…show me. Imagine I'm an unwanted potential suitor.'

Slowly she stood, tucking her feet back into her shoes.

'I'm pleased to make your acquaintance,' she said, bowing her head. He saw she didn't hold eye contact for more than a second and looked about her with a distracted air.

'It is a pleasant evening, is it not?'

'Indeed.'

'Are you enjoying the ball?'

'It is diverting, although quite a crush.'

James paused and Caroline nodded her head slowly.

'I'm keeping the conversation superficial, an exchange of pleasantries, but not allowing it to go any deeper.'

'There's only so long a man can comment on the weather or the social event. If you keep the conversation superficial, no matter how much he's interested in you he will eventually just move on.'

'It's true.' She chewed on her lip as if remembering her behaviour the last few years.

'You use single-word answers or short sentences, you give nothing of yourself away.'

'But what if I have nothing interesting to say?'

He laughed, only stopping when he realised she was being completely serious.

'Cara, you're anything but boring.'

'With you, perhaps, but I'm used to you.'

'You make me sound like an old piece of clothing. Comfortable.'

'That's how you make me feel.'

He wasn't sure if it was meant to be a compliment or not, but he didn't really want to be like an old piece of clothing to Caroline.

'Invite them in, let them get to know you. When they ask questions, tell them how you really feel rather than giving some meaningless platitude.'

'No platitudes,' Caroline said softly. 'And a proper smile.'

She looked up at him then and smiled again and James felt the world around them tilt slightly, as if he were standing on uneven ground. Impulsively he reached out and caught her hand, feeling her soft fingers beneath his own. He'd brought it halfway to his lips before he caught himself and by then it was too late to hide the intended gesture. With a flourish he turned it theatrical, planting a kiss beneath her knuckles.

'You'll be the toast of the ball tonight.'

'The Tevershams'?' Caroline groaned.

'You're attending?'

'I told my mother last night I wished to find a husband, to marry this Season. She promptly declared we would attend *every* ball, every dinner party, every social occasion until I had a wedding date set.'

He laughed, imagining Lady Yaxley's delight when she heard Caroline's announcement. As an only child Caroline would be the only one to give Lady Yaxley grandchildren and he knew she delighted in fussing over young children.

'So, yes, I'll be attending the Tevershams' ball and any other ball these coming few weeks. Will you be there?'

'I will. I need to see my pupil in action.'

Caroline looked at him in horror.

'I'll be discreet,' James assured her.

'You're going to glower.'

'I've never glowered in my life.'

'Well, you're going to distract me, then.'

'You won't even know that I'm there.'

She looked as though she were about to say more, but then shut her mouth quickly.

'I should probably leave soon.' Caroline sighed, flopping back in the chair. She looked comfortable, as if she belonged in his study, and for an instant he had a flash of what it might be like if he did ask Caroline to be his wife.

Clearing his throat, he stood quickly. He must be coming down with something—he'd had far too many uncomfortable thoughts this morning. First that flash of desire and now this comfortable, contented feeling he got when imagining Caroline in his house, legitimately, as his wife.

'I'll call your maid,' he said. It was just an anomaly, a one-off occurrence. He needed a few hours away from Caroline and when he saw her next everything would return to normal.

Caroline blinked, as if surprised to have been dismissed, even if gently. Then she nodded and stood, smoothing down her skirts.

'What is our next lesson?' She waited until he returned to the room and then turned to face him.

'You don't need any lessons on dancing, but perhaps tonight we could practise your subjects of conversation when a gentleman asks you to dance.'

'No more small talk,' she said with a smile. She reached out and took his hand, waiting for him to meet her eyes, then squeezing. 'Thank you. Perhaps with your help I will be a married woman by this time next year.'

'The men of London are fools if they don't rush to propose.'

Chapter Six

Dear Georgie,

How are you? Thank you for your last letter—I was so eager to hear all your news, although I'm sure everything has changed now seeing as it took almost a year for the letter to reach me. How are the children? I long to see James, Amelia and Thomas—do they look any more like you as they get older or do they still favour their father in looks?

Recently I've been wanting to see you even more than usual. I wish for your wise counsel and advice.

I've decided to marry. It might seem like a rushed decision, but I've been thinking about it for quite some time. I have to admit the idea has been growing for the last six months at least.

I think I've accepted nothing is ever going

to happen with James—really accepted it. I will always love him—I don't think you can ever rid yourself of true love, can you? Still, I need to move on with my life, to build something new. As I grow older I realise I want a family. I want a horde of lively, beautiful children and the only respectable way to make that happen is to find a husband.

So that is my aim this Season. I am not overly fussy—he doesn't have to be young and handsome, just reasonably kind, and happy to give me some modicum of freedom.

Caroline paused in her writing, reading back what she had written. She thought back to when she and Georgina had been giddy debutantes, convinced the men of their dreams would swoop in and whisk them away in a flurry of romance and adventure. It had happened for Georgina, although Caroline wasn't so naive to think it had been easy—her friend had given up a lot to start her life with Sam Robertson. She'd left her friends, her family, her country behind, but it was still a happy ending.

Blinking back the tears, Caroline picked up her pen again. She *would* get her own happy ending, just perhaps not the one she'd always dreamed of. A life of simple contentment was her aim now.

As you can imagine, Mother is ecstatic. I've only just informed her of my plans and already she has a courtship and wedding planned out.

Tell me, Georgie, do you think I'm doing the right thing? I know I've always said I will not marry, I won't settle, but as I get older it seems I want different things.

This will make you laugh—James has taken it upon himself to be my tutor in attracting suitors. He tells me that he has had every technique tried on him, so he knows what is effective.

He is completely oblivious to the bitter-sweet irony of his teaching me how to seduce another man, but I am determined this will be the year that I finally give up this infatuation and build something for myself which isn't based entirely on dreams and wishes.

Perhaps by the time this letter reaches you I will be a married woman.

Write to me, Georgie. I long to hear all your news.
With everlasting affection,
Caroline

She signed her name with a flourish. She always found writing letters cathartic, especially to Georgina. Although Georgina's departure had been the event that had brought James into her life Caroline still missed her friend sorely. They corresponded a lot, but the months it took for the letters to reach the other side of the world meant it felt more like writing in a diary than to another person.

As she folded the letter in half and slipped it into the envelope the door to her bedroom opened and her mother bustled inside, stopping abruptly as she saw Caroline seated at her little writing desk.

'Whatever are you doing?'

'Writing a letter to Georgina.'

'At a time like this?'

Caroline raised her eyebrows, but didn't say anything. She loved her mother dearly, every last bit of her—the dramatic exclamations and the over-the-top worries as much as the kind heart and the staunch defence she mounted if anyone dared to criticise anyone important to her.

'Twenty minutes, in twenty minutes we leave for the ball where you may meet your future husband.'

'You make it sound rather dramatic, Mama.'

'It is important, Caroline. Now let me look at you.'

Obediently Caroline stood up. She was wearing a brand-new dress, a beautiful royal-blue silk gown that swept majestically from a high waist to the floor. The bodice area had tiny gold flowers embroidered all over it and a gold sash separated the bodice from the silk skirt. Silently Caroline thanked her mother for understanding that whites and pastels, the traditional colours for debutantes and unmarried young women, washed her out and made her look pale and unhealthy. After years of conforming she had decided she would wear what suited her rather than what was expected. The result was pleasing, even to Caroline's self-critical eyes. Her maid had also done a fantastic job with her hair, coiling the long strands into elegant curls that cascaded over her shoulders and down her back, and pinning up the front to accentuate the blonde in her hair.

Again most young women would wear their hair up tonight, with tight curls arranged around their faces, perhaps a ribbon for decoration.

'You look beautiful,' Lady Yaxley said, tears welling in her eyes.

'You're sure about my hair?'

'Absolutely, my darling. It suits you. Besides, not quite the same things are expected of you as if it were your first Season.'

Caroline looked at herself in the mirror, checking each angle critically, and was surprised to find she was pleased with the result. It might have been a cutting remark two evenings before, but Rebecca Preston hadn't been wrong when she'd described Caroline as angular. Her face was a little too thin, her nose a little too pointed, her body a little too sharp without the soft curves gentlemen seemed to prefer, but tonight even she found it difficult to be too critical of her appearance.

'Just remember to smile,' Lady Yaxley said as she came up behind Caroline. 'You look radiant when you smile.'

Caroline thought back to that morning when James had told her exactly the same thing. Quickly she tried to suppress the memory. Tonight she had vowed she would not think of James, at least not until she saw him later in the evening. Tonight she would be completely focused on the eligible gentlemen, those elusive unmarried few who might be looking for a wife.

The ball was well underway when Caroline walked in, arm in arm with her mother. Lady Yaxley had firm ideas of the correct etiquette for attending any social function and arriving at least an hour after the start time was essential in her opinion. It was late enough that most of the important people would have just arrived, but not so late that they might have dispersed to other areas. The perfect time to be *seen*.

Caroline felt an unfamiliar flutter of nerves as they stepped into the ballroom. It was beautifully decorated, lit with two huge chandeliers filled with candles. The walls were partially mirrored and it gave the sense of the ball stretching to infinity with a vast number of guests. The candlelight also reflected off the mirrors, giving the whole room a warm glow. She tried to focus on the beauty of the decorations, but instead found her eyes flicking from left to right. For a long time the most she'd had to worry about when attending a ball was whether she would have to make small talk with someone she didn't like, but now there was so much more at stake.

'Courage,' she murmured to herself. She was going to need it. Tonight was the first night she was actually going to make an effort, the first night in a very long time that she was going to try to be attractive to potential suitors rather than scare them off. If it didn't work, it would be a great blow to her confidence. At least when she didn't try she couldn't be rejected.

'There are a lot of people here tonight.' Lady Yaxley's eyes hadn't stopped moving across the crowd. Caroline nodded, unsure where to start. Normally she would dart through the crowd until she found one of her friends and then spend the evening talking and laughing and socialising with the young women and their husbands, but tonight she felt as though she might need a different approach. 'Remember, smile, make eye contact, but most of all have fun, my darling. The courtship can be the most exciting part of a relationship.'

Lady Yaxley patted her on the arm and then let go, disappearing into the crowd behind them in a matter of seconds. For a moment Caroline felt completely alone, but after a moment of panic she straightened her back and tipped up her chin. *This* was what she'd been born for.

'You look like you're contemplating running away.' James's deep voice came from over her shoulder. His breath tickled her neck and she felt that heavy pull of anticipation she always did whenever he was near.

'I wouldn't dream of it,' she said, turning with a smile.

For a moment he just looked at her, his eyes flitting from top to toe and back again, seemingly taking in every last detail before he shook his head slowly.

'Cara, you look ravishing.'

She wished she didn't feel such pleasure at his words, but the warm flush that spread through her was unmistakable.

'Everyone's eyes will be on you tonight and quite rightly so.' He spoke slowly as if he couldn't quite find the right words. Shaking his head, he looked over her again. 'You look beautiful.'

'It's just a new dress and something a little different with my hair.'

'Whatever it is, it works.'

She slipped her hand through his proffered

arm and allowed him to escort her through the crowds. Part of her just wanted to enjoy this moment, but she forced herself to let her eyes dance over the other guests, trying to single out anyone who might be of interest to her.

'Dance the first dance with me. It'll give everyone the chance to see you out there in the middle of the ballroom. After that I will leave you to be inundated with requests for the next dance.'

Before she had a chance to answer the musicians struck up the first notes of the next dance and James led her to the dance floor. It was a lively country dance and already the couples were lining up in preparation for the march. Caroline took her place in the line of women with James standing opposite.

'What a *brave* look,' Miss Preston said as she came hurrying over to take the space next to Caroline, a bewildered young man trailing behind her.

'Brave?'

'Your hair. I mean it in the most complimentary of ways, of course, but it is certainly different.'

Caroline smiled serenely. She was beginning to see how Miss Preston worked, giving her condescending compliments and barely concealed insults to undermine whomever she was talking to.

'Thank you,' Caroline said. 'I dread being dull in any fashion. I was talking to the Duke and some of his friends and they said sometimes they find it difficult to tell the young ladies apart, with their identical hairstyles and pale, insipid clothing. I would never want to be part of that, to look like nothing more than a sheep blending into a flock.'

Miss Preston glanced down at her white gown, her mouth momentarily setting into a hard line before she recovered her composure.

The couple at the top of the line began the march, moving swiftly in time to the fast music as they paraded through the middle of the other dancers. James caught her eye just before it was their turn to parade, then gripped her hand and swept her through the middle aisle between the dancers. Caroline felt all eyes on them and forced herself to smile despite the nerves deep in her belly.

As they reached the other end Caroline slipped her hand from James's and took her place again in the line of ladies. It was another few minutes until the march had finished and the dance could begin properly, with Lady Teversham calling out the steps from one side of the dance floor. It was a lively dance, with much partner swapping, and as the tempo quickened again and again and again Caroline found herself forgetting her nerves and enjoying the dance. She laughed as she missed a step, skilfully whisked around to the correct position by Lord Hauxton, feeling his eyes on her as she weaved through the dancers to her next partner.

Only when she felt her face glowing and her chest heaving did the music stop and James found his way back to her side.

'*That* was fun,' she said, hearing the rasp in her voice.

'You dance well, Miss Yaxley.' Lord Hauxton came up beside them and took her hand, planting a kiss on her knuckles. Caroline had always found him quite a serious man, at least since his wife's death. Normally he was quiet, reserved, and this forward behaviour took her by surprise.

'Thank you, it was such a fun dance.'

'I had to come over and speak to you to tell you I think you look particularly lovely tonight,' Lord Hauxton said.

Caroline felt James shift beside her and glanced

in his direction. He was glowering intently at his friend.

'Is something wrong with Heydon?' Milton bent his head in as if they were co-conspirators in some dastardly plot.

'He does look a little queer,' Caroline said, glancing theatrically again at the Duke. She turned to him. 'You're glowering. You assured me you never glowered.'

'I'm not glowering.' His glower intensified.

Milton smiled. 'Sorry to say, Heydon, Miss Yaxley is right. That is an impressive glower you have on your face.'

'I'm not glowering.'

'Perhaps we should leave Heydon to his glower,' Milton said, offering her his arm. 'Would you care to take a stroll around the ballroom with me?'

'That would be delightful, Lord Hauxton.'

She slipped her hand into the crook of his elbow, looking over her shoulder one last time at James. He was watching them walk away.

'Heydon is rather protective of you.'

'I think he thinks of me as a sister.' It was the heartbreaking truth. Caroline had always thought of James as the only man she would ever love, whereas he looked on her affectionately as the sister he'd never had.

'He's still glaring at us.'

'I wonder what scandalous things he's imagining we could get up to in a crowded ballroom?'

Lord Hauxton laughed, drawing looks from the people they passed.

'Do you know we've never properly spoken?' He guided her through a crowd of people and towards the open doors at the end of the ballroom. Caroline felt a waft of cool air, getting colder as they stepped through the doors and into the night beyond. The terrace was well lit, with groups of people escaping from the heat of the ball, but Milton chose their spot on the terrace carefully, in full view of the ballroom so neither of them could be accused of any scandalous behaviour. 'We've exchanged a few pleasantries, certainly socialised in the same circles, but I cannot recall ever spending more than a few minutes in your company, Miss Yaxley.'

Caroline was about to utter some inane reply when she remember James's advice.

'I find that is true for many of the people I'm acquainted with. In society we seem to talk about the weather, exchange small titbits of gossip, but there are very few people we actually talk to properly. Even though we've probably been at the same events tens of times, perhaps even hundreds.'

'Why do you think that is?' Lord Hauxton leaned in a fraction as if truly interested in her opinion.

'The divide between men and women for one. At these balls it is very public, your every move is scrutinised by everyone else. It will be noted that we took a stroll together, that we spoke for a little time. Once is nothing unusual, but to form a connection, a friendship, we would have to speak a fair few times and *that* would be commented upon.'

'So you think we avoid those sorts of situations?'

'I do. I think often it is too much effort to fight other people's preconceptions, their judgements, so we don't put ourselves in those situations. Which means meaningful connections aren't made.'

'A shame,' Lord Hauxton murmured. 'Yet you and Heydon have managed to defy convention and maintain a friendship despite public scrutiny.'

'One of the very few exceptions,' Caroline agreed. 'And not without its own boundaries. We never dance more than one or two dances together, always ensure we are properly chaperoned, yet the gossips still talk.'

'So you think if we took the gossips away more men and women would be friends.'

'Undoubtably. I know many would argue men and women have different interests, different approaches to the world, but I think the best friendships are based on more than just shared experiences. With some people there is just an affinity, an understanding, a deeper connection.'

'Although shared experiences can bond you closer together.' Lord Hauxton smiled at her and Caroline felt herself smiling back. There was no flutter in her stomach, no race of her pulse, but perhaps that was for the best. She was enjoying herself, enjoying his interest in her, and if he didn't make her heart pound then it just meant she could keep a clear head.

'I won't deny that.'

'With the eyes of the crowd in mind, perhaps we should go back into the ballroom, but I wonder if you would save me a dance later this evening?'

'I would like that.' Caroline slipped her hand into the crook of his arm and allowed him to lead her back into the ballroom. When she was safely ensconced with her mother he bowed and bade her farewell.

'Lord Hauxton?' her mother asked speculatively, raising a perfectly shaped eyebrow.

'Lord Hauxton,' Caroline confirmed with a nod. A perfectly pleasant man, just what she had declared she was looking for.

James was above skulking in dark corners and pulling unsuspecting people into deserted rooms, but still he found himself loitering behind a handily placed overgrown fern in the hallway of the Tevershams' house. He'd been there for only a minute, planting himself in the spot when he worked out it was the way to the card room. Thirty seconds later he was rewarded by Milton sauntering past, a smile on his normally serious face.

Slipping out, he grasped Milton by the arm, watching as surprise turned to bemusement as he pulled his friend into a darkened room.

'This is a little secretive,' Milton said as the door closed behind them.

It took a few seconds for James's eyes to adjust to the darkness but when they did he saw he was in a relatively small room with some comfortable chairs and an unlit fire.

'You took Miss Yaxley outside,' James said, hand on the door handle to ensure they were not disturbed.

'I did. Interesting woman. I can see why you're friends with her.'

'What are you doing?' James could hear the unreasonable edge to his voice.

Milton regarded him for a long moment and then flopped down into one of the chairs. 'You're not normally an unreasonable man, Heydon, don't start now. You told me Miss Yaxley is looking for a husband. I am in search of a wife. You have no designs on the woman yourself. I can't see why you would object.'

'You're looking for a wife?'

'I'm a widower. Emily died three years ago, I think it is about time I married again.'

Heydon nodded, feeling pleased that his friend had found the strength to move on after the devastating events of three years previously when he'd lost his unborn child and his wife in one awful evening.

'You should marry again,' he said quietly, 'But you can't think Cara… Miss Yaxley is the one for you?' He wasn't sure why he was quite so opposed to the idea of his two friends becoming close.

'Why not? You should think of it as a compliment. I value your judgement. You're always saying that she's the only woman you enjoy spending time with.'

James was beginning to feel unreasonable. In truth he should be pleased. Milton was one of his closest friends, a man he both liked and respected. He knew the man had doted on his first wife, treating her as an equal in their partnership. Milton was wealthy, titled, a useful member of society. All these things pointed to him being a good candidate for a husband for Caroline, yet he still felt as if it were all wrong.

'Do you think you would be suited?' he asked, the edge ebbing out of his voice.

'I barely know the woman, but she seems good humoured, kind, sensible. I'm not proposing I rush into anything, but I can't see why we wouldn't be suited.' Milton gestured for James to take the armchair opposite and they sat together in the dark for a few minutes, both lost in their own thoughts. 'I'm not looking for the same sort of love that you are, Heydon. I loved Emily, but I would be lying if I said I loved her at the beginning of our marriage. I liked her, enjoyed her company, but the love came with time.' Milton looked at him thoughtfully. 'If you do not wish me to pursue Miss Yaxley, then I will step away, out of respect for our friendship.'

Heydon shook his head. He could not ask that of the man. The more he thought about it, the more he realised they would probably be perfectly happy together. Even though Milton was not the right man for Caroline, but she had told him exactly the same as Milton—she wasn't looking for love, just someone who she could build a life with.

'Forgive me. I find myself a little protective of Miss Yaxley. In the same way I would be if she were my sister.'

'Nothing to forgive. Now shall we see if Teversham keeps any decent brandy in any of these cupboards? I can't stomach another glass of punch.'

Chapter Seven

Caroline eyed the colourful table filled with an assortment of desserts. Everything looked so appetising and after an evening of dancing not only were her feet sore, but her stomach was growling with hunger. She took one last look and then stepped away. The ribbon around the waist on her new dress was pulled tight to best show off her figure and she didn't think she would fit an éclair or pastry into her stomach without feeling horribly uncomfortable.

'Surprisingly good food,' James commented as he sauntered over, picking up one of the delicious-looking eclairs and taking a bite. She glared at him, not for the first time envying his more practical outfit with nothing constrictive around the stomach area.

'I wouldn't know.'

'You haven't tried anything?'

'No.'

He raised an eyebrow. Caroline was not normally so reserved when it came to anything sweet.

'I'm strapped into my gown a little tightly,' she said eventually. For a moment he looked at her, really looked at her, his eyes sweeping over her body, taking in the way the dress clung to her curves. Caroline felt the heat begin to rise from her core, overwhelming in its intensity. This was how she'd always dreamed of him looking at her, rather than the familiar glances he normally bestowed, as you did with something you were inordinately comfortable with. She'd noticed it earlier in the evening, when his eyes had raked over her body and he'd told her she looked ravishing, and now he was doing it again.

James cleared his throat. 'It may stop you from eating eclairs, but the effect is quite entrancing.

'Entrancing?'

'I'm sure you've seen most of the gentlemen this evening have been stealing glances when you walk past.'

Caroline had noticed. She'd received such attention when she was a debutante, fresh faced and eager to make an impression. Then she and

Georgina had spent hours getting ready for the balls, trying on different gowns and getting their maids to do their hair again and again until it was just right. As the years had passed Caroline had grown tired of the time it took to curl her hair, especially as she'd resolved not to marry—it hadn't seemed so important to have every last aspect of her appearance perfect.

Now she was reminded of the little boost in confidence it gave her to know her dress swished in just the right way and that her hair hung perfectly down her back. It was probably a shallow thing to feel, but the truth of the matter was much of a person's first impression of you came from how you looked. If that was a positive impression, then it made the follow up so much easier.

'I saw one or two looking,' she admitted. With a glass of punch in her hand and the swell of music behind them, she was feeling suddenly brave and stepped in a little closer. 'What is it about my appearance that is entrancing?' She spoke with an air of innocence, her eyes wide as she waited for James's answer.

He cleared his throat again and Caroline felt an unfamiliar rush of anticipation. It was as though tonight he was seeing her as a woman for the first time, not just his comfortable friend.

Waving his hand vaguely to encompass her entire body, he raised his eyes to meet hers.

'Blue suits you,' he said eventually.

'But I've worn blue before…'

His eyes flitted down again, lingering on her body before he answered. 'Not like this. The dress emphasises your curves. Then falls away into a sweeping skirt that makes a man imagine…' He trailed off.

'Imagine?' Caroline prompted.

James lifted his eyes to meet hers, holding them for a long moment before he continued. 'Imagine what is underneath.'

'Oh.' She knew he was doing just that, perhaps for the first time ever, and she felt a shiver of pleasure at the thought.

'I must apologise for the crassness of all men,' he said, his eyes still not leaving hers.

'I hardly think I can blame you for how all men think.'

'That would be unfair.'

She didn't want to move, didn't want to break this magical moment. They might be standing in a ballroom filled with people, but it was as if they had all faded away and it was just the two of them floating in wonderful solitude.

'And it is useful to know how men think,' she said, taking another step towards him. A few more inches and it would be viewed as inappropriately close, but Caroline felt like stepping over the boundary anyway. Instead she tilted her head so she was looking up at him. 'You can be my guide.'

'I'm not sure I should be revealing the secrets of our sex.' He smiled at her then, the grin he reserved just for her, and Caroline felt her legs wobble underneath her.

'What if I promise not to tell?'

'You know I've never been good at saying no to you. What do you want to know?'

Caroline considered. There were so many things she wished she knew, but most of them were personal to James and not something that applied to all men.

'My mother always told me a man is more interested in a woman's qualities than her appearance, but I've always thought that is untrue. The pretty girls are always married off first no matter their personalities.'

'Men are superficial fools,' James said with

a wry shake of his head. 'We *know* it is more important to have a woman we can converse with, we can laugh with, that we could build a life with, but our rebellious minds have different ideas. It's all rather primal. For men I think we are more visual than women, at least at first, until you get to know someone.'

Caroline felt the carefree exuberance seep out of her and she took a step back. The reality of her situation came crashing back into her consciousness. Tonight James had been affected by her appearance, but normally he did not notice her. One night was not going to change anything.

With a deep breath she steeled herself for the familiar disappointment, then looked up at him with sunny smile and looped her arm through his.

'Walk with me for a moment,' she said, dipping her head low so he couldn't see the loss of the smile and the tears now brimming in her eyes.

He obliged, strolling around the periphery of the ballroom, talking quietly so only she could hear. It was as if he could sense her sudden melancholy and fought it with a string of wry observations about the ball and their fellow guests. It was late, well into the early hours of the morning now, and the crowd was beginning to thin out, leaving only the most dedicated of couples on the dance floor for the final dance.

As the music died away Caroline squeezed his arm, then walked purposefully away. She was done for this evening, ready for her bed, ready to let sleep wash away the mounting feeling of disappointment.

'I saw you dance with Lord Hauxton,' her mother said softly. Caroline laid her head on her mother's shoulder and allowed herself to think back over the evening. If she was being fair to herself, she would call it a resounding success. She'd been inundated with requests to dance and not just from the husbands of friends who knew she liked to be asked. She'd spent the evening waltzing and reeling and talking and laughing. It had been fun, more fun than she'd allowed herself to have at a ball for years.

Then there was Lord Hauxton, serious but kind. Lord Hauxton, who hadn't asked anyone to dance since the death of his wife three years earlier, but tonight had stepped on to the dance floor with her. He'd spoken softly, listened to her opinions and made it clear it wouldn't be the last time they conversed.

'He was very attentive.' She was pleased, even if she had to keep reminding herself of the fact.

'You did very well tonight, Caroline darling. I think we will have no problem finding you a husband this Season.'

Caroline yawned. She wanted nothing but to fall into her soft, comfortable bed, pull the covers up to her chin and sleep until the sun was high in the sky.

'The Duke was also very attentive this evening,' her mother said, measuring the words cautiously.

Caroline was careful not to let her body react. She wasn't sure if her mother knew of her infatuation with James. Lady Yaxley was astute and had always been involved in Caroline's life, much more than most parents she knew. It wouldn't surprise Caroline if her mother knew of her feelings for James, just as it wouldn't surprise her that she'd allowed Caroline her privacy over the years.

'We spoke a couple of times. It is good to have him back from the Continent.'

Lady Yaxley sighed, a heartfelt sound that

made Caroline sit up and look at her mother. 'I had hoped…' She inclined her head as if trying to find a delicate way to phrase the sentence. 'I had hoped he might realise what he is missing. Or what he will miss when you marry.'

Caroline gave a little shrug. She knew if she spoke now she was at risk of all the pent-up emotions flooding out and she wasn't sure if she was strong enough for that this evening.

'We will still be friends.' She could hear the quiver in her own voice and knew if they continued talking about James she was at risk of bursting into tears.

'That's not what I meant, darling. I had hoped he might offer for you himself.'

Caroline opened her mouth to answer, but found nothing would come out. The words felt trapped in her throat as if thick honey was sticking and holding them.

'I know how you feel about him,' her mother said quietly, squeezing Caroline's hand. 'And he may not feel the same way, but I do think you would be very happy together.'

'I'm not what he wants.' Caroline bit the inside of her lip, hoping the pain would stop the tears, but it didn't work and the salty droplets were soon streaming down her cheeks.

'Sometimes men can't see what's right in front of them.' She wrapped an arm around Caroline and hugged her tight. 'It doesn't mean you're any less wonderful, any less perfect.'

The carriage bumped over a rut in the road and Caroline felt her mother hug her closer to her. She closed her eyes for a moment, trying to find some inner strength to bring her out of this moment.

'Just remember there are many paths to happiness,' Lady Yaxley said sagely. 'Which is why I think you're doing the right thing. And not just because I want grandchildren.'

'You and Father didn't love each other when you first met, did you?'

Lady Yaxley laughed. 'Goodness, no. I could barely stand him. He was young and arrogant and hadn't seen enough of the world to be comfortable in it yet. I didn't much like him for the first few months of our acquaintance, but with time we both matured and now I can't imagine life without him.'

Caroline nodded, knowing she was partly still trying to convince herself.

'Life is what you make it, my sweet. You are a naturally happy person, a joy to be around. You will make a success of your marriage whomever you decide to give yourself to. Remember that.'

'I will.'

The carriage drew to a stop outside the front door of their town house and after a few seconds the door was opened and the footman helped first Caroline and then her mother down. They hurried inside, out of the cool night air, and Caroline quickly bade her mother goodnight.

Chapter Eight

Cursing under his breath as he looked at the clock, James threw off his bedsheets and stood. It was only six o'clock in the morning, and after the ball he hadn't got to bed much before three, but sleep was eluding him and every moment he lay in bed tossing and turning he grew more and more agitated.

Pulling on his trousers, he dropped to the floor and began the regime he'd honed over the years to keep his body fit and conditioned. Exercise had a way of cleansing the mind and he hoped after a few rounds his muscles would be screaming and the troublesome thoughts in his head would have quietened.

Caroline. She was what was bothering him. As he'd fallen into bed a few hours earlier he'd welcomed sleep, only to find it plagued by entirely inappropriate images of his closest friend.

He'd dreamed of her in that striking blue dress, hair cascading freely around her shoulders, but instead of a background of the ballroom she was in his bedroom, beckoning him towards his bed. He'd woken with his body hard and filled with desire and every time he closed his eyes he now saw the Caroline of his dreams inviting him to step closer, to touch her, to taste her.

Pushing himself harder, he felt the exquisite burn in his arms as he pushed up and down again and again. He continued until his arms felt as though they might collapse beneath him before moving on to his legs, but still the images of Caroline haunted him.

'Control,' he murmured under his breath. Control was something he prided himself on, one of his strengths. He never showed his irritation when an ambitious mother interrupted a private conversation to thrust her daughter in his direction nor allowed any of the more militant tenants on his estate to rile him when they asked for unfair concessions. He was skilled at hiding his true feelings from the public eye, only letting those who were close to him to glimpse what he really thought on a variety of matters. The issue was Caroline knew him better than anyone else.

She would notice the change in him immediately, notice he acted differently around her.

He could picture her stepping in close, her breasts brushing against his arm, her head tilted up so her eyes met his. He could almost feel her soft breath, the sharp inhalation as he wrapped his hands around her and pulled her body in to his.

With a groan James straightened, then dropped to the floor. It seemed one round of exercise wasn't enough to banish the inappropriate thoughts.

Pausing at the bottom of the steps leading to the front door, James glimpsed the familiar figure of Milton through the window. He frowned. The man was taking things too fast, he'd only danced with Caroline a few hours earlier and now he was here at her house, pressing his suit.

Taking the steps two at a time, James knocked on the front door, stepping inside as a footman opened it.

'Good afternoon, Redwood,' he said, passing the young man his coat.

'Good afternoon, sir. Shall I announce you?'

'No need. I know the way.' He strode through

the hall and pushed open the door to the drawing room, blinking as he took in the only two occupants of the room.

Caroline was sitting in her normal place in the corner of an elegant sofa. Facing her, in a chair that was pulled close, was Milton. They had their heads bowed together, talking quietly, only looking up when he stepped into the room.

Lady Yaxley was nowhere to be seen. Caroline's mother was often a little lax with her chaperoning duties where James was concerned, but he'd imagined her to be more thorough with any other gentleman. *Anything* could be happening in the drawing room.

'Your Grace,' Caroline said, a sunny smile on her face. She looked radiant, her cheeks flushed and rosy and her eyes shining. 'What a lovely surprise.'

'Miss Yaxley,' he said stiffly, nodding a greeting to Milton. 'Milton. I didn't expect to see you here.'

Milton opened his mouth to answer, a half-amused, half-puzzled expression on his face, but at that moment Lady Yaxley came breezing into the room.

'Good afternoon, Your Grace,' she said, coming over to James and giving him a motherly embrace. 'What a lovely surprise.'

'I will leave you to your new visitor,' Milton said, directing a smile at Caroline. 'Until tomorrow.'

James waited until Milton had been shown out before he spoke again. 'Tomorrow?'

'Lord Hauxton has invited me to accompany him and his sister to the opera.'

'You don't like the opera.'

Caroline shrugged. 'He's not to know that. Anyway, I haven't been for almost a year, perhaps I will enjoy it this time.'

'Perhaps.'

'Come and sit,' she said, sitting back down herself and patting the seat of the sofa next to her.

James sat, feeling his leg brush hers. Caroline didn't seem to notice, turning to him with a sunny smile.

'I didn't expect to see you today.'

'I found myself eager for your company.' In truth, he had agonised over the decision of whether to pay a call on Caroline. He felt as though he needed to see her to prove to himself the dream and his reaction to her yesterday had been anomalies. That she was the same old Caroline, not this new seductress his mind had cast her as.

'Lord Hauxton is a friend of yours, isn't he?' Lady Yaxley said quietly. For a moment he'd forgotten she was there in the room with them.

'Yes. A good friend.'

'He's a good man?'

James nodded. He couldn't lie as much as he felt inexplicably compelled to. 'He's a good man. One of the best.'

Lady Yaxley nodded, satisfied.

'I thought perhaps…' James began, but was interrupted by the door opening and Lord Mottringham stepping into the drawing room.

'Lord Mottringham to see Miss Yaxley,' the footman intoned, stepping back out of the room. Caroline stood, smoothing down the skirt on her pale pink dress.

'Ah, you have company,' Mottringham said, his voice gravelly.

'Come in and sit down,' Lady Yaxley said graciously.

'I won't stay long,' Mottringham ran his hand over the bald dome of his head, then started to fiddle with his moustache. James realised he was nervous and remembered Caroline's words a few days ago—that Mottringham had once been interested in offering for her hand in marriage. 'Actually I was hoping to have a moment alone with Miss Yaxley.'

Caroline's eyes widened and he felt her fingers digging in to the material of the sofa between them. He had the urge to reach out and take her hand, to reassure her that he wouldn't abandon her to whatever Lord Mottringham wanted to propose, but he knew it wasn't his place.

'A moment alone,' Lady Yaxley echoed. 'Of course. Perhaps you would be so kind as to accompany me for a stroll around the garden, Your Grace,' she said, turning to him.

James hesitated. Caroline's fingers had edged closer to his and brushed the edge of his hand. He could see the tension in her shoulders, the breath she hadn't released in her chest.

'Surely a chaperon…' he began.

Lady Yaxley waved away her hand. 'The door will be left open and I am certain Lord Mottringham has no nefarious intentions.'

She stood, leaving him no choice but to accompany her.

Outside James lingered for a second, watching as Lord Mottringham sat down in the place he'd just vacated. He sat close to Caroline, too close, and James was about to rush back into the room when Lady Yaxley gently tugged on his arm.

'My husband has known Lord Mottringham for many years,' she said quietly, her tone reassuring. 'He is a valiant man, a good man. He would never compromise Caroline.'

They walked through the hallway, into the bright morning room at the back of the house and out through the glass doors into the small garden beyond.

'He's friends with your husband?'

'Good friends. Lord Mottringham also has an estate near ours in Hampshire.'

'He's too old,' James said bluntly. He wasn't normally so free with his opinions, but he felt shaken. Caroline had declared her intention to marry and had told him it didn't much matter to her who her husband was. Now Lord Mottringham was no doubt asking her to be his wife. It would be the wrong decision for her to accept, but she might not see it. He was too old, too bumbling, too dull.

'Many young women are perfectly happy with

an older husband.' Lady Yaxley seemed calm and unperturbed.

'He wouldn't make her happy. He doesn't *know* her.'

'Caroline is an extraordinary young woman.' She held up her hand laughing. 'I know I'm biased, but she is extraordinary. She will make her own happiness.'

James grimaced. She might well do, but the idea of Mottringham touching her, taking her to his bed, made him feel nauseous.

'I doubt she will give him an answer today.' Lady Yaxley paused to take a sniff of the last solitary rose on a healthy-looking bush in the corner of the garden. 'She will wait, see what develops with Lord Hauxton and give Mottringham his answer in a few days.'

They took another lap around the garden in silence, James glancing back over his shoulder every few seconds to check if Caroline had emerged.

'How about you, Your Grace? Have any young ladies caught your attention this Season?'

James thought of Caroline, of his reaction to her and the inappropriate thoughts that kept swirling in his mind.

'No.'

'Lady Whittaker told me you are close with her daughter.'

James shuddered. If he wasn't careful, he was going to get trapped by the Preston family into an arrangement he really did not want.

'I'm not a great admirer of Miss Preston,' he said slowly. 'But she is proving rather tenacious.'

'Caroline doesn't like her,' Lady Yaxley confided. 'She hasn't said, but I get the impression she's been on the receiving end of a couple of catty remarks.'

He grimaced, remembering he still hadn't asked Caroline to accompany him to the Prestons' house for dinner. She wouldn't thank him for the invitation.

At that moment Caroline appeared on the grass, stepping out through the glass doors from the morning room. She looked flushed, but not distressed, and James immediately knew it had unfolded just as Lady Yaxley had predicted. He felt some of the tension seep from his body and he smiled the first genuine smile to cross his lips all day.

'He proposed,' Caroline said as he crossed the

small patch of grass towards her. 'I told him I would consider his proposal.'

'You must consider carefully. Take a few days, but don't keep him waiting too long.'

'I will, Mama.' Caroline linked her arm through James's and together they began to stroll across the grass, neither saying anything until Lady Yaxley had gone back inside.

'Two days ago you announce your intention to marry and today you received your first proposal,' James said with a half-smile. 'You must have an excellent teacher.'

'He is adequate, I suppose. Although he can't claim any glory for this proposal. I haven't conversed with Lord Mottringham since we started my lessons.' She glanced back over her shoulder to where her mother was hovering by the door. 'Do you have time to go for a stroll? I feel restless, and Bertie will be better behaved if you come, too.'

They collected Bertie from his comfortable bed downstairs before heading out. They'd just stepped out of the door when Henrietta came hurrying up the steps, her mother still halfway down the street.

'Good,' Henrietta said. 'Play along.'

Beside him he felt Caroline stiffen with surprise, but noted she obliged without question as Mrs Harvey came up the steps.

'Caroline has asked me to accompany her and the Duke on a little walk,' Henrietta said, breezing back past her mother. 'We may be a while. It's such a glorious day.'

'Thank you,' Henrietta said as they rounded the corner out of sight of the house. 'I thought I was never going to shake her off.'

'Your mother?' Caroline was incredulous.

'I know, I know, I'm terrible.' Henrietta looked over her shoulder to check no one could see, then planted a kiss on Caroline's cheek and began to hurry away. 'When you get home, tell Mama I had a headache and I've returned home to rest.' With that Henrietta was dashing off along the pavement, leaving Caroline stunned and Bertie barking at her departure.

'That was unusual,' James murmured next to her. 'I wonder where she's going in such a hurry.'

'It can't be anywhere reputable.' Caroline felt as though her stomach were sinking inside her. She thought of all the times she had asked Henrietta to lie for her, to pretend they were together when Caroline wished to spend time alone, or, more recently, with James. She hadn't thought to ask where Henrietta was going, what she was doing with her freedom. She'd always ensured Henrietta had her maid with her, but perhaps she should have been doing more. 'Come on.' She gripped James's arm and pulled him along next to her, following in Henrietta's footsteps.

'We're following her?'

'Yes. I need to see where she's going. What I've been helping her get away with.'

'She's probably just off to meet a young gentleman she has an affection for.' James's voice was too reasonable for this situation. She wanted panic and indignation.

'That's what I'm worried about,' Caroline retorted.

All of a sudden James swept her against the railings, his body brushing up against hers as he spun around. Despite the very public location Caroline felt a rush of desire as he stepped in closer, but as quickly as he'd pressed her against the railings he'd stepped away, leaving her feeling bereft and shaken at the same time.

'She didn't see us,' James said as they started along the pavement again. He was walking fast, his head down, but eyes searching keenly for Henrietta and any clue as to where she might be going.

This was one of the reasons Caroline loved him so much. He jumped into any situation with her without complaint, trusting her judgement, helping her where others might hesitate or distance themselves.

'Where is she going?'

Henrietta was heading out of Mayfair to the less salubrious area to the north-west. To Caroline's knowledge she had no friends or acquaintances in Paddington and there was no good reason for Henrietta to be walking in that direction.

They followed her across a couple of roads, dodging the carriages and horses, then had to pull up abruptly as they rounded a corner and she was only a few feet away from them, standing in front of a door as if waiting to be let in.

From the position they were standing in Caroline couldn't get a glimpse of whoever opened the door, all she saw was the swish of Henrietta's skirts as she swept inside.

'What now?'

Caroline considered. She knew they should

leave Henrietta to her secrets, but she felt responsible for her cousin, knowing she had been too caught up in her own dilemmas to realise her cousin was creeping off to a liaison of her own.

'We have to get a look inside.'

'Just stop and think about this for a moment, Cara.' He turned her to face him and for a moment she forgot where they were or what they were doing there. 'Do you really want to go barrelling into an unknown situation? Perhaps in this case ignorance is the best outcome.'

She shook her head. If Henrietta was meeting someone unsuitable, at least she would know. That way she would be able to discuss it rationally with her cousin and hopefully make her see the danger in what she was doing.

'I need to do this.' She took a step and immediately James was at her side. She had never doubted he would accompany her. He might caution or counsel her against her actions, but even when she went against his advice he never abandoned her. Quickly they went around the corner and tied Bertie up out of sight, Caroline crouching down and promising the lively dog that they would be back soon.

They walked arm in arm to the door Henrietta

had disappeared through a few minutes earlier. Caroline raised her hand to knock, but as her fist met the wood the door creaked open a few inches, revealing a darkened hallway beyond.

Caroline looked at James and he shrugged, pushing the door open wider. There was no one in sight, no one to stop them slipping into the hallway and pulling the front door closed behind them.

It took a moment for her eyes to adjust to the darkness, but when they did she blinked in amazement. The dark hallway was dusty and had an air of genteel neglect, with a thin layer of dust on the few pieces of furniture, but the walls were covered from floor to ceiling in paintings and drawings in all different styles. There were large canvases in expensive-looking frames showing beautifully painted landscapes next to small but intricate charcoal drawings of people and animals.

'What is this place?' Caroline whispered, aware of every noise in these unfamiliar surroundings.

James stepped forward, motioning for her to stay where she was. Silently he padded down the hall, pausing by a half-open door and peering inside. When he was satisfied there was no one in the room he motioned for her to come join him.

They stepped inside and Caroline looked around in confusion. Set up on one side of the room was a large easel surrounded by a palette and paintbrushes and facing it a *chaise longue.*

'I don't understand…' she whispered. It looked like an artist's studio, somewhere set up for artists to come and paint, bringing their models to lounge on the sofa while they captured their likeness.

As the only plausible explanation came to her Caroline felt her hand shoot to her mouth.

'No.' She wasn't easily scandalised, she didn't think the rules that governed society were particularly sensible. Too many things were seen as scandalous in her opinion, but *this* was difficult to accept. Henrietta posing for some artist, some man, could ruin her completely.

'There might be another explanation,' James said quietly, taking her hand in a reassuring manner.

'What?'

'Perhaps she is visiting a friend. Or perhaps the whole residence isn't artists' studios.'

'We need to find her. To see for sure.' Caroline

had picture after picture racing through her mind of Henrietta lounging back on a couch such as this, perhaps semi-clothed, modelling for some handsome and charming young artist. Even if she was fully clothed, with buttons all the way up to her chin, it was still hardly a reputable place for an unmarried young woman to be spending her time.

'We'll probably be caught. Then Henrietta will know you followed her.'

'I don't care. I need to do this.' She had to see exactly what was going on, only then could she confront her cousin and try to make her see how foolish she was being.

James looked at her for ten seconds, as if assessing how serious she was, then his lips transformed into a rueful smile. 'If we get caught and handed over to the magistrates for trespassing, then I reserve the right to use your stubbornness as my defence.'

'I'm not stubborn. Just forceful.'

He motioned for her to fall in step behind him and together they crept out of the room and back into the hallway. One by one they checked the downstairs rooms, most of which were set up in the same configuration as the one they'd been inside.

'She's got to be upstairs,' Caroline whispered, setting one foot on the bottom step and wincing as it creaked loudly. They both stiffened, listening for sounds of movement above them, but all remained quiet.

Carefully they made their way up the old staircase, pausing whenever there was a particularly loud creak from the ancient wood. At the top was a narrow landing with four doors leading off, all slightly ajar. Caroline peeked inside the first door, withdrawing quickly as she saw the old woman who'd answered the door to Henrietta sitting inside, rocking backwards and forward in a rocking chair and humming as her knitting needles clicked together rhythmically.

The next two rooms were empty, both with easels and various pieces of furniture that Caroline supposed could be used as props.

'Last one,' James murmured as they approached the final door.

Caroline knew she had to be the one to look inside, knew it had to be her and not James, but even so she hesitated. It still wasn't too late to walk out the front door and leave Henrietta to her secrets.

'Better me than someone else,' she whispered to herself, resting her hand on the wood of the door and pushing it open just a fraction.

Caroline's eyes swept over the room. There was an easel and paints, the same style of *chaise*—this one with a woman reclining on it. And the artist standing in front of the canvas, back to the door.

For a moment she couldn't move, it took too much of her to try to understand what she was seeing. There was a woman reclining on the *chaise longue*, dress slipping off her shoulder in a scandalous fashion, but it wasn't Henrietta. Henrietta was standing in front of the canvas, palette in hand, painting in bold, confident strokes.

Backing away, Caroline knew this wasn't how she wanted her cousin to have to tell her about her art. She wanted to be out of here, far away, to have time to gather her thoughts and then she could gently probe Henrietta.

'We need to leave,' Caroline said quietly, gripping James by the hand. As they started for the stairs there was a noise from the first room, the one that the old woman had been sitting and knitting in. Before Caroline knew what was happening James had whisked her into one of the other empty rooms, pulling the door closed behind them. Quickly he guided her behind a folding screen, probably in the room for the models to get changed behind, but providing a little welcome cover for their hiding place. Hanging up behind the screen were a few dresses, silky and sumptuous, and Caroline supposed they must be for the models to wear while they were sitting for the artists.

He pressed a finger against his lips and together they listened for the sounds outside the door. Caroline was acutely aware of how he had pressed her up against the screen, his body hard against hers. She could smell his cologne, that sweet mixture of lavender and citrus that made her want to bury her face in his shoulder and pull him even closer. As usual he seemed completely unperturbed by their closeness, not even noticing when his hand brushed against her breast as he manoeuvred himself into a better position.

'Times up,' the old woman said, her voice muffled by the wall in between the two rooms.

Henrietta's voice was softer, harder to make

out, but from what Caroline could hear she thought her cousin was protesting.

'Not my fault you were forty minutes late. You had the room until five o'clock. It's five o'clock now. I'll store away your canvas and have it ready for you at the same time next week. I suggest next week you are on time.'

A few minutes of rustling and scraping next door followed and then the sound of retreating footsteps.

'Shall we try to creep out?'

James shook his head, motioning for her to stay silent for just a few minutes longer. Caroline felt him stiffen as the door to their room opened and there was the sound of footsteps heading inside.

She glanced up, taking in his serious expression, his strong jaw and his dark eyes, and had the overwhelming urge to raise up on her tiptoes and kiss him. The urge was only there for a second, but it was almost enough. She felt herself moving up towards him, her body brushing against his, sending exquisite jolts of pleasure across her skin.

She caught herself as he looked at her, meeting her eyes with his own, and for a moment Caroline fancied she saw something akin to desire flare in him, but knew she was only imagining it.

The footsteps receded and the door closed and Caroline was just about to exhale in relief when she heard a key turn in the lock. With panic in her eyes she looked up at James, but he'd stepped away, turning so she couldn't see his face.

'We're locked in.'

He put a finger to his lips, waiting for another minute before speaking. 'It would seem so.'

'Don't sound so calm.'

'There's really no point in panicking.'

'Of course there's a point in panicking,' Caroline said, crossing her arms and stepping away.

'And that would be…?'

'It makes me feel better.'

James laughed, a low, throaty laugh that cut right through her, making her momentarily forget their predicament. He took a couple of steps closer to the window, pressing himself against the wall before looking out to the street below.

'I'm not sure if this makes it better or worse,' he said.

'What?'

'The old woman has left. Locking the front door behind her.'

Caroline groaned. Now they were trapped behind two locked doors with no hope of escape.

'How could it make it better?'

'At least we won't be discovered.'

'I think I want to be discovered. Just think of the scandal if I'm missing all night. My mother will be so worried, she'll wake all of London trying to find me.' It wasn't an exaggeration. If Caroline failed to come home, her mother would initially remain calm, but as the hours passed and there was no word from either her or James then she would raise the alarm and refuse to let anyone rest until they were found.

'I'm sure it won't be that bad.'

She levelled him with a look that told him he should know better.

'There might be some other scandal to entertain the *ton* in the coming few weeks.'

'More salacious than me and you trapped in an artist's studio in Paddington all night together?'

'Perhaps not.'

Caroline sank to the floor, feeling desperation wash over her. Finally she had decided to marry, to move on with her life, to find a husband and hopefully start a family. She even had a few gentlemen who seemed interested in doing just that and now they would be scared off by this terrible incident.

A fat tear rolled down her cheek followed by another and another. James sank down to the floor next to her and wrapped an arm around her shoulder.

'Don't cry,' he said softly, reaching up and wiping the tears away. It was an intimate gesture, one more suited to a husband or a lover than a friend and Caroline felt the familiar ache in her heart as she imagined what life could be like if he just loved her in a different way.

He kissed her on the top of her head, stroking her hair, his body leaning against hers.

'I won't let them ruin you.'

Caroline sniffed, trying to stem the flow of tears.

'I don't think even your influence could keep all the gossips in London quiet.'

'If the worst happens, then we'll just have to marry.' He said it nonchalantly, completely unaware of how his casual words ripped at her heart.

Slowly she straightened up. She knew she should keep her mouth shut otherwise she might say something she would regret, something that might reveal her true feelings.

'The worst?' she asked, cursing her mouth for not listening to her brain.

'If we're discovered having spent the night together.'

Caroline let out a strange, half-strangled laugh, her hand flying to her mouth to cover the sound.

'I promise your virtue is safe with me,' James said.

'I am well aware,' Caroline muttered under her breath, quickly pushing herself to her feet and walking to the other side of the room. She needed to put distance between them, to calm herself. Especially if they were going to be stuck in here all night.

'I don't think it would be a disaster,' James said, oblivious to her discomfort.

'What?'

'If we were forced to marry.'

Caroline spluttered. It was not ladylike or attractive, but she just couldn't help herself.

'You disagree.'

'No.'

'No?'

'Yes, then.' She just wanted him to be quiet, or talk about something else, anything else.

'This was meant to reassure you,' James said with a frown. 'I just wanted to tell you I wouldn't let a scandal ruin your chances of getting married. If your other suitors stepped away because of the scandal, I would marry you myself.'

'I'm not a charity case,' Caroline said stiffly.

'No, of course not.'

'I don't need you to marry me out of pity.'

'That wasn't what I was suggesting.'

'Wasn't it?'

'No. Damn it, Caroline, can't a man be chivalrous any longer?'

'It is not chivalrous to tell a woman you would only wish to marry her in the direst of circumstances.'

'That's not what I said.'

'It's the truth. The only thing that would force you into marriage with me is a scandal of monumental proportions.'

'That's not fair, Cara.'

She knew it wasn't fair, but her head was spinning and her heart breaking all at the same time.

He took a step towards her, then another. When it became apparent she wasn't going to fight him off he strode across the rest of the distance between them quickly, taking her by the arms and waiting until she looked him in the eye before he spoke.

'Any man would be lucky to have you as his wife, Cara. *Any* man. Including me.'

She looked up at him, aware that there were fresh tears in her eyes. 'You don't mean that.'

She didn't want to hear his answer, didn't want to see the expression on his face or pity in his eyes so she quickly shrugged him off, sidestepped around him and headed back towards the window, busying herself with jiggling the window fastenings to see if they would give way.

'Let me try,' James said softly as he came up beside her.

She stepped aside, still not trusting herself to look at him. She already felt like a fool and knew if she said any more it would jeopardise their friendship. It only worked as well as it did because James had no idea whatsoever of her feelings for him. If he knew she loved him, that he was the first thing she thought about when she woke up and the last thing she thought about at night there would be a new awkwardness between them and she didn't want that.

'I can get the window open.' He pulled it up a crack and peered out. 'But the street is busy below. We should wait until it gets dark and make our escape then.'

Caroline peered out of the window to the ground a good twelve feet below.

'Do you think we can drop down without injuring ourselves?'

'I'll go first so I can catch you, or at the very least cushion your fall.'

Caroline chewed her lip. It would be better than being absent all night. The streets would probably be quieter by seven or eight. By that time her mother would be worried about her lateness, but she wouldn't have summoned a search party. Caroline could claim an injury, something James had needed to tend to, perhaps, and they might just get out of this situation without any repercussions.

She nodded, feeling the relief seep through her.

'Looks like you won't have to marry me after all,' James said softly. He began pacing around the room, looking at the various pieces of artistic equipment. 'Now what shall we do with the next two hours?' he mused, flashing her a grin.

Caroline couldn't help herself, for a moment

she imagined all the wonderful ways they could spend two hours, and most of them involved James's lips pressed against her skin.

'Can you paint, Cara? Or draw?'

'Barely. I had lessons when I was younger, but my teacher eventually gave up and told me to stick to music as my art form.'

'I dabbled a little when I was in Rome.' He picked up a tin of charcoals and fingered them for a moment. 'Model for me.'

'Here? Now?'

'Have you got anything else to do for the next two hours?'

'No-o-o,' she drew out the word.

'Come on, then, have a seat, recline back and imagine you're in a Rubens painting.'

Her eyes flicked to the silky dresses hung up behind the screen. She wanted to pose for him in one of those, not her insipid day dress. If he was going to look at her, really look at her, she wanted to be more exotic and alluring than plain old Caroline Yaxley in her own dress.

James followed her gaze, his eyes widening a fraction as he worked out what she was thinking.

'We do have a couple of hours. If you wanted to get changed…'

'I shouldn't.' It was unnecessary and vain. James had seen her enough times to know what she really looked like—changing into a revealing dress wasn't going to change his views on her.

He took a step towards her, the irresistible smile on his lips, the one he knew she couldn't say no to.

'What's the worst that could happen?'

'Do you really want me to answer that?'

She bit her lip, considering. Nothing bad *could* really happen. They were locked in here, it wasn't as though they were about to be discovered. She took a step towards the folding screen. Caroline felt the surge of excitement inside her. Just for the next couple of hours she was going to be daring and carefree and she would leave the sensible part of herself behind.

'No peeking,' she instructed.

'You're really going to do it? I was joking.'

'I want to see what you can do,' Caroline said, knowing he would love the challenge in her voice.

James tapped his foot on the floor rhythmically. He knew women's clothes were unnecessarily complicated, but it was taking Caroline an age to get changed behind the screen. He could hear the rustling of material, the swishing of fabric as it brushed against skin. Unbidden, an image of Caroline shrugging off her dress came to his mind and James felt himself begin to grow hot. These past few days, ever since that moment in the study when he'd had the urge to kiss her, he'd been plagued with inappropriate thoughts about his friend. Normally he wouldn't react whenever her hand brushed innocently against his, but now he felt as though his skin were on fire at every innocent touch.

And now they were all alone in a locked room and Caroline was stripping off only a few feet away. He could imagine the cotton of her dress falling off her shoulders, pooling at her waist before she wriggled her hips and it dropped to the floor. He *knew* she would be wearing some form of undergarment, but in his imagination her skin was completely bare, bare and rosy and warm.

He groaned, standing and pacing around the small room, trying to distract himself from the images racing through his mind. Perhaps this hadn't been a sensible suggestion. He hadn't thought she would agree. Caroline was adventurous and daring, more so than other women of his acquaintance, but she was also innately sensible. And stripping off in a strange building, even if every door in the place was locked, wasn't an entirely sensible decision.

She stepped out from behind the screen and James let out a low whistle.

'You like it?'

The dress was a deep red, the colour of seduction, with a full silky skirt and a tight, low-cut bodice. Flimsy bits of material acted as sleeves, but they had been cut too large and sat off the shoulder seductively. It was more skin than he'd ever seen Caroline reveal and he found he couldn't tear his eyes away. To add to the effect she had unpinned her hair, letting it fall loose around her shoulders.

'Where do you want me?' she asked innocently, the words making James taut with desire. He took a step towards her and then with a momentous self-resolve he stopped where he was, knowing if he got within touching distance he might do something that would ruin their friendship for ever.

It's Caroline, he told himself, trying to pair this vision of seduction in front of him with his normally so-ordinary friend. No, not ordinary, that was unfair, that was selling her short. Caroline was much more than ordinary, she was fun and mischievous and loving, but she wasn't *this.*

'The *chaise longue,*' he managed to get the words out after a few seconds. She seemed to glide across the floor as if her feet were barely touching it. He watched as she settled herself on the edge, perching as if she were in a drawing room full of well-to-do ladies.

'Perhaps I should recline.' Then she smiled and James felt the world stop wobbling under his feet and right itself again.

'You look…different.'

'Hardly a compliment,' she said, raising her eyebrows. 'I was hoping for something more than different after struggling with these fastenings for ten minutes.'

'I could have helped you.' The words were out before he even knew what he was saying. He could just imagine his fingers trailing down her back and tugging on the ties that held the silky dress in place.

Caroline blinked in surprise at his words. It wasn't as though they always spoke to one another formally, but he hadn't ever flirted with her before. He shook his head, aware he must look as if he were having a little mad episode, but for the life of him he couldn't think why he hadn't ever flirted with her before.

Your friendship, the remnant of the sensible part of him was quick to remind him. Friendship, a one-of-a-kind friendship that would be ruined if he acted on even one of the thoughts that was racing through his head.

'Then I really would be a ruined woman,' Caroline mused, but much of the tension from a few minutes ago had gone from her voice.

'No one would know.' James's voice was low and he saw how Caroline responded to it. The slight widening of her eyes, the way her chest rose and fell a little more quickly.

He took a step towards the *chaise longue* and then another. Part of him was screaming to back away, to send Caroline behind the screen to change back into her normal clothes, but he knew he wasn't strong enough to do that.

'Lie back a little,' he instructed, watching as she reclined, her eyes never leaving his. 'Good.' He reached out, only hesitating a moment before he gripped hold of her ankle, bare underneath the silky fabric of her skirt, and lifted it on to the edge of the *chaise longue*. Her skin was warm and soft and he had the urge to trail his fingers up to her calf and beyond, but with iron self-control he stopped himself. 'Are you comfortable?'

She nodded and he noticed the flush to her cheeks and the sultry parting of her lips. It wasn't just him, she was feeling something between them, some spark, the irresistible pull of desire.

Slowly he leaned over her, thinking how easy it would be to kiss her, but instead gently pulling the loose coil of her hair over her shoulder so it fell over one side of her chest.

'Perfect,' he murmured, stepping back.

He retreated behind the easel, selecting a charcoal from the tin and beginning to draw. Every so often he would stop and look at her, noting the angle of her head and the fullness of her lips, committing it all to paper.

All the time he was drawing he found himself wondering what it would be like to kiss her, to take her in his arms and tumble back on to the *chaise longue* together.

'How is the drawing?' Caroline's voice pulled him abruptly from his thoughts.

'Hmm.'

'That doesn't sound promising.'

'I may have overestimated my ability.'

She laughed and he wondered how he had never seen her beauty before, how he'd only just noticed how desirable she was. They had been friends for five years and she was the woman he'd spent the most time with, ever. Surely he should have noticed the enticing way she smiled and the intriguing sparkle in her blue eyes.

You're a fool, he told himself, repeating it time and time again. It sat heavily on him, this thought that the only reason he was attracted to her now was because she was suddenly unavailable. Caroline had decided to marry and all of a sudden he was finding her almost irresistible. It was an uncomfortable thought, one that didn't say much for his unconscious decision making.

'Can I see?'

'Not yet. Give me chance to fix it.'

'My foot is going to sleep.'

'Stop wriggling, woman. You're hardly the perfect artist's model. Bertie would sit still for longer.' With his words they both fell still and silent for a moment and then together rushed to the window.

'Can you see him?' Caroline's face was pressed close to the glass.

'No. I can't hear him either.'

They had tied Bertie to a post just around the corner, out of view in case Henrietta had been in a position to catch a glimpse of him. In the drama that had followed they had forgotten about the lively dog that was no doubt growing frantic at their absence and was probably now terrorising the street.

'We need to get out of here.'

James watched as she started pulling at the ties that held the dress in place, letting the strands run through her fingers as she loosened off the bodice. He knew he should step away, or at the very least look away, but instead he took a step towards her.

'Let me,' he said, feeling her body fall completely still underneath his touch. Gently he unlaced the ties, feeling his self-control waver every time his fingers brushed against her skin. When the dress was loose, only held up by Caroline's hands at her front, he took a shuddering breath and stepped away.

It was a passing desire, nothing more. He'd desired many women in his life and it wasn't worth losing five years of friendship over.

You could have her. He silenced the voice. He

could. He could marry her, wake up to his best friend and the woman he was currently finding irresistible, each and every morning. It was a tempting thought, but he knew he couldn't do it. He loved Caroline, but not in that way. He'd promised himself long ago he would hold out for true love, even if it meant staying a bachelor until he was seventy. Caroline deserved to be more than second-best.

He waited as she changed, busying himself with the window catches, waiting until she was ready to pull up the window and look down into the street below. It was quiet, with the occasional person hurrying past into the failing light.

'Are you ready?' He stepped back to the easel, rolling up the charcoal drawing he'd made of Caroline and tucking it inside his jacket.

She nodded, looking down into the street with an expression of determination mixed with apprehension.

'We'll have to be quick. If someone sees us climbing out of here they may well raise the alarm and I don't fancy explaining to an angry mob that we weren't up to anything nefarious.'

'I'll be quick,' she promised.

With one last look up and down the street

James swung his leg out of the window. He gripped hold of the sill and began to lower himself, feeling the burn in his muscles and glad of the exercises he did every morning and the hours spent at the boxing club. As soon as he was as close to the ground as he could get while still holding on he let go, pushing out from the wall at the same time. He landed lightly, feeling a judder through his knees, but immediately he knew he hadn't done any damage.

Looking up, he saw Caroline's face in the window and marvelled at her courage as she swung herself out without any hesitation. She was as quick as he had been, lowering herself before looking back to ensure he was ready for her.

'I'll catch you.'

She pushed off, landing on him heavily and with her in his arms he took a few staggering steps back.

'Oi, stop,' a voice called out from the other end of the street.

They both instinctively turned towards it, then before the man could move, James set Caroline on her feet, grabbed her hand and began to pull her along. They ran, stopping only to untie Bertie who barked happily as they approached and then ran alongside them wagging his tail furiously.

Only when they were half a mile away did James let them slow their pace. Caroline turned to him, her face glowing from the exertion, her grin the widest he'd ever seen it.

'We made it.'

'And it's not even that late.'

'Thank you,' she said, squeezing his arm.

'I can't take you home like this.'

Caroline raised a hand and grimaced as she felt the free flow of her hair over her shoulders. She looked as though she'd spent the afternoon being ravaged. Although James had only fantasised about doing just that, he felt guilty all the same.

'I'll take you to my house. We can send a note to your mother and make up some story of why you've been delayed. That should give you time to make yourself look more like you did when you left this afternoon.'

Caroline nodded and slipped her hand back into the crook of his elbow. As they walked along he realised his plan meant being once again alone with Caroline in a private space and he felt the thrum of anticipation, even though he knew nothing could ever happen.

Standing in front of the mirror, Caroline jabbed a pin into her hair and grimaced. Her lady's maid, Anna, made it look so easy when she swept Caroline's hair up into a neat coil, taking just a few minutes to make her look presentable.

'It's impossible,' she muttered, selecting another pin and pushing it into her hair. Tentatively she took her hands away and almost growled in frustration as the strands tumbled down around her shoulders again. 'Can you put something in the note that would explain why my hair is unpinned?' she called to James.

He was sitting in his study, writing a note to be delivered to Caroline's mother to explain why they had been out for so long. Knowing James it would be short and to the point, and all the more convincing because of it.

'Shall I blame the horde of marauding pirates or the mischievous flock of geese?'

'I hope you're going to come up with something more convincing than that.'

'I have merely said there was an accident and we have been detained, but no one is harmed.'

Simple, to the point. Although she would have to come up with the details to satisfy her mother's curiosity later.

Caroline took two more pins and stuck them into her hair, regarding the result with a grim displeasure. It would have to do. She turned and entered James's study, flopping down into one of the armchairs while he arranged for a footman to deliver the note.

'You will have to stay another twenty minutes,' he said as he came back into the room. 'Otherwise you'll arrive too soon after the note.'

It wasn't a hardship spending twenty minutes in James's comfortable study, even when she should be worrying about what she was going to say to pacify her mother when she finally returned home.

'We could use the time to start your next lesson.'

'What is my next lesson?'

'You're going to the opera with Milton tomorrow night, aren't you?'

She nodded. It wasn't her favourite place to go for a night out, but he'd asked and she had accepted in the spirit of furthering their acquaintance.

'Then perhaps we should work on a little flirtation in close quarters.'

Caroline swallowed, remembering the look in his eyes as she had emerged from behind the screen in the artist's studio, dress falling off her shoulders and hair flowing down her back. It would be dangerous to accept his proposal, but she knew she wouldn't be able to resist.

'Surely there is little I can do. The opera is a very public place, there are eyes watching you from every direction.'

It was the truth, the opera was as much about socialising as it was enjoying the spectacle on stage and there would be plenty of gossip aimed in her direction when she arrived on Lord Hauxton's arm.

'On the contrary, there is much you can do. How you sit, how you lean in, those little touches that can be fleeting, but filled with meaning.'

Reaching out, he pulled her to her feet and as Caroline stood, their bodies brushed together. She wasn't sure if she imagined it or if he lingered just a moment too long before stepping away. He led her over to his desk and motioned for her to sit in the chair behind it, before manoeuvring the one on the opposite side to be placed next to her.

'Imagine you're watching the opera. The scene on stage is intense and I lean in to murmur something about one of the performers.' He moved closer, his lips almost brushing her ear and sending delicious shivers down her spine. 'Impressive range.'

It took all her effort not to lean back into him, not to hope his arms would encircle her and pull her towards him.

'How would you react?'

She steeled herself, rallying. With a little half-smile she made eye contact, swaying in even closer and touching her hand fleetingly to his. 'And such presence,' she murmured. 'I haven't seen a performer captivate an audience like this in a long time.'

James's lips parted and for a second she thought he might kiss her, but then he abruptly pulled away. 'You told me you didn't know how to flirt,' he said with his customary smile. 'I think you will have no problem captivating any man's attention.'

She couldn't tell him that everything came so easily when he was around, that her heart might be pounding in her chest, but still she found it easy to talk to him. The little touches, the eye contact, all of it felt so forced, so awkward with anyone but him.

'I get nervous,' she said, sitting back, trying to create some distance between them to see if it would help her concentrate.

'When you get nervous just imagine it is someone you are comfortable talking to. Your cousin, perhaps, or me.'

His words cut through her and she had to turn away to hide the anguish on her face. He truly had no idea that she would be sitting there at the opera wishing it was him accompanying her, wishing it was him she was flirting with. Even with her best intentions to move on with her life she knew every conversation, every encounter with a potential suitor, would be overshadowed by James's presence.

'I should go,' she said, standing abruptly. 'The note should have reached my mother by now and I don't want her rushing round here to accompany me home.'

'I'll walk you.'

'No, I'll be fine on my own.'

'Nonsense.' He was already halfway out to the

hall to call for their coats. Caroline hesitated, then followed. She knew the sensible thing was to give in. It was dark out and there was no way James would ever jeopardise her safety by letting her walk home by herself. This part of London was safer than most, but that didn't mean a young lady should venture out alone after dark.

'Ten more minutes,' she reassured herself. Ten more minutes and then she could shut herself in her bedroom and cry into her pillow for the life she would never have.

Chapter Nine

It was cold outside, with a frost already beginning to form on the grass of the little green spaces and parks as they walked past. Caroline pulled up the collar of her coat to shield her neck from the worst of the icy temperatures and moved a fraction closer to James to share some of his warmth. One hand was resting on James's arm, the other held Bertie's lead, with her lively dog walking sedately for once, tired out by all the excitement of the day.

'I love evenings like this,' James said, looking up at the sky. Caroline also looked up. There were no stars visible, as was normal in London. It was one of her favourite things about returning to Hampshire, being able to look out of her bedroom window at night and see the constellations. Tonight the sky was clear and the moon bright above them, but not a single star was visible.

'Do the stars look the same in Italy?' She had often wondered this, late at night when she would stare at the sky and imagine James looking up at the same sky thousands of miles away. Sometimes she would allow herself to indulge in her secret fantasy, imagining she was strolling arm in arm with James through the piazzas of Florence or meandering over the bridges in Venice.

'They do. Although it certainly isn't as cold as this out there.'

'You've never been in the coldest months.'

'True.' James might love to travel and spend as many months away from England as at home, but he didn't shirk his responsibilities. He always came back for the winter months when Parliament was in session and spent time touring his estates and sorting out any problems his estate managers brought to his attention. Caroline knew he left his cousin, a young but very capable man, in charge while he was away. 'I can't really imagine ice on the canals or snow covering the Colosseum.'

'Tell me about Italy again,' Caroline prompted quietly.

James looked at her, affection in his eyes, but she wondered if there was a hint of pity there, too, as if he knew the closest she would ever get to foreign travel would be his stories.

'You would love it, Cara, the people, the countryside, the sights. It is a country filled with passion and beauty and serenity.' He paused as they rounded the corner and had to wait for a carriage to trundle down the road before they could cross to the pavement on the other side. 'My favourite place I've ever been is a sleepy little village called Positano. It is nestled on the hillside of the Amalfi coast and it looks as though it has come straight from an artist's imagination.'

She loved the slightly dreamy, faraway look he got in his eyes when he was recounting the details of one of his trips.

'The streets are steep and cobbled and the houses painted in pastels. In the squares and piazzas, the locals drink coffee and watch the world meander on, happy in the knowledge they live in one of the most idyllic places in the world. And the sea…it's a blue like I've never seen before, deep and inviting and beautiful.'

'Do you swim in the sea?' Immediately she regretted the question—even before he answered she could imagine him stripping off on a rocky outcrop and diving naked into the water.

'In that heat, with the cool water so inviting, it would be foolish not to.'

'I've only been to the seaside twice so I'm no expert, but I'm guessing they don't have bathing machines in Positano like they do in Brighton.'

He threw his head back and laughed. 'No, I think the Italians would think we English make a simple swim in the sea far more complicated than it should be.'

'But surely men and women aren't allowed to swim together.'

James shrugged. 'They have areas of the beach where the men swim and areas for the women. That's not to say that late at night there isn't some blurring of those lines.'

That right there was another fantasy that Caroline knew would torment her when she was alone at night. She could almost see a version of herself slipping into the warm Italian sea to join James for an illicit midnight swim.

She coughed to try to cover her embarrassment and was mortified to see James looking at her with a knowing expression on his face.

'You're imagining it, aren't you?'

'Imagining what?'

'A late-night swim with a gentleman you favour.'

She shook her head violently and knew he would be able to see through the protestation. If she'd been less flustered she would have laughed and made some joke about the temperature of the water killing any ardour she might feel, but she knew it was too late to try that now.

He dropped his voice lower even though there was no one else nearby to overhear. 'Swimming to the edge of the cove with nothing between the water and your skin, knowing at any moment his body could brush against yours.'

Caroline felt a deep yearning like she had never felt before. She wanted what he was describing so badly, wanted just one moment in the water with James, with him desiring her as much as she did him.

She glanced up and hesitated, almost losing her footing despite the even pavement they were walking on. Not for the first time this evening she saw desire in James's eyes as he looked down at her and with a jolt of pleasure she knew he was imagining the same thing as her. Imagining it *and* desiring it.

He cleared his throat and looked as though

he were about to say something, then cleared his throat again. 'There's a secluded little cove twenty minutes from Positano, you have to climb over the rocks a little to get there. The locals tell me if you swim in the waters of the cove at midnight with a woman your souls will be bound together for eternity.'

'You didn't take anyone for a swim there?'

'No. I don't think I could impose myself on anyone for eternity.'

'You know half the women in London would do anything to be bound to you for one lifetime, let alone eternity.'

'They would do anything to be bound to my title and my money,' he corrected her.

Caroline blinked, hit by the sudden realisation of how lonely life must be for James. She'd seen time and time again people treat him differently because of his title and status. They were overly polite, but in doing so were overly superficial. He had hinted before he had only a small handful of true friends, people who wanted to socialise with him not for the connections he could bring, but for the pleasure of his company alone. She'd known all of this, but somehow hadn't been able to see how it influenced so many parts of his life.

'Is that why you travel so much?'

He turned to her with a question in his eyes.

'To meet new people, people who don't *know* you're probably the richest man in England, people who don't treat you differently from any other English gentleman on the Continent—it is liberating.'

'I always thought it was because of Georgie.'

James frowned. 'Lady Georgina?'

'I thought you cared for her more than you let on, that her decision to run away to Australia hurt you deeply despite what you said and that was why you went away so much.'

Over the years he'd revealed only a little about his short engagement to Georgina. He'd always told Caroline it hadn't been love, that his resolve to hold out for a woman he had that instant connection with had wavered and Georgina had been a suitable candidate for a wife. When she had come to him to break off their engagement, he had encouraged her to follow her heart and be with the man she loved. Still, Caroline had always wondered, always feared, that there had been more to his feelings than the respect and mild affection he proclaimed he felt for Georgina.

'Lady Georgina was an amiable woman, but

I wasn't overly upset by the ending of our engagement. Besides, I have been going off on trips across Europe since long before I met you and Lady Georgina.' He smiled at her, a smile that made her heart squeeze in her chest. 'With no intent of undermining Lady Georgina's character, the best thing to come out of my short engagement with her was my friendship with you.'

He paused, turning his body slightly so he was facing her. Caroline saw they were at the corner of her street, only a hundred feet away from her front door. As always she didn't want the time with James to end, especially after all the revelations of the last few minutes.

'You are very dear to me, Cara,' he said, reaching out and trailing his fingers down her cheek in an intimate gesture that took her breath away. 'Sometimes I wonder…' He trailed off and looked away, shaking his head as if deciding not to continue with the thought.

For a moment she wondered if he was going to kiss her and the disappointment washed over her as he stepped away.

'I should get you home.'

In silence they covered the short distance to her front door.

* * *

James felt Caroline slip her arm from his as they reached the steps leading up to her front door. He still couldn't believe what he'd been about to say. He needed some space, some distance from Caroline and the intense urges he was having today.

'Caroline darling,' Lady Yaxley called as she flung open the front door. She must have been watching from the window, waiting for them to walk up the street. He squinted back into the darkness wondering if she had seen them pause on the corner, seen him lean in as if he'd been about to kiss Caroline. 'I've been so worried. What happened?'

Bertie bounded up the steps and disappeared into the house, barking loudly. Caroline's eyes followed her dog and a look of relief crossed over her face.

'An incident with Bertie, Mama. You know how excitable he gets with the ducks in the park. His lead got caught and then as he was struggling to free himself he knocked Lord Heydon into the Serpentine.'

Lady Yaxley gasped, but James could see she

was trying to hide a smile. 'Were you harmed, Your Grace?'

'Only my pride, Lady Yaxley. And sometimes it is beneficial to a man to be reminded that, no matter his status, he can still be knocked to the ground, or in this case the water, by an overenthusiastic dog.'

'Luckily we were in a quiet area so not too many people saw His Grace go for his little swim.'

'Luckily,' he murmured. It was an inventive story, with just enough absurdity to make it paradoxically unlikely to be made up.

'You must come in, Your Grace.'

'I don't want to impose.' By the time he'd finished his protestation he'd already been ushered inside and directed to a warm seat by the fire. Bertie looked up at him with lidded eyes and James gave the dog a rub on the head.

'He's a monster,' Lady Yaxley said, looking at the bloodhound with undisguised love in her eyes.

'But he's our monster.' Caroline crouched down beside Bertie and stroked his back. 'Whatever happens we mustn't tell Father about this. He thinks Bertie is too unruly as it is.'

'I'm sorry for the lateness of the hour,' James said, flashing his most endearing smile. 'Your daughter was kind enough to accompany me home so I might change before we returned here. Of course I ensured we were properly chaperoned at all times.' He thought back to the moments in the artist's studio and his house, moment after moment where they had been unchaperoned and alone. Multiple moments where he had wanted to kiss Caroline, to pick her up and carry her to his bedroom and ravish her just as he did in his dreams.

'I'm just glad you are both unharmed. Will you stay for a brandy, Your Grace? Or a glass of wine.'

'A brandy would be much appreciated. Warming.'

Lady Yaxley rang for the footman and quietly asked for a brandy. While she was occupied Caroline came and took the chair beside him.

'Not bad,' he murmured. 'Certainly an inventive story.'

'I thought it was inspired.'

'Although your mother might question why no one saw a dripping wet duke walking through Hyde Park this afternoon.'

Caroline sucked her bottom lip into her mouth as she considered this.

'How easy do you think it would be to start a rumour that you were pulled into the Serpentine?'

'Far too easy. The gossips don't care where the information comes from, it's the thrill they get from spreading it they like.'

'Can your ego take an imaginary dunking?'

'I think I'm able to withstand it.'

'Thank you. I am indebted to you once again.'

'I'll have to find some interesting way to redeem your debt.' As soon as he said the words he imagined a thousand things he would like Caroline to do. Most involved very little clothing and a lot of time spent in bed.

He forced himself to look away, to focus his gaze on the flickering flames, waiting until his eyes were almost watering before he allowed himself to glance back at Caroline. Today had been a strange day, undeniably enjoyable despite the drama, but certainly unsettling. He had almost kissed his best friend more times than he cared to admit and the burgeoning desire he felt for her was increasing every moment they spent together.

Lady Yaxley came and joined them by the fire, smoothing down her skirts as she sat. A moment later the footman reappeared with a glass of brandy which he handed over to James.

Quickly he took a gulp, enjoying the warm burn as the liquid travelled down his throat. He would just drink his brandy, make his farewells and leave, giving him time and distance away from Caroline to remind himself of the madness of his desires.

'Did your hair get loosened in the park somehow?' Lady Yaxely asked, her eyes narrowing slightly as she took in Caroline's attempts to pin her hair back neatly.

There was a pause and he saw Caroline's eyes widen a fraction as she tried to work out a reasonable explanation for her needing to re-pin her hair.

'Bertie,' James said, giving a serious shake of his head to accompany the word. 'He jumped at you when he got out of the water and somehow you knocked your hair with your arm.'

'Bertie has been busy today,' Lady Yaxley murmured.

'Thank you for your hospitality, but I must excuse myself and return home. It has been a most eventful day.'

Caroline accompanied him to the front door. As he stepped outside he thought about turning back and brushing a kiss on her cheek, but with Lady Yaxley already suspicious he knew he would never get away with it. Instead he straightened his back and strode off down the road, resisting the urge to look back.

Chapter Ten

'I served in the army for five years,' Lord Hauxton said as they rode at a sedate pace through Hyde Park.

'You did? Surely that's unusual for an earl?'

'It is, but I was no great rebel, protesting against the path my father had mapped out for me, I'm afraid. I wasn't born to inherit. When I went off to the army I had two older brothers in robust health.'

'What happened?'

'There was a fire at our ancestral home. Both my brothers were in residence, as well as my parents. I was away with my regiment at the time.'

'I'm so sorry. To lose everyone all at one, that's terrible.'

'It is. I still sometimes find myself thinking I'll just go and ask one of my brothers for advice on this matter or that.'

She didn't doubt Lord Hauxton had always had a serious character, but a life marred by so much tragedy explained a little why he had a reputation for only seldom smiling in company. Although she had found him to be a pleasant companion, fascinating to talk to and interested in her views.

'I've been lucky,' Caroline said, bringing her horse in a little closer to Lord Hauxton's as she spoke. 'I haven't lost many people in my life. Although I do understand what you mean by sometimes reaching for someone who isn't here. I had a friend, a very good friend, who left the country five years ago. She was like a sister to me and even now when I don't know what to do I think I'll just pop around to her house and ask her.'

'Lady Georgina,' Milton said after a moment. 'I remember her.

'Although in my case I suppose I am lucky in that I can still write to her.'

'It's not quite the same, though—although putting pen to paper can be cathartic it isn't the same as the back and forth you get when someone is right in front of you.'

They rode on for a few minutes in silence and Caroline stole a glance at the man riding beside her. He was an accomplished horseman, attractive and eloquent. He was more than she had dared to hope for when she had decided to start her search for a husband.

Unbidden, an image of James flashed into her mind and she had to resolutely push it away. It wasn't fair to compare Lord Hauxton to the man she'd loved for five years. Milton did have one advantage over James, though—he seemed interested in her romantically.

She thought of the spark of something that looked very much like desire in James's eyes as she'd stepped out from behind the screen in the artist's studio. He'd looked at her in a way he'd never looked at her before, hungry and primal. She'd watched as he'd wrestled with himself as he'd taken hold of her ankle and then felt the crushing disappointment as he'd moved away.

For days she'd been plagued by images of that look of desire in James's eyes, trying to work out if she'd imagined it and, if not, what it meant.

Nothing, she told herself for the hundredth time. It meant nothing. It was just something to distract her from Lord Hauxton, from what was important.

'I was planning on inviting you to the opera again next week,' Lord Hauxton said as they turned their horses and started to head back through the park, 'but I think you are not altogether too keen on it.'

Caroline was about to protest, but then decided against it. 'No, I've never really warmed to it,' she confessed. 'I know most people love it and I admire the singers greatly—I often wish I could sing with a tenth of their range—but the whole opera experience is not my favourite way to spend an evening. I'm sorry.'

'There is nothing to apologise for. Everyone has different interests, different likes and dislikes.'

'You like the opera, though.'

'I do, but I can see how it wouldn't appeal to everyone. And I happen to believe that it is healthy in a friendship or a relationship to have different interests and differences of opinion.'

Caroline quickly glanced sideways. It was the first time Lord Hauxton had mentioned a relationship between them, even though it was quite clear where his intentions lay. In the past four days she'd seen him three times. First when he'd come to call on her on the afternoon she and James had become trapped in the studio. Then the following day at the opera and now today for this ride through Hyde Park. Her mother was becoming increasingly hopeful that a proposal might be forthcoming before the end of the month and even Caroline couldn't deny things were moving forward quicker than she ever imagined possible.

There was no quickening of her pulse at that thought, no surge of joy in her heart, but she reminded herself for the hundredth time that it didn't matter.

'Good afternoon, Lord Hauxton, Miss Yaxley.'

Caroline had to turn around to see who had joined them, he'd approached from behind quietly.

'Lord West.'

She didn't know Lord West well, despite him being another of James's friends. He lived in the very male world of the *ton*, eschewing the dancing at the balls he attended for the card rooms, or more often, if James was to be believed, preferring to spend his time in some of the less salubrious taverns south of the river.

'Pleasant day for a ride,' Lord West said, manoeuvring his horse into step beside Caroline.

'It is indeed, Lord West. Are you out riding for pleasure?'

'My wife has her relatives visiting,' he said, lowering his voice and leaning in conspiratorially. 'I decided a little fresh air would do me the world of good before jumping back into the fray.'

Caroline had to suppress a smile. Although she did not know Lord West well, she had heard snippets of information about him from James. She remembered James saying he was dissatisfied with his wife—a young woman Caroline had met on a handful of occasions who was pretty, but forceful in nature.

'I'm sure it can't be all that bad,' Milton murmured.

'I can assure you it is. Perhaps you'd like to take my place, Milton, and I'll spend the rest of the afternoon in the park with Miss Yaxley.'

'I think your wife might notice the wrong man had returned to her,' Caroline said drily.

West looked at her for a moment and then threw his head back and laughed.

'Do you know, Miss Yaxley, I think she might, but whether she would complain would be another matter.'

'You do your wife a disservice, West.' Milton's voice was low but serious and Caroline saw the thrum of tension pass between the two men.

'You're right, of course. Shouldn't speak badly about the wife in public. Shame she doesn't afford me the same courtesy—*everyone* has heard how much she regrets our marriage and how she wishes it was Milton or Heydon who'd proposed.'

Caroline shifted uneasily in her saddle and glanced sideways. West was swaying backwards and forward ever so slightly and she realised he was well on his way to being inebriated. From the frown on Milton's face he was aware of the issue, too, and was trying to work out how best to deal with it.

'Ah, here he is. The man every wife secretly wishes they were wed to.'

Caroline looked ahead, seeing James appear through one of the gates to the park on horseback. She felt a nervous energy begin to surge through her. She hadn't seen him since the evening they'd spent locked together in the artist's studio and immediately she was taken back to that moment when he looked at her with desire in his eyes.

'Good afternoon,' James said lifting his hat as he approached. She noted the minuscule frown line between his brows as he looked at each of the three of them in turn. 'If I was a suspicious man, I would think this some sort of conspiracy.'

'Milton and I have decided you've been keeping Miss Yaxley to yourself for far too long,' West lurched a little on his horse as he spoke, causing both James and Milton to lean forward in their saddles as if ready to pounce. 'She's a delightful creature.'

'Woman,' Caroline corrected him not quite under her breath.

'Spirited,' West continued.

'Also like a horse.' Caroline knew she should keep quiet, but West was beginning to irk her and she'd never been good at holding her tongue.

'I have a feeling what you see is what you get with Miss Yaxley, unlike many women who hide behind a veneer of loveliness, only for you to find the harridan beneath once you're already shackled.'

'Enough,' James said abruptly. 'Stop before you insult Miss Yaxley any further.'

'A compliment, my dear fellow,' West slurred. He was more intoxicated than Caroline had first realised and she momentarily forgot her annoyance at the man as he swayed dangerously in his saddle. She might not like him, but she didn't want him to break his neck falling from his horse.

'Hardly a compliment to your wife.' Milton had moved closer to her, their legs almost touching now and as she looked over he motioned for her to take a tighter grip on her reins. 'In case the fool does something stupid and scares the horses,' he murmured.

Caroline did just that, taking the reins and ensuring she had a stable seat on her mare's back.

'Milton, I trust you will see Miss Yaxley safely home,' James said, his voice taking on the authoritative air Caroline always thought of as his ducal tone. 'I'll ensure West makes it home without breaking his neck.'

'You'll do no such thing. I'm having a splendid time with my dear friends and Miss Yaxley.'

'We are not,' James said bluntly.

He signalled to Milton to escort Caroline away, but as she nudged her horse forward West shot out a hand, moving much quicker than she thought a man in his cups should be able to.

In a flash of movement James vaulted down from his horse, grabbed the bridle of West's mount and at the same time pulled his friend from the saddle.

'You don't touch her.'

'What business is it of yours?' West slurred. 'She's hardly your concern. It's Milton making advances. Unless—' He broke down into a cackle of laughter. 'Unless you're cuckolding Milton even before he's married her.'

'Stop staggering,' James said, holding West by the lapels of his jacket for a second as the other man regained his balance. Caroline watched in horrified fascination at the suppressed anger radiating from James's body. 'Apologise to Miss Yaxley. At once.'

West turned to her and Caroline felt some of the tension begin to ebb out of her. If he apologised, that could be the end of it. She doubted West would have much of a friendship with either James or Milton going forward, but at least no one would do anything stupid.

After a long few seconds West spun back to face James, lunging forward as if about to punch him. West was slow and James's reflexes meant he easily dodged out of the way of the blow.

'Tomorrow. At dawn. On the Heath.' West stumbled to one side as he said it.

'No,' Caroline whispered. It was ludicrous, and

the last thing she wanted was someone getting hurt in her name.

'Be reasonable,' Milton said and Caroline noticed his hand was resting on her horse's neck, calming the mare in the tense situation.

'You, too. I'll have you both.' After a failed attempted to remount his horse West stalked off leading the animal behind him.

For a moment all three remained silent, stunned by the turn of events.

'What just happened?' Milton asked, shaking his head in disbelief.

'He's drunk. He'll realise what a mistake he's made once he sobers up.'

Caroline could see James was still tense with anger, but he controlled it well.

'You won't fight?' Caroline looked first at James as she spoke, forcing herself to turn and include Milton in the question.

'I doubt West will go through with it.'

'That's not an answer.'

'I will not have him dishonour you,' James said quietly. He held her gaze for a long moment and Caroline felt her heart begin to pound in her chest.

'It is not worth dying for.'

'Heydon is right. West will retract once he sobers.' Milton smiled grimly. 'And if he doesn't he's a bigger fool than I ever gave him credit for.'

'I will call on him later this afternoon.' James remounted his horse and flashed her a reassuring smile, even though his eyes were still serious. 'And I will let you get back to your ride.'

Caroline watched as he turned his horse around and trotted off, her heart sinking with the knowledge that if West did not retract both James and Milton would face him on Hampstead Heath in the morning.

'Shall I escort you home, Miss Yaxley?'

'Thank you.' After everything that had happened Caroline did feel as though she needed to be alone to think it through, to see if she could come up with some solution to stop any of these wooden-headed men getting hurt.

Chapter Eleven

'Did you speak to him?' Caroline asked the moment the carriage door opened. 'Is it all straightened out?'

James had to suppress a smile at her eagerness, although he didn't like the lines of worry on her face.

'He would not admit me. His footmen had strict instructions not to even let me in through the front door.'

'No.' She sat down on the seat of the carriage opposite and slumped back, despair in her eyes. 'You can't go, James. Promise me.'

'You know I can't do that, Cara.'

'I don't want you to get hurt. Not for a meaningless insult.'

'Not meaningless. If he repeats that comment, it will become rumour and you know how dangerous rumour can become.'

'No one will believe it.'

'They don't have to believe it, not really. They will spread it and distort it and it will harm you in one way or another. Milton is a good man, but he has his pride, and your other suitors will certainly be less understanding.'

'I don't care.' She had tears in her eyes and he could tell it was costing her a great effort to stop them spilling over on to her cheeks.

'I care.' Gently he reached forward and took her hand. 'I have no family, no wife or children. No brothers or sisters or parents. No one to protect, but I do have you. What sort of man would I be if I let someone harm the person I care about the most?'

She looked at him with her large blue eyes and he felt something tighten inside him. Without thinking through the consequences he slipped from his seat and joined her on the cushion opposite, conscious of how his legs were pressed against hers in the narrow space.

'Don't cry.' He reached up and wiped the tears away. 'Nothing bad will happen to me. West was a poor swordsman at school and hasn't picked up a blade in years and I doubt he is any handier with a pistol.'

For a moment she searched his face, looking for reassurance, perhaps, and James was overcome with the sudden urge to kiss her. It would be so easy to bend down, to pull her in even closer to his body and kiss her until they were both breathless.

Even as he had the thought he felt his body swaying towards her, felt the irresistible pull drawing him in even closer. Caroline's eyes widened just a fraction and that small movement was enough to bring him back to his senses. He couldn't kiss her and especially not right now when she was upset and vulnerable.

Clearing his throat, he quickly moved back to the seat opposite, all the time cursing the ongoing urge he had to gather her up in his arms and ravish her right here in the carriage. He now understood why society insisted on chaperons for even the most mundane of situations—it seemed he couldn't be left alone with Caroline without almost doing something foolish.

Foolish? his subconscious asked the question. Would it be foolish to kiss Caroline? Certainly he didn't want to do anything to sully her reputation and even an unwitnessed kiss might somehow damage her innocent status. Still, as he'd just told her, he cared for her more than anyone else in the world and enjoyed her company more than anyone else, too.

She was getting married, but she wasn't promised to anyone just yet. It wouldn't be difficult to persuade Caroline to marry him instead of Milton or Mottringham, it wasn't as though she loved either of them. The idea of waking up next to her in bed every morning made the desire flare afresh inside him and he had to take a deep breath to steady himself.

He wished he had a brother to talk to, or a friend who wasn't invested in the scenario. Normally he would discuss a dilemma with Caroline or Milton, but he could hardly confess to either of them his burgeoning desire.

'I want to come.' Caroline was looking at him with a steely expression and it took him a moment to remember what they had been talking about. 'To the duel. I want to come.'

'No.'

'Let me rephrase. I am coming—it is up to you if you escort me there or not.'

'You could get hurt.'

'Don't you dare use that argument on me. *You*

most likely will get hurt. If you insist on fighting for my honour, I will be there to see it.'

'Your mother will never allow it.'

'Of course not. I'm not planning on telling her.'

'You will never get out of the house undetected before dawn.'

'You let me worry about that.'

'Cara, I'm doing this to protect your reputation. If you go missing or are seen on the Heath at dawn unchaperoned with three gentlemen, then there will rumours afresh.'

'Will you pick me up or do I have to find my own way there?'

'Please.'

'If you insist on going, then I insist on accompanying you.'

'We're a pair of fools,' James murmured quietly as they drew up in front of the Prestons' town house. It was impressive, with fat pillars flanking the door and the paintwork in immaculate condition. The house was large by London standards, taking up almost a quarter of one side of the street.

'Tell me again why we're here,' Caroline said with a grimace.

'By the machinations of a very cunning woman. And you're here to protect me.'

Caroline snorted, sitting back in her seat signalling her reluctance to get out of the carriage.

He stepped down first, turning back to help Caroline down the step before offering her his arm.

'The things I do for you,' she said quietly.

It was true, she was an extraordinary friend. For a moment he faltered, missing his step. She had always been an extraordinary friend, loyal and steadfast. He thought back to the moment in the studio when he'd almost kissed her, to the warmth and anticipation in her eyes. Again in the carriage she hadn't looked shocked or appalled when he'd leaned in that little bit too close—instead a wonderful anticipation had thrummed between them.

Surely not.

He glanced at her, thinking of all the moments they'd shared together, and wondered if the platonic friendship he'd been so sure they had was entirely that.

'Your Grace,' Lady Whittaker gushed, coming down the front steps to greet them, 'and Miss

Yaxley, we are delighted you could come to our humble little dinner party.'

Miss Preston was standing next to her mother, looking stunning and fresh faced in a pastel-pink gown, her hair pulled back with ringlets falling around her shoulders. James couldn't deny she was beautiful, but there was a hardness in her eyes and on occasion even a flash of cruelty.

'Thank you for the invitation,' Caroline said as they entered the house, Lady Whittaker showing them into the well-lit drawing room. Lord Whittaker was waiting for them inside with another elderly gentleman who James had met on a couple of previous occasions. He was Lord Whittaker's younger brother, a retired high-ranking officer in the army, and it looked as though he were the only other guest present.

James watched, half-amused, half-dismayed, as Colonel Preston expertly introduced himself to Caroline and manoeuvred her off to the other side of the room, leaving him alone with Miss Preston.

'I'm so pleased you could come this evening.' Miss Preston stepped in closer and he caught the sickly-sweet scent of roses in her perfume. 'I have been waiting with anticipation for our next meeting ever since you were so kind as to walk me home from the park.'

'Indeed,' James murmured, already wishing the evening could be over.

'We have a few minutes until dinner is served, perhaps you would like to accompany me for a walk about the garden.'

'It is dark, Miss Preston, and cold.'

'I don't mind the cold. And I have you to protect me from whatever lurks in the dark.'

'I would hate for you to trip and hurt yourself, it would mean having to cut the dinner party short.'

'Oh, I wouldn't want that, although I am very steady on my feet.'

He forced a smile, wondering if it was too late to run out of the door. He'd thought Miss Preston would be more subtle in her attempts to engineer a situation where they were alone, or at least wait until they'd eaten.

'Miss Yaxley, Colonel Preston, accompany us on a stroll around the garden,' he called over.

'There is no need,' Miss Preston said, a touch of petulance in her voice. 'We're all friends here, no one is going to think anything of us going for a walk by ourselves.'

'I'd love some fresh air,' Caroline said and in that moment he could have kissed her. Instead he gave her a surreptitious wink and ensured she and the Colonel were following before he stepped out on to the terrace with Miss Preston.

Thwarted in her efforts to get him alone, Miss Preston was silent for the first couple of minutes they were outside. It was late October, the night sky dark and the air damp, not the most pleasant evening to be taking a stroll around the garden, and James found himself wishing for the warmth of his fire in his study and a large glass of brandy to chase the chills away.

'I hear you've been to Europe recently.' Miss Preston had positioned herself even closer to him and as they walked her body brushed seductively against his. James surreptitiously moved a couple of inches to the side.

'Yes, Italy. A fascinating country, have you been?'

She screwed up her nose. 'I don't travel well and I'm not sure I would like to travel somewhere so *uncivilised*.'

James laughed, then realised she was being serious. 'Italy isn't uncivilised. There is more history, more culture, more *civilisation* there than anywhere else I've ever been.'

'Really?' She sounded as though she were forcing the note of enthusiasm in her voice.

'In Rome there are historical ruins on every street corner, reminders of the great empire. It's not just the capital either, even the little provincial towns have the grandest churches and monuments you could imagine.'

'Are you talking about Italy?' Caroline stepped up her pace and pulled the Colonel along with her.

'We are. Miss Preston does not see the appeal. I'm trying to convince her otherwise.'

'It would be different if you were my guide,' Miss Preston said and as she looked up at him she actually fluttered her eyelashes.

He thought he heard Caroline scoff and had to suppress a smile. Miss Preston might be considered the diamond of the Season, but she was far from the most skilled seductress he'd come across in his time. Her compliments were clunky and sometimes even downright awkward and her flirting was too obvious.

'Shall we go back inside?' Caroline suggested, shivering as she looked up at the overcast sky.

'Let me accompany you.' Colonel Preston stepped forward, volunteering his services.

'We will stay for a few more minutes.' Miss Preston gripped hold of his arm as James went to follow Caroline and the Colonel.

'Come, Miss Preston, I would never forgive myself if you caught a cold.'

'I wish to have you to myself just for a minute,' Miss Preston said, stepping in closer. 'I am so pleased you could come to our intimate little dinner party.'

He didn't say he'd been left little choice. Of course he could have refused—he was a duke, even the rudest of behaviour would eventually be excused—but he had been brought up to be polite and often found it hard to shake the habit even if the results were to his detriment.

'I'm very much looking forward to getting to know you better this Season,' Miss Preston said. 'I hope I'm not alone when I say I feel a spark between us, a special something?'

James tempered his response. He reminded himself she was only eighteen, young and inexperienced in the world. She was trying to force something that wasn't there, buoyed by the attention she had received in her first few weeks as a debutante into thinking her appearance made her irresistible to all men.

'Miss Preston,' James spoke carefully, measuring his words, 'I have no doubt you will receive a multitude of proposals this Season, but I feel it would be irresponsible of me to lead you to think there was something between us.'

He watched as the smile fell from her face, the confusion and hint of anger replacing it slowly, making her look even younger.

'I have no plans to marry and I would hate for you to focus your attention on me when you could be looking at more receptive gentlemen.'

'You have no plans to marry?' Her hand had slipped from his arm and she was shaking her head in disbelief. 'Everyone wishes to marry. Whether it be for companionship or money or advantage. *Everyone* wishes to marry.' Her voice rose on the last few words and James held out a placating hand.

'Not everyone.' It was a lie, of course, but easier than explaining the truth to her. He would want to marry if the right woman came along. The woman who made his heart sing the very first time he laid eyes on her. The woman he was fated to be with. He wasn't even sure if that woman existed, but he did know it was not Miss Preston.

'Yes everyone. You're a duke, you have to produce an heir, or at the very least you should want to.' She looked at him with utter disbelief in her eyes. 'It's her, isn't it? I knew there was something *unsavoury* about your relationship.' She shot a look at where Caroline and the Colonel were standing just inside the doors to the drawing room.

'Don't forget yourself, Miss Preston,' James said, his voice hard. She took an involuntary step back, still looking between him and Caroline, her lips curling.

'You would prefer *her* to me?'

James wanted to tell her that he would prefer almost anyone to her and that she and Caroline were so different they shouldn't be even spoken about in the same sentence, but he knew it would make things worse. He had a feeling Miss Preston had a vindictive nature and although his title and status meant he was untouchable, Caroline was not.

He began walking away, striding briskly to the steps that led back up into the drawing room. Before he reached the door he felt Miss Preston's hand on his arm, pulling him round.

'You would prefer her to me?' she repeated.

He studied her face, saw the anger and entitlement and unpleasantness. 'Yes.'

'But she's—'

James cut Miss Preston off. 'That is quite enough,' he said curtly, walking away. 'Thank you for your hospitality, Lady Whittaker, Lord Whittaker. Unfortunately we are going to have to cut this evening short. Please accept my apologies.' He spoke as soon as he stepped back into the house, walking over to Caroline and taking her by the arm.

'What?' Caroline whispered, but he just shot her a warning glance. There would be plenty of time to explain when they were in the carriage.

'Is something amiss, Your Grace?' Lady Whittaker's face was pale, her eyes darting to where he'd left Miss Preston on the terrace alone.

'Thank you for the invitation,' James said, not waiting to be shown out, instead hurrying down the steps with Caroline by his side. Only once they were in the carriage did he sit back and catch his breath.

'What on earth was that about?' Caroline asked,

her eyes wide as he thumped on the roof and the carriage sped off down the empty street.

'Miss Preston declared her interest in me, I told her it would never happen.'

'Just like that?'

'I didn't see the point in tiptoeing around the subject. It's not as though my feelings are ever going to change.'

Caroline looked at him in disbelief for a moment, then laughed. 'Why the hasty exit?'

'I needed to leave before I said something I couldn't take back.' As he'd stood outside the drawing room door with Miss Preston asking him if he truly preferred Caroline to her, he'd felt angry. Angry at the way the young woman had dismissed Caroline's worth, how many people seemed to dismiss her worth. If he'd stayed, especially if she'd pressed him further on the issue, he would have been overcome with anger.

'She was disparaging about you.'

'She always is.'

'Exactly.'

'I suppose we should be thankful there was no one else outside the family present.' Caroline settled back on her seat, chewing her lip. 'Perhaps they will think it too embarrassing to tell anyone we walked out of a dinner party without even the scantest explanation.'

'She's just a child,' James said out loud—it was the sentence he'd been repeating to himself over and over again.

'What?'

'Miss Preston. If we didn't leave, I would have railed at her and it would have been unfair because she is just a child. An unpleasant child, but a child all the same.'

'She's eighteen.'

'Until a few weeks ago she would have been closeted away at the family estate, listening to the opinions of just a few people, learning to regurgitate them. She hasn't mixed with enough people to form opinions of her own.'

'What did she say to you?'

'She wouldn't believe I would choose you over her.'

'Choose me? You haven't chosen me at all.'

He looked up sharply, trying to see if he could detect a hint of reproach or sadness in her voice, but her expression was neutral, her face giving nothing away.

'She assumed the reason I didn't want her was

because I was in some sort of illicit relationship with you.'

There was silence for ten seconds and then Caroline burst out laughing.

'What's so funny?'

'You do realise that half the *ton* think the same thing? They don't understand our friendship and so they decide to imagine it to be something it's not, even if the idea is ludicrous. We might be careful, James, so there is no scandal, no evidence of bad behaviour, but the gossips like to speculate all the same.'

'Ludicrous?'

She paused, looking at him, her eyes staying fixed on his.

'Ludicrous,' she repeated. He watched as her tongue darted out to moisten her lips and saw the flicker of something she was trying hard to repress in her eyes. She was good, he had to give her that, he could only detect the flash of desire now because he was searching for it. He wondered how long she had been hiding it, how long she'd felt something more than the platonic friendship they'd started with. His own desire for her had been mounting for the past couple of weeks, but he was beginning to suspect Caroline's might have been burning for longer.

The idea made him feel equal parts uncomfortable and surprised. He prided himself on seeing the world as it was, on his observational skills. If he hadn't realised Caroline's true feelings for him, then he was not the man he thought he was.

Without thinking he reached out and trailed a finger down her cheek, feeling the warmth of her velvety-soft skin. He had the sudden notion that he wanted to run his fingers over every inch of her body, to see if the skin was as silky soft everywhere. He could imagine trailing his fingers over her collarbones and then down on to her chest, capturing her breasts in his hands, savouring the moment as he got to know every single part of her.

'Cara…' he began, not knowing what else he wanted to say, but just needing to say her name.

'James.' She looked up at him and he felt the desire swelling inside him and before he could stop himself, he swayed forward and kissed her. His hands came up and laced through her silky hair, pulling her gently in towards him. Her lips were warm and sweet and he wondered why he hadn't done this before, why he didn't spend his whole time kissing Caroline.

She was still for a second and then seemed to melt into him, letting out a little contented sigh. One delicate hand came up to rest on his chest, her fingers gripping his shirt.

He kissed her and kissed her, unable to stop himself, unable to listen to the small voice of reason telling him to pull away. She was receptive in his arms and under his lips and he could think of nothing but how she felt and how she tasted.

With one hand still tangled in her hair, he let the other drop to her cheek, caressing the soft skin. Only when they lurched over a rut in the road did they spring apart, both breathless and wide eyed at what had just happened.

The silence stretched out before them as James tried to wrestle with the urge to take her in his arms again, conscious that a second kiss would tangle his thoughts even more than they were already.

He was just leaning in, unable to resist, when the carriage slowed to a halt and Caroline's eyes widened in surprise as she looked out the window.

'We're home,' she whispered, her hands flying to her messed-up hair.

'I'll tell Tomlinson to take us for a ride around the streets so you have time to fix up your hair,' he said, wondering how sinful it would be to mess it up just a little more first.

His suggestion came too late, with the door to Caroline's house already opening and the footman stepping out to open the door of the carriage. Frantically Caroline began fixing her hair, jabbing the pins in with such ferociousness that he winced in sympathy at the pain. It was the second time this week she was arriving home with her hair messed up because of him. If they weren't careful, someone was going to notice.

When the carriage door swung open she didn't seem as poised and perfect as she had at the beginning of the night, but she at least didn't look as though she had been half-ravaged in the back of the carriage.

Before she stepped down Caroline glanced at him, confusion and a hint of sadness in her eyes. He knew he should say something, should explain or reassure her—anything would be better than this silence—but he found himself lost for words. He didn't know what the kiss meant, he didn't know how he felt about Caroline, didn't even know if this had been a moment of madness or a manifestation of some deeper feelings.

She didn't look back as she disappeared inside the house, leaving James feeling deflated and unsettled.

Chapter Twelve

She hadn't slept a single wink, so it wasn't hard rousing herself before dawn to dress and creep from the house. By the time the clock showed half past five James had not called for her and she had to assume he wasn't going to. Perhaps he had forgotten after the excitement of the night before or perhaps he was trying to stop her from attending the duel by making it harder for her to get there.

She felt guilty about creeping out unaccompanied, but she knew she had to be there. The night before she had written a short note to her mother, explaining she had woken early and gone out for a ride and now she folded this note in half and left it on the little table in the hallway before slipping out through the kitchen to the side passage and to the front of the house that way. Outside, Richard, the young boy her parents employed to run errands and help in the kitchens, was waiting with her horse. She'd asked him yesterday to fetch her horse from the stables where he was kept while they resided in London and have him saddled and waiting for her so she could make a speedy exit. Now all she needed to do was find her way to Hampstead Heath in the dark.

She'd ridden out that way before and knew it would take about an hour with the streets more or less empty and no obstructions. Hampstead Heath was huge in area, but she had discussed the matter with Henrietta, who despite her young years seemed to have much more practical experience than Caroline, and she'd directed her to a spot on the southern edge of the Heath that was popular for duels.

She'd only been riding for five minutes when there was a shout behind her. Caroline felt her heart begin to thump in her chest as she turned and looked, wondering if she should just spur her horse into a gallop to outrun any danger.

Emerging out of the darkness on horseback was a figure clad in an elegant riding habit and hat, her posture perfect and a wide grin on her face.

'You look as though you've seen a ghost,' Henrietta said.

'What are you doing?' Caroline couldn't believe her cousin was out here in the street before dawn.

'Accompanying you.'

'You can't.'

'Of course I can. Mother doesn't rise until at least ten and I've bribed my maid to inform her I went for an early stroll with you when she does emerge. Now we're just two young women out for a civilised ride, nothing scandalous about it, rather than you skulking through the darkness on your own.'

'I wasn't skulking.' Caroline said, unable to take her eyes off Henrietta. 'Who are you?' she murmured. She loved her cousin—despite the six-year difference in their age they had grown close over the last few months—but Caroline was beginning to realise that there were hidden depths to Henrietta. She wasn't like most eighteen-year-olds, at least not the superficial personas they let the others see at social occasions.

'A loving cousin,' Henrietta said with a mischievous smile and nudged her horse forward in the darkness. 'We'd better get moving or the duel will be over before we reach Hampstead.'

'As the older cousin I feel as though I should be doing more to discourage you from attending...'

'Rest assured, nothing you could say will stop me. Now tell me all about what happened to make the Duke leap to the defence of your honour again.'

'He didn't leap,' Caroline muttered, feeling the familiar churning in her stomach that welled up every time she thought of James fighting on her behalf. If he got injured... She shook her head. He was cautious, astute and physically fit, he had the odds on his side.

'Tell me about it anyway.'

'I was out for a ride with Lord Hauxton,' Caroline began, seeing the gleam in her cousin's eyes and knowing she wouldn't get through the story without at least a dozen interruptions.

'Lord Hauxton, he's the one who wants to marry you?'

'He hasn't asked.'

'And he's friends with the Duke?'

'Yes.'

'How wonderfully interwoven.'

'What do you mean?'

'Well, Lord Hauxton is probably going to propose to you.' Henrietta held up a gloved hand to stop Caroline's interruption. 'And he's friends with the Duke, who is the man you *wish* would propose to you.'

'No… I…' Caroline said, but was silenced by a knowing look from Henrietta.

She chewed her lip, wondering if everyone knew her deep, dark secret. A few days ago her mother had told her she knew of Caroline's feelings for James and now it seemed Henrietta knew as well.

'It's nothing to be ashamed of. He is rather dashing, all tall and dark and handsome. And rich. Although he's a little on the old side.'

'He's only forty-one.'

'So you admit it?'

'He's a friend,' Caroline said stubbornly. 'A very good friend.'

'A friend you wish would warm your bed every night.'

'Henrietta,' Caroline said, scandalised. Her cousin shouldn't know of such things. Caroline was sure she'd been much more innocent at eighteen.

'There's no need to pretend otherwise, there's hardly anyone here to overhear us.'

The streets were deserted and they were moving at a good pace through London. Caroline looked about her, aware she was in an area she had only passed through on a couple of occasions, but instead of feeling nervous about the ride she could only feel petrified at the ordeal that was to come.

'Does everyone know?' Caroline queried softly.

'That you're in love with the Duke?' Henrietta shrugged. 'I think everyone assumes you must be, or thinks you're having some sort of scandalous affair, but no one *knows* you've been head over heels in love with him for years.'

'Good.' The idea of people speculating about her feelings made her uncomfortable, but it was better than everyone knowing for certain she was in love with a man who would never love her back.

'Does he know?'

Caroline shook her head. She thought back to the kiss they'd shared the night before, her entire body flushing with warmth at the memory. It had been a moment of madness, one spliced with sheer pleasure. She'd seen the way James had been looking at her the past few days, seen the way his eyes flicked to her lips, the way he'd found innocuous little ways to touch her. She didn't dare hope it meant anything, not anything more than a passing desire anyway.

Liar, she admitted to herself. She did hope. She hoped and dreamed and wished. Five years she'd known James, five years of imagining what it would be like if he took her in his arms and kissed her. Then last night it had happened.

'I think he may suspect,' Caroline said slowly. 'He didn't, until recently, but I think he might have a notion I have deeper feelings for him than I have let on.'

'But he doesn't feel the same way about you?' Henrietta's question was gentle, but it made Caroline shift uncomfortably none the less.

She thought of the desire in his eyes, the look of possessiveness as he'd kissed her She could still feel the softness of his lips on her own as if the kiss had been mere seconds ago, not hours.

Caroline bit her lip before forcing herself to look straight ahead. She wouldn't delude herself into thinking the kiss had been anything more than an outpouring of desire. 'He likes me, cares for me as a friend, but he does not love me.'

'You've loved him for a long time, haven't you?' Caroline was surprised by the empathy in her cousin's voice and wondered when the little scrap of a girl she had run around the gardens with had grown up into a thoughtful and empathetic young woman.

Taking a deep breath, she nodded. It was the first time she'd admitted that she'd been besotted with James since they'd first met, outside of her letters to Georgina. They were cathartic, but suddenly she wished to tell someone who could respond immediately, who could understand how she felt each and every day. 'I've loved him since the day I met him.'

'Perhaps you should tell him. He can't act unless he knows the depth of your feelings.'

'Knowing James, he'd ask me to marry him.'

'Isn't that a good thing?'

'No,' Caroline said emphatically, emphasising her view. 'I don't want him to marry me out of some sort of misplaced sense of obligation.'

'Even if it meant you got to spend every day with the man you loved?'

'I want him to be happy and I think he *could* be happy with me, but what if we married and then he fell in love with someone else? He'd be tied to a woman he didn't love, unable to follow his heart.'

'He's at least forty, it hasn't happened so far,' Henrietta said.

Caroline squared her shoulders. 'I've accepted I need to move on from the Duke. We will be friends and nothing more, just like we always have been.'

'I heard a rumour you've been seen with Lord Hauxton on quite a few occasions.'

'He seems a very nice man.'

'Nice,' Henrietta snorted. '*That's* what young girls dream about when they're looking for a husband.'

'I think nice is underrated. I'm going to have to live with whomever I marry for the rest of my life.'

'I know.' Henrietta sighed heavily.

'What about you? You're eighteen, there must be someone who has caught your eye?'

'No.' Her reply was a little too quick, a little too firm, so immediately Caroline was intrigued. She wondered if it were related to Henrietta's sessions in the artist's studio she went to weekly or if it were another secret altogether.

They rode in silence for a few minutes, Caroline trying to ignore the cold that was permeating through her riding habit. There were swirls of fog in the distance as the buildings thinned and they could see flashes of the countryside beyond.

'Whoever decided to make duels so inconveniently far out of London?' Henrietta murmured as they finally spotted the edge of the Heath.

'I suppose it keeps them out of the public eye.'

'Far less likely to be caught,' Henrietta conceded, 'but awkward to get to so early in the morning.'

'How do you know so much about duelling?' Caroline asked as Henrietta guided them round the edge of the Heath before selecting a path into the interior. Without her cousin she would already be hopelessly lost and probably would be still riding round at midday having long missed the duel.

She shrugged, 'I've been to one or two.'

'One or two? How on earth have you been involved in one or two duels?'

'Sometimes I socialise with a slightly volatile group of people.'

'So is it one or two?'

'Four.'

'Four?'

Henrietta nodded.

'These are artists, aren't they?'

'How do you know that?'

'I saw you go into that house the other day, the one where you hire the room for an hour and paint.'

Henrietta looked at her suspiciously. 'You followed me?'

'No. Well, yes. But I was worried about you.' She hadn't wanted to tell her cousin she knew her secret like this, she'd hoped Henrietta would confide in her and there would be no need to reveal she'd followed her.

Henrietta cocked her head to one side for a moment as if weighing up whether to be angry, then she smiled. 'Do you know, I've been going there to paint for almost a year and you're the only person ever to find out.'

'Why *do* you go there to paint? Surely you could paint at home—your mother would encourage it.'

'Watercolours, paintings of flowers or scenery or perhaps a tame little portrait.' Henrietta wrinkled her nose up with disgust.

'What do you paint?' Caroline heard the hint of unease in her own voice.

'Life. Real life.' There was a shine to her eyes

that Caroline had never seen before and it made her yearn for something of her own. Henrietta was passionate about her painting, she continued even if doing so meant risking her reputation. It must be rewarding to have something like that.

Caroline was just about to ask more about it when Henrietta pointed through the darkness to a huddle of figures half-camouflaged by the trees. Cautiously they turned their horses towards the group, wanting to be sure it was James before they alerted the men to their presence. Any stranger out here could be up to no good and Caroline didn't fancy getting in their way.

As they rode closer Caroline felt some of the tension seep from her shoulders as she recognised James and Lord Hauxton standing shoulder to shoulder. Both men were frowning deeply at her as she approached, although it was James who moved first.

'What the devil do you think you're doing here?'

'I told you I would come.'

'I didn't think you would be so foolish when it came to it.'

'Nor I you,' she said coolly.

'I told you last night I have no choice.'

'Of course you do. It just happens not to be a choice you wish to take.' Caroline looked around, noting the first streaks of dawn appearing on the horizon. It was quiet on the Heath, eerily so, with the only noise coming from the uneasy shifting of her horse. 'He's not here.'

'I wouldn't celebrate just yet. West is notorious for being late.'

Caroline peered out at the rolling hills of the Heath, trying to make out anyone approaching through the pale light. She knew she should go over and greet Lord Hauxton properly, but the nerves in her stomach were making her tense and she felt as though she were frozen in place.

'Miss Yaxley.' Lord Hauxton approached, saving her from having to move. 'You're here.'

'Yes.'

'I would never presume to tell you what you should and shouldn't do...' he said with a soft smile. 'But should you really be here?'

Grimacing, she shook her head. 'I hoped I might help you all to come to a peaceful conclusion.' In truth, she wasn't so vain to think she could influence these three men when they seemed so set on this path, but she'd needed to be here, to see everything unfold with her own eyes all the same.

'He's here,' Henrietta said from her position behind Caroline.

Everyone turned, watching West approach with another man riding alongside him.

'He's brought a second,' Milton said flatly. 'But no doctor.'

West halted fifty feet away, the other gentleman continuing on without him.

'Good morning, Your Grace, Lord Hauxton.' He nodded to each of them in turn, pausing with a frown as he took in Caroline and Henrietta. 'Mr Harcourt.'

Mr Harcourt cleared his throat a couple of times, looking uneasily at the two men.

'I was hoping there might be a way to settle this amicably.' He spoke softly, his accent a barely audible lilt of the west country smothered by aristocratic tones.

'West wants that?'

Caroline felt her hopes begin to rise and felt her hand grip hold of the reins even tighter as she waited for Mr Harcourt's answer.

Mr Harcourt grimaced. 'Lord West has not stopped drinking since demanding this duel.'

There was a moment of silence as they all regarded the man standing in the distance, then Caroline heard herself gasp as she saw the pistol he was brandishing in his hand.

'Enough.' James strode up the hill towards West, his shoulders squared and gait stiff, as if ready for battle.

It took Caroline a few seconds to realise he was actually going to walk up to a man wielding a pistol and confront him. She watched in amazement before coming to her senses and slipping out of the saddle. She had to stop him, she had to save him.

As she made to run after James she felt a firm hand on her arm.

'Let him go,' Milton said. 'He's got a sensible head and quick reflexes, I doubt an inebriated West will even get the chance to wave his pistol in Heydon's direction. Besides, you'll just distract them.'

Caroline knew he was right, but almost carried on up the hill anyway. It went against her nature to stay still and do nothing, so she found herself shifting from foot to foot.

As James stopped a few feet away from West, Caroline took a deep breath in and held it. Without even realising she was doing it she began making silent bargains for James's safety.

If he comes through this unscathed, I'll do more for charity. If James lives, I'll be a better daughter. If he survives, I'll tell him how I feel.

Henrietta had slipped from her horse, too, and was now standing beside Caroline and silently she gripped her cousin's hand in support. Despite Lord Hauxton's words a nervous energy radiated from him and his gaze hadn't left his two friends across the Heath.

They were too far away to hear what James was saying, but the careless wave of the pistol in West's hand made all four of them gasp with fear of the sound of the shot that might follow. Instead James took a step towards his friend, and then another, and to Caroline's surprise he held out his arms, with West collapsing into them.

Her eyes still didn't leave the pistol in West's hand, not until she saw James take it from the sobbing man and throw it into the undergrowth a few feet away.

With a glance at Lord Hauxton, who nodded in

agreement, they hurried across the Heath, Henrietta and Mr Harcourt trailing behind. When they reached James, West was still sobbing, his head buried in James's shoulder.

'I'm so sorry,' he kept repeating, the words slurring into each other. 'I'm so sorry.'

James motioned for Harcourt to approach and Caroline strained to hear the soft words he said to the man before handing West over to him, no doubt to make sure he got home safely.

'What did you say?' Caroline had waited until West was out of earshot to pose the question, but she couldn't wait any longer.

James let out a long exhalation and she could see the lines of tension on his face. His demeanour might have been calm, but she could tell the whole predicament had shaken him.

'I reminded him of our friendship and asked him what was really troubling him.'

Caroline blinked. She'd imagined something much more profound, although it had undeniably had the desired effect. Neither James nor Milton had needed to face their friend in a duel and no one had got hurt.

'He's had a bad few weeks. His wife…' James

trailed off. 'Suffice it to say he has not been thinking clearly. He apologised for what he said about you and will come and see you to apologise in person when he has himself straightened out.'

'I'm just glad no one was hurt.'

Caroline caught Henrietta's glance in her direction and realised she was standing far too close to James for propriety and the hand she had laid on his forearm was too familiar.

'Shall we return to London?' Henrietta prompted, a note of forced jollity in her voice. 'Lord Hauxton, perhaps you'd be so kind as to help me mount my horse.'

'We shall follow,' James called after them as Henrietta steered Lord Hauxton towards the horses.

For a moment they stood in silence, the enormity of everything they needed to talk about gaping out in front of them. James took a step towards her and for one wonderful second Caroline thought he was about to take her in his arms and kiss her, out here in the open, declaring to the world that she was the woman he wanted to be with, the woman he couldn't keep his hands off. Then he hesitated, ran a hand over his face and looked away across the Heath to where their horses were tied.

Chapter Thirteen

'It seems you had a wasted trip,' James said quietly. He had the urge to reach out and tuck the stray strands of hair back behind her ears, but instead balled his hands into fists to stop them from moving.

He didn't like feeling so uneasy with Caroline, so off balance. She was the one person in the world he always felt at ease with, the one person he felt as though he did not need to stand on ceremony with. And now as he looked at her, he was lost for words.

'Not wasted. I'm glad there was no duel. It was a foolish challenge and this is a far better ending than anyone getting shot and maimed. What did you really say to make him change his mind?'

'Nothing really. I reminded him of our friendship, of the man he truly was. He broke down into tears.' James shrugged. 'His wife is having an affair and he is finding the revelation hard to cope with. He moans about her all the time, but I think he really loves her.'

'No wonder he's in such a state.'

'Still no excuse for what he said to you.'

It was Caroline's turn to shrug. She was not like many young ladies who would revel in the drama swirling around her. Caroline preferred the quiet life, the easy path.

He swallowed, knowing he was going to have to address the awkwardness that hung between them. The problem was he didn't know what to say. He couldn't tell her the kiss had been a mistake because he'd enjoyed every single second of it and was finding it hard not to reach out and pull her in to another embrace every moment they spent together.

He couldn't bring himself to do the right thing either. No one had seen the kiss, no one suspected they'd crossed over the line between friendship and scandal, but he knew. And he was *supposed* to be a gentleman. By rights he should be taking her by the hand and asking her to marry him.

'We should get back,' Caroline said, narrowing her eyes as she watched Henrietta and Milton ride into the distance. 'I'm going to be in enough trouble as it is.'

'Just one more minute, then I'll escort you home,' James said, dropping his voice low.

Caroline's eyes flicked up to meet his and he saw confusion and the hastily concealed flash of hope. If he was any kind of man, any kind of friend…

'Last night,' he said, clearing his throat.

She looked at him, her face blank, waiting for him to continue. She wasn't about to make this easy for him, to step in with a gush of reassurance that they needn't think about it again.

'In the carriage…'

Caroline nodded slowly. 'We kissed.'

'We did.'

'People do kiss,' she said softly.

'They do.' His eyes darted down to her lips, impossibly rosy and inviting, and he found himself thinking of kissing her again. 'All the time.'

She shivered and he took advantage of the moment to step in closer and place a hand on her back, conveying some of his body heat to her—it felt as though he had enough to share.

'Sometimes when two people are close it can be difficult to see the boundaries between what is acceptable and what is not,' he said in a speech that he'd rehearsed in his head. It sounded a lot less impressive out loud.

'What is not acceptable, James?' Her voice caught in her throat.

'Two friends, two platonic friends, probably shouldn't kiss.'

'Probably not,' she agreed, never taking her eyes from his. They were impossibly blue and lovely, the centre just next to the pupil a touch darker than the rest. They were eyes he'd spent many hours looking at—how was it he hadn't been captivated before now?

'I should probably apologise.' He didn't want to apologise, didn't want to say it had been wrong when it had felt right.

'Please don't apologise.' Caroline reached out hesitantly with a gloved hand, laying her fingers gently on his chest. 'In that moment, for a few seconds it felt right. I felt it and you felt it. There is nothing wrong with that.'

'You are an extraordinary woman, Cara.' Many women would be demanding he do the right thing and marry her or would be cold and indignant. Caroline, as usual, had made things easy for him, had acknowledged the kiss, but shown him it wasn't something they needed to change their friendship over.

It has changed, though. He rubbed his forehead, trying to dislodge the thought, but couldn't. He would never be able to forget that single second when Caroline's façade had slipped and he'd seen the years of longing hiding underneath. And he would never be able to forget how she'd felt as he'd held her in his arms, how she had fitted perfectly against him. No, nothing would ever be the same again, no matter how hard they tried.

'We really should get back,' she said, dropping her hand from his chest and stepping away, breaking the invisible rope that was pulling them together. He should have let her go, should have just watched her walk away to her horse, but instead he caught hold of her hand as she turned and pulled her firmly back to his body.

'One more won't make a difference,' he murmured, more to himself than her as he lowered his lips on to hers. For an instant she was stiff under him, unyielding, then he felt her relax just as he was about to pull away. He brushed his lips against hers again, tasted the sweetness and heard a low groan escape him as she pushed in closer.

Under his hands her body felt just right, her skin satiny soft, her hair silky smooth. He had visions of tumbling her down in the undergrowth, not caring about the dampness of the earth or the leaves that would stick to them. He just wanted to feel her body writhe underneath him, to touch where he'd never been allowed to touch before.

Unable to stop them, he felt his hands rise and caress her back, the bare skin of her neck, her shoulders, then one hand dropped down to her breast and he felt her shudder.

'James,' she whispered as he pulled away just a fraction. It was a plea, an entreaty, to carry on and he knew he could not refuse her. Still kissing, they sank down, James feeling the wet grass beneath his knees, but was too far gone to care. Caroline's arms snaked around him, pulling him back, and she laid on the ground, then they were in the position he'd been dreaming of these last few weeks, her body warm underneath him, inviting him in.

It would be so easy to take what he wanted, what they both wanted, to strip her bare in the cool morning air and explore her body. He knew they would both enjoy it, the desire that had been simmering between them was a testament to that, but would they regret it?

He kissed her, a gentle kiss on the lips that was achingly tender. If they went any further, he'd have to marry her. Searching for some response in himself to that thought, he pulled away just a fraction.

'James, we need to stop,' Caroline said softly but firmly, wriggling out from underneath him. Her face was a mask, her expression serene, but he knew she was hiding her true emotions. 'We can't do any more, not here.' She paused, closing her eyes before continuing, 'Not ever.'

'Caroline, I…'

It was a relief when she interrupted him as he didn't know what to say. His body screamed for him to brush away her protestations, to kiss her again until she realised they were *meant* to be together, that their bodies were incomplete without one another, but there was that little nagging doubt, and he knew that was no way to treat his best friend, his Cara.

'I think I need to get home.' She scrambled to her feet, brushing the mud and grass off her riding habit with a grimace, turning away as she picked leaves off her skirt. She was quick, but not quick enough to hide the tears in her eyes.

In that moment he hated himself, hated that he couldn't be the man she wanted, the man she deserved. Caroline deserved the very best to adore her, to worship her, not a man who couldn't even propose after he'd almost ravished her.

'Marry me, Caroline,' he said, blurting the words out.

That made her stiffen, frozen to the spot, a long thirty seconds passing before she turned to him.

'Don't,' she said, her voice taut with anger. 'Don't ask that when you don't mean it.'

'Of course I—'

'No. You don't.'

He reached out for her, but she backed away, the tears streaming down her face.

'Caroline, I never want to hurt you.'

She looked at him without speaking for a long moment, then turned and fled. He was so stunned that at first he didn't move and she was already halfway back to the horses by the time he started to sprint after her. He marvelled at how she vaulted into the saddle, using the branch of the tree to help her up, then cursed as she started to gallop away before he had even reached his own horse.

'Caroline,' he shouted, mounting in one fluid movement. It would only take one stumble, one spot of uneven ground, and she would be hurtled from the saddle and at this speed would likely break her neck.

Even with his body bent low over Nelson's neck and his heels urging more and more speed from the horse, he didn't catch Caroline up until they were almost back at her house and the morning crowds in the street forced her to slow her pace.

'Wait,' he called as he came up beside her.

She'd stopped crying, but there was an unmistakable pink tinge to her eyes and her hair was flying wildly behind her. He couldn't deliver her home like this, but more importantly he couldn't leave things between them like this.

'James,' she said, drawing in a long breath, making her voice judder as she said his name. 'I think it would be for the best if we didn't see each other for a little while.'

'No.'

'I can't do this.' The tears were back in her eyes and all he wanted to do was reach out and embrace her. He almost didn't recognise the sad, stiff woman in the saddle and he hated that he was the reason for her distress.

'Caroline...'

She shook her head. 'I can't do this, James. Please. If you care for me, just leave me alone, just for a little while.'

He almost protested again, but saw the sincerity in her eyes and nodded. 'If that is what you want.'

'It is.'

She urged her horse on suddenly, leaving him behind once again, but this time he didn't try to catch up, instead following her at a distance of fifty feet, ensuring she got home safely.

'You're a fool, Heydon,' he muttered to himself.

Chapter Fourteen

Caroline glanced in the mirror in the grand entrance hall and grimaced, wishing she hadn't caught the reflection of herself. She looked gaunt, drawn, and even the little touch of rouge her mother had rubbed into her cheeks before they'd left the house didn't do anything to make her look any more appealing.

'We can go home at any time,' her mother whispered, squeezing Caroline's arm. On the other side Henrietta stood, glaring at anyone who approached, her way of showing solidarity with her cousin.

'Thank you.'

It had been a week since the duel that had never happened, a week since the kiss on the Heath. A week since James had oh, so casually asked her to marry him. She'd spent the week shut up in her room, pleading a multitude of ailments that her mother hadn't questioned too closely. Caroline knew her mother suspected something less physical was the cause of her seclusion, but she had left Caroline to it without too many questions.

Part of her wished she was still in her bedroom now, huddled under the covers and pretending the outside world didn't exist. In the end, though, being alone with her thoughts had felt like self-imposed torture as she analysed every moment of their relationship since she'd met James five years ago.

'Lord Hauxton dropped a note in saying he would be in attendance tonight,' her mother said quietly and Caroline could see her eyes flitting over the other guests as she searched for the man she hoped her daughter would marry.

Lord Hauxton. The real reason she'd hauled herself up out of bed and put on the pretty lavender dress and let her maid pull and clip her hair into a fancy style. He'd sent a note each day enquiring about her health, after she had let it be known she had caught a chill. He was quietly persistent without being pushy.

You need to move on, she'd told herself so many times, and now here she was doing just that. Moving on with her life, past James, and grasping the future with both hands. Lord Hauxton was her future.

Her mother gave her one last final hug and then headed off into the crowd of guests, leaving Caroline and Henrietta together. A second later Miss Preston appeared, her expression serene, looking radiant as always.

'Miss Yaxley, Miss Harvey, how thrilling you are here tonight.' It was over-effusive, even when said with a hint of sarcasm, and Caroline felt a wave of nervousness roll over her. She and James had walked out of an intimate dinner party with her family with no good excuse and that had been after James had rebuffed Miss Preston's advances in the garden. She wasn't naive enough to think Miss Preston would let the matter go, she was too petty for that.

'Miss Preston, I trust you are well.'

'Very well, thank you. Very well indeed.' She could almost see the evil grin on the young woman's face. 'I'm sure I will see you throughout the evening.'

Caroline smiled weakly, wondering how she had been unfortunate enough to garner the attention of the most vindictive debutante of the Season.

They watched her glide away and Caroline could tell Henrietta was pulling a face without even looking sideways.

'Is it compulsory to be that horrible if you're that beautiful?'

Caroline laughed. 'It does always seem to be the attractive ones.'

They strolled arm in arm around the periphery of the ballroom, watching the couples in the centre dance a waltz, mesmerised by the movement and the music. By the time they had reached the far end of the ballroom the dance was just coming to an end and the couples beginning to step away from one another, creating a little swell of a crowd. Perhaps that was why she didn't see him coming.

'Miss Yaxley,' James said, bending into a low bow, before greeting Henrietta. It was Caroline's eyes he held though, Caroline he lingered over.

'Your Grace.'

She might have thought the intervening week had strengthened her resolve, but one look into his dark eyes and she felt all the familiar hopes and dreams come rushing back.

'I hoped I might see you here tonight,' he said quietly.

'I'll just...' Henrietta didn't even bother to finish the sentence, instead slipping away and leaving them alone in the corner of the ballroom.

'I was worried about you after...' he paused for a moment as if searching for the right words '...after Hampstead Heath.'

'I caught a chill, nothing more. I'm much better now.'

'Nonsense,' he said, leaning in so no one would overhear him. 'You're more robust than that, Cara.'

She glanced up at him. That was a mistake. His eyes were filled with warmth and concern and she could feel herself slipping back into her old role as his best friend, secretly hiding her love.

'You're right. I needed some time to myself.'

'And did it help?'

She shrugged. Her emotions had been all over the place, her resolve swinging from deciding she would move on and accept another man's proposal and never see James again to worrying she would be lost without his friendship.

'I never knew I was so indecisive,' she said.

'Is there a decision to make?'

She didn't answer.

'I meant it last week, Cara,' he said, his voice low so no one else could hear, 'when I asked you to marry me.'

'Stop it,' she muttered, glancing around. She placed a hand on his chest and physically pushed him away from her, albeit gently. It was too much, here in the crowded ballroom, and she needed him to stop confusing her.

'Cara, wait a moment.' He caught her by the hand and she breathed deeply before turning back to him.

'You don't love me, James,' she said quietly, holding his eyes so he knew how serious her words are. 'You don't love me and you are a man who believes in love. What sort of a friend would I be if I agreed to marry you, when the woman you love could be making her way into your life as we speak?'

She reached out and laid a hand on his arm, then forced herself to take a step away.

'These past few weeks have been…hard. I care for you, I value our friendship, but I think I stand by what I said last week. I need some time apart from you, some time to build my own life.'

'I don't understand.' James's expression was

serious and Caroline had to resist the urge to reach out and smooth the frown lines between his eyes.

'No, you probably don't. But will you do it for me?'

He was silent for a long moment and then gave a single nod. Reaching out, he took her hand in his and then raised it to his lips and placed a kiss just below her knuckles.

'I'll be here for you whenever you need me,' he said quietly.

Caroline forced herself to turn and walk away, feeling her heart squeeze inside. She was walking away from the man she loved, after he'd asked her to marry him for the second time. Perhaps she was the biggest fool in the world.

'Cara, wait,' James called after her.

She spun, almost knocking into him he'd come up so quickly behind her.

'One last dance.' He looked at her with such a serious expression she knew she could not refuse. 'One last dance and then I will fade away.'

As he spoke, the first notes of a waltz were played by the quartet of musicians and Caroline knew she could not refuse him. One last dance, one last farewell, then she would put James and all the hopes and dreams she'd wished for over the years from her mind.

'One dance,' she agreed, holding out her hand. Even through her satin gloves she could feel the warmth of his hand, the strength of his fingers as he led her to an empty spot on the dance floor, and she felt her movements become fluid and easy. No matter what else passed between then they still had their history. The hundreds of dances they'd danced together, the thousands of hours spent in one another's company.

'Close your eyes,' James murmured to her, holding her firmly, just the correct distance from his body. She did, allowing her own to sway to the music and placing herself entirely in his hands as they danced. Her feet responded to even the lightest pressure on her waist by James, allowing him to change her direction and spin her past the other dancers. Caroline felt a peculiar calm as they moved, they were in complete harmony, bothered by no one else and focused entirely on the pleasure of the dance.

'Tell me we don't work well together,' James said as the last notes of the waltz sounded and Caroline let her eyes flicker open.

'We work well together,' she admitted.

'You won't stay away too long?'

Caroline swallowed hard, trying to keep her composure. She didn't want to spend any time away from James, not a single second, but if anything, their dance had shown her how necessary it was for her to get a little distance. When he was near he was all she could think about, all she could feel. If she was ever going to move on with her life she needed to be able to think clearly.

'Not too long.' She smiled sadly at him, then with a heavy heart turned and walked away.

There wasn't a lot of point in him staying much longer. The only reason he'd come tonight to the Deveauxs' ball was to see Caroline and now she had requested he give her some time away from him. That was like a spear to the heart, piercing and painful, and he'd almost called out as she'd walked away from him.

Instead he'd let her go, not knowing if he was a fool or a gentleman for respecting her request. The last half an hour he'd circled the periphery of the ball, fending off any attempts to engage him in conversation and instead keeping Caroline in his sights, albeit at a distance.

He felt hollow inside, as if he'd just lost part of

himself. When she'd asked him for some space a week earlier he thought it would be temporary, but today he got the impression she was saying goodbye and that hurt more than he could have ever imagined.

This past half an hour he'd watched her socialise, although he could tell the customary spark was missing from her eyes. She'd danced with one young gentleman, but hardly conversed with him throughout the reel, and she'd spent much of her time staring blankly into the distance as if lost in her own thoughts.

Now, though, he felt a stab of jealousy as her face lit up as Milton entered, making straight for her, taking her hand and kissing it before smiling a familiar greeting to Lady Yaxley. She was pleased to see him and James had to admit to himself that it rankled. *He* was the one who made her laugh and made her smile, who she wrote to when he was away and who she arranged her day around when he returned.

Reminding himself jealousy was not a noble emotion, he watched the interaction between Caroline and his friend, trying to feel pleased when she smiled at something Milton said or he laughed at one of her observations. After a minute he turned away in frustration. Tonight had not gone well, perhaps it was time to slip away and go and have a quiet drink at his club instead.

'I hear congratulations are in order, Your Grace,' Mr Deveaux said as he almost barrelled into James.

'Congratulations?'

'The rumour is you've finally decided to settle down and get yourself a wife.'

'What rumour?' James felt a cold dread seize hold of him. Surely no one could have overheard the whispered proposal in the corner of the ballroom. And if they had they couldn't have mistaken Caroline's 'no' for anything worth celebrating.

'You and Miss Yaxley. Congratulations.' Mr Deveaux thumped him on the back and then walked away, leaving James staring after him with his mouth open.

Other guests were looking at him, most smiling in that way people had when they thought you were in receipt of happy news.

With a growl of frustration he turned back to where Caroline had been a moment before and strode across the ballroom.

'We have a problem,' he said, not even taking the time to greet Milton.

Caroline blinked a few times as if she couldn't quite believe what she was seeing.

'Good evening,' Milton said pointedly.

'No time for that. We have a problem.'

'What?'

'There is a rumour...' He swallowed, glancing between Caroline and his friend. 'A rumour that I am engaged.'

'To whom?'

'Congratulations,' Lady Whittaker almost shouted as she glided over. 'Shall we toast the happy couple?'

Caroline's eyes widened and James saw the colour drain from her face. People were turning towards them, their eyes flitting between Caroline, him and Milton, smiles fixed to their faces.

Shaking her head, Caroline locked eyes with him, as if pleading with him to do something. He gave her a half-smile. He would do anything for her, anything to save her from this embarrassment, if only he knew what.

'Oh, I'm so happy for you, dear, what a wonderful announcement,' someone else said, resting their hand on Caroline's arm.

'What wonderful news.'

'It'll be the wedding of the year.'

Caroline was now a sickly green colour and her breathing rapid and shallow. He wanted to reach out to embrace her, but that would only make matters worse.

Milton was studying him, eyes narrowed ever so slightly, a protective hand on Caroline's back.

Almost imperceptibly James shook his head.

'Please,' James said, raising his voice to be heard over the dozen people gathered round offering their empty congratulations. 'Ladies and gentlemen, there has been a mistake.'

He couldn't say they weren't getting married, it would seem like a rejection of Caroline, a statement that he didn't think her good enough. Perhaps he could make light of it, say he had offered, but she had turned him down. If only he could know what would be best for her.

'Indeed there has,' Milton spoke up. 'Miss Yaxley has indeed received proposals this Season…' he smiled at her, making it clear to the crowd that he was one of the gentlemen who had proposed '…and as is a woman's prerogative she is taking some time to consider her options.'

'Whoever she chooses will be a very lucky man,' James added.

A murmur went through the crowd, excited and almost disbelieving. They would be the subject of gossip at the breakfast table for weeks to come, at least until some foolish debutante got caught doing something she shouldn't.

Caroline summoned a smile to her face, but anyone who knew her would be able to tell it was forced. She took Milton's arm and together they hurried away from the crowd, away from the watching eyes. Away from him.

Chapter Fifteen

'That wasn't how I hoped to ask you,' Lord Hauxton said as they stood together at the very end of the terrace. A lantern was burning bright a few feet away, but their distance from the house meant they were still in semi-darkness.

Caroline looked at him, not comprehending for a moment. So much had happened in the last few minutes that she felt as though her mind was still racing to catch up.

Lord Hauxton stepped closer, angling his body so he shielded her from the view of anyone watching from the ballroom.

'To marry me. That wasn't how I hoped to do it.' He smiled at her and Caroline felt a warmth towards him. It wasn't the same burning heat she felt for James, but perhaps that wasn't a bad thing. At least she could think rationally when Lord Hauxton was around. 'I'm quite a traditionalist, I had hoped to speak to your father and then take you somewhere pleasant to propose, but I was forced to show my hand early.'

Damn Miss Preston and her rumours. Caroline knew it had to be her, no one else would be as cruel to spread gossip about a fake engagement between her and James. If Lord Hauxton hadn't stepped in, they both would have been humiliated.

'Thank you,' she said quietly. 'You didn't have to do that. I appreciate it. You're a kind man, Lord Hauxton.'

'I saw your face when you realised what people were saying.'

Caroline dreaded to think what her expression must have been. She'd felt as though the ground were shifting and breaking beneath her feet. To hear people congratulate her on an engagement to James was like having someone read her most private thoughts and then shout them out to the world.

'I think it was Miss Preston's doing,' she said quietly. 'She does not like me and the Duke rebuffed her advances last week. I'm sure this was her petty revenge.'

'To humiliate you both with a story of an engagement that you would then have to deny?' He was watching her carefully and Caroline wondered how much he had guessed. Lord Hauxton was an astute man and he'd seen her and James together on a number of occasions. The whole of society wondered about their relationship, but Lord Hauxton had seen their interactions first hand.

'Exactly.'

'Heydon looked as though he were ready to jump in there and defend your honour. To propose himself.'

Caroline nodded. 'He's a good friend and it wouldn't sit well with him—the idea I was targeted because he rebuffed Miss Preston a little too harshly.'

Milton nodded, then took another step closer, reaching out and gripping her hand in his.

'I know our acquaintance has only been brief,' he said quietly, 'but I think we would be well suited. I think I could make you happy and I know how important that is in a marriage.' He paused, giving her hand a little squeeze. 'I know it is a big decision. Take a few days to think it through.'

She searched his face, but couldn't see anything but kindness there. Not for the first time she wished she felt something more for this man. He was generous and good and selfless and she wished she could throw her arms around his neck and declare she would marry him without any hesitation. Instead this would be a practical decision, one made with her head and not her heart, and a little part of her felt as though Lord Hauxton deserved more than that, he deserved more than a wife who was in love with someone else.

'It is a big decision, although I have enjoyed the time we've spent together so far. I will not lie and say this wasn't where I hoped our acquaintance might lead.' It wasn't a yes, but it was an indication of her final answer. She might be foolish in matters of the heart, but underneath it all she was a sensible woman and the sensible decision here would be to marry Lord Hauxton. He was exactly the kind of husband she had hoped for when she had decided to settled down and marry a few weeks ago.

He leaned forward and brushed a kiss on her cheek, delicate and unassuming. Immediately Caroline thought of James, of the passion-filled kisses they'd shared. Quickly she pushed the thought away. It was Lord Hauxton out here on the terrace with her. Lord Hauxton who was offering her a future. Lord Hauxton who truly wanted to marry her.

'I should return you to the ball, unless you would rather I arrange for your carriage to take you straight home?'

Caroline considered. She didn't wish to hear the whispered speculation about her or see the furtive glances as everyone talked about the multiple proposals she was apparently considering. People would talk whether she was in attendance or not and perhaps it was time to be kind to herself and retreat home.

'I think I will go home,' she said after a moment.

'Very well. I will ask for your carriage to be brought round. Will your mother accompany you?'

Caroline hesitated. Her mother was chaperoning Henrietta tonight, so unless Caroline dragged her cousin from the ball, too, it would be impossible for her mother to accompany her home. Besides, a little peace wouldn't be a bad thing. She had a proposal to consider.

They walked back through the ballroom together and Caroline felt all eyes on them. It made her glad of her decision to return home and she wondered if perhaps she might eschew social occasions until she had given Lord Hauxton his answer.

Only once she was safely ensconced in her carriage did she relax, forcing herself to think of something other than the two men who had been occupying all her thoughts these last few weeks.

Chapter Sixteen

James knew she wouldn't be strolling through Hyde Park in the early afternoon, but he still went anyway. He might not understand her request for space, but he was trying his very hardest to respect it. He hadn't been to her parents' town house, hadn't attended the social events he knew she was meant to be going to, but he couldn't seem to stop himself from heading into Hyde Park every afternoon *just in case.*

If he came across Caroline in the park, he would know it was because she wanted to see him.

Four days and there had been no sign of her. Either Bertie was going crazy being shut up in the house for so long, or Caroline had found another spot to walk her beloved hound.

He'd just crossed one of the bridges over the Serpentine when he heard a familiar excited bark. Unable to stop the smile from spreading across his lips, he spun, the smile falling when he saw Lady Yaxley struggling with the excitable dog.

'It would seem you have an admirer,' she said as Bertie jumped up and started trying to lick his face.

James crouched, taking time to give the dog a rub behind the ears and down his back, rewarded by the powerful thump of his tail as he crowded in closer.

'You thought I was Caroline,' Lady Yaxley observed quietly when James finally stood back up. 'She doesn't often let anyone else walk Bertie.'

'True.'

'And she does frequent Hyde Park around this time most days.'

'I know.'

James looked at Lady Yaxley, wondering if she had chosen this time and this spot to walk Bertie, knowing she would run into him.

'Walk with me, Your Grace. I find Bertie is more tiring than I had imagined.' She handed him the lead and James felt the familiar weight and tug as Bertie lolloped along next to them.

'Is Caroline well?' He spoke quickly, unable to stop himself.

'She is, thank you for asking. And you, are you well?' Lady Yaxley fixed him with her penetrating stare that James could imagine had wrestled many secrets from her daughter in her youth. Her eyes were the same brilliant blue as Caroline's and just as intense.

'Yes, thank you.'

'I must confess I worry about you, Your Grace.'

'You worry about me?' James almost stumbled he was so surprised. His own parents had passed away years ago and he had no immediate family. No one to worry about him apart from the closest of his friends.

'Of course I do.' She was smiling at him in a motherly way. 'You've been in our lives for a long time, Your Grace, and I see you as part of the family.'

He felt a flush of guilt. She wouldn't be saying this if she knew how badly he'd treated Caroline. If she knew about the kisses and the inappropriate thoughts he couldn't stop himself from having.

'That's very kind.'

'I hope you will understand then why I am worried about you.'

Bertie tugged on the lead, but James barely registered. Lady Yaxley's expression was entirely serious, her forehead creased into a frown and her eyes troubled.

'I'm sure you're aware of Caroline's new resolve to find herself a husband.'

He murmured something indecipherable, waiting for Lady Yaxley to continue, to show where she was going with this.

'She is getting older and I think she realised she wanted a family, and a husband to share her life with. Even if it meant eschewing the idea of marrying for love.' Lady Yaxley patted his hand and he wondered how much she knew. She was an astute woman and Caroline had always said it was hard to keep anything from her mother.

'It is an understandable sentiment,' James said quietly.

'One that I am led to believe you don't share?'

He cleared his throat. He wasn't used to discussing affairs of the heart, even theoretical ones, with anyone, let alone the mother of the woman he was rather messily entangled with.

Lady Yaxley paused, waiting for him to turn

and meet her eye. 'Caroline tells me your parents were blessed to fall in love at first sight, to know immediately they were destined to be together.'

'They were very happy together.'

'I'm sure they were. Just as Lord Yaxley and I are very happy together. Our marriage was arranged and, when I first met Lord Yaxley, I could hardly stand to be in the same room as him.' She smiled, a smile filled with genuine warmth. 'He grew on me over time and now I would be lost without him. He's my constant, my partner, my love.'

James didn't know Lord Yaxley as well as his wife as the older man didn't often come to London for the whole Season, preferring the quiet of the estate in Hampshire, but on the occasions that he'd met him he'd been pleasant and warm in manner. He'd always thought Lord and Lady Yaxley well suited.

'There's a lot of different sorts of love in the world, Your Grace. The slow-building, slow-burning kind and the lightning strike of instant infatuation. Both are equally valid and I would hate to think of you missing out on love because you were holding out for just one specific type, when another could be even more rewarding.'

He opened his mouth to reply, to say something, but no sound came out. Lady Yaxley was looking at him with a sadness in her eyes that cut into him. He believed she really did want him to be happy, to find love.

Bertie barked, pulling on the lead, and even with his strength James was tugged forward. He took a couple of steps, glad of the distraction. Of course he wanted love, he wanted it more than most men he met. Most were perfectly content with marrying a woman they barely knew for money or advantage or because they thought she would make an adequate wife. He actually wanted love, wanted that heart-clenching, head-spinning emotion his parents had talked of.

'I don't want you to be lonely when Caroline is gone,' Lady Yaxley said as she caught up with him. 'Things will change, of course they will. I'm sure you and Caroline will still be close, but she will have a husband, eventually a family. I like to think perhaps the same would suit you.'

'I'm certainly not against the idea of settling down.'

'You're just waiting for the right person.' Lady Yaxley suppressed a sigh. It was refreshing to have someone talk to him so openly and honestly even if it was a little uncomfortable. Caroline did, but most others were too aware of his status and his influence to tell him what they really thought. 'Lord Hauxton has proposed to Caroline,' she said, changing the direction of the conversation.

He felt Bertie's lead slipping through his fingers and only his quick reflexes saved him from having to chase the lively dog into the Serpentine.

'That's good,' he said, his voice betraying the lie. Even to his own ears it sounded forced and untrue.

'She hasn't accepted yet. Apparently he told her to take a few days to consider things, was quite insistent. I suppose he wants to make sure she is completely decided.'

It seemed as though his own proposal hadn't been discussed with Lady Yaxley.

'Lord Hauxton is a good man.'

'So I am told.'

'You think she will accept?'

Lady Yaxley didn't look at him as she answered, instead inspecting the flecks of mud on her boots. 'Unless someone else proposes then I should imagine she will. As you say, Lord Hauxton is a good man, he will make a decent husband.' The rest of the sentence hung between them unsaid, but James knew Lady Yaxley was implying that he would make a better one. If only she knew. 'We are going to the Wellingtons' house party in Suffolk tomorrow, I understand Lord Hauxton has obtained an invitation. She will probably give him her answer then.'

James felt a weight settle upon his shoulders. He didn't want her to marry Milton and he hated how selfish that made him.

'I'm sure the Wellingtons would be delighted to have you in attendance. You are a duke and that matters to most people. I could let it slip to Mrs Wellington that you would like an invitation.'

It would be foolish to go. He should stay away from Caroline, just as she had asked, let her make her decision about her future without any further interference from him.

'Caroline asked for a little space when I saw her last.'

'Sometimes we ask for what we think we want, rather than what we need. I'll send you a little note once I've contacted Mrs Wellington.'

James couldn't bring himself to say no. He

knew nothing could change between him and Caroline, but perhaps if he could see her one last time before she became engaged they would both be able to convince themselves they were doing the right thing.

'Good, that's settled then. I should be getting Bertie back home, but I hope I will see you tomorrow.'

Watching her as she strolled along the path, James wondered what exactly she hoped to achieve by pushing him into Caroline's orbit once again.

Knocking on the door, he waited, listening for the sounds of movement inside. It took a minute, but soon the door was inching open, a small pale face looking out.

'Good afternoon, sir.' The maid looked relieved to see him standing on the door and James wondered if he'd scared the young woman with his insistence that no one else be admitted.

'How is he?' He stepped inside, handing over his coat.

'He seems well, sir.'

James walked through the hall and pushed open the door to the small room beyond, letting his eyes adjust to the gloom before he ventured inside.

'I didn't expect you to visit again so soon,' West said, his voice clear and crisp. It was a relief not to hear the words slurred by the effects of alcohol.

'We're worried about you.'

James hadn't spoken to Milton in the last couple of days, he'd been avoiding him since the Deveauxs' ball, but he knew Milton was worried about their friend, too.

West murmured something quietly, then stood to greet him. As James shook his hand he let his eyes flicker over his friend. The day's worth of stubble had been shaved off and his hair washed and combed into neat waves. He was fully dressed, even wearing a perfectly tied cravat. Everything from his posture and clothes down to the look in his eyes had improved over the last few days.

'I think the time for worrying is almost over,' West spoke quietly. 'Although I do appreciate your concern, especially after...'

After the duel, or the threat of one. For a moment James had been livid with his friend, livid for the insult to Caroline, livid for putting lives at risk, livid for not being the man he thought he was. Then he had paused, looked deeper, seen the pain and hurt that had driven the change in West and realised his friend needed help, not recriminations.

James sat down in the empty armchair by the fire and stretched out his legs. It was cold and damp outside today, the sky grey and the streets slippery with fallen leaves. A respite in the warmth was welcome and he felt himself relax a little as the heat from the fire began to thaw his cold extremities.

'Have you decided what you're going to do?'

West shook his head, but James noted he didn't look anywhere near as desolate as he had when he'd asked him that question a few days ago.

'The way I see it I've got two options: either I give Emma an ultimatum, tell her she isn't seeing that man again, or I decide I don't wish to have a wife who loves another man.'

'Divorce?'

West grimaced. Even in extreme cases divorce was unpalatable. 'Separation. She can live in the country and I will stay in town.' James heard the catch in his friend's voice and remembered his drunken words. West loved his wife, even now after finding out she had been conducting an affair for much of their short marriage. It would be hard for him to push her away with any finality.

'Does she know you know?'

'No. At least I don't think so.'

It was hard to give any advice. James had never been married, let alone to a wife who was then having an affair. It was the greatest of betrayals, but he wondered if his friend could ever truly be happy again if he hadn't at least tried one last time with his wife.

'Perhaps you owe it to yourself to sit down with Emma and at least try to see if there is a solution.'

Silently West nodded, then clapped his hands together.

'Enough about my depressing woes. Tell me how your little love triangle fares.'

James raised an eyebrow. 'Love triangle?'

'You, Miss Yaxley and Milton.' He counted them off on his fingers as he spoke.

'Hardly a love triangle.'

West just looked at him as if waiting for him to accept the truth.

'I ran into Lady Yaxley on my walk in Hyde Park. She tells me Milton has proposed to Caroline.' He tried to say it nonchalantly, as if it were merely a piece of news he was passing on, but he could hear the edge in his voice, feel the stab of regret in his stomach.

'And you're here with me and not with her?'

'It's her decision to make.'

West looked at him for a long moment, shaking his head. 'You do know the girl is head over heels in love with you. She has been for years.'

James didn't answer. He knew there was something there between him and Caroline, but he still couldn't quite believe she'd been in love with him for all that time and never let anything slip.

'You're forty-one, Heydon, hardly a young man. You've been waiting for the perfect woman for twenty years—why not settle down with someone who will make you happy instead of looking for someone who might not exist?'

'It wouldn't be fair on Caroline.'

'Nonsense. She'd be married to the man she loves and you would be married to a good woman. What is more fair than that?'

He closed his eyes, wondering if he should confess that he had asked Caroline to marry him. Poorly, it had to be said, as an afterthought to the kiss and the desire that coursed through him. It was hardly surprising she had refused, it hadn't been a large romantic gesture.

'I asked her,' he admitted.

West sat staring at him for a minute and then let out a low laugh. 'And she refused?'

'It was not how I imagined proposing to a woman. It was hurried, rushed.'

'After some indiscretion?'

James stayed silent.

'No wonder she refused. No woman wants to be proposed to purely out of a sense of duty. Especially a woman who has other options available to her.'

'I should just leave her and Milton to it,' James said.

'That's going to be hard, seeing them together at social occasions, watching their wedded bliss at dinner parties and the like. Your friend and the woman you care for most in the world.' West's words were spoken quietly, but had a certain sting in them. James studied his friend and saw genuine concern in his eyes. He was pushing him to try to get James to act before he allowed something he would regret to pass.

'Perhaps I'll move abroad. Permanently.' Of course he wouldn't, no matter how appealing the idea of travelling without worrying about his responsibilities. He was a duke and with that came his estates and land to manage, tenants to oversee and his duties as a peer of the realm. These past few years he had managed to get away with frequent trips abroad, but he had still spent at least half of the last five years in England and that was how it had to be. There would be no moving abroad, no running away.

'Listen to yourself. You're thinking of moving abroad to save yourself from having to see Miss Yaxley married to another man. Surely that tells you all you need to know.'

Standing, James walked over to the fire, holding his hands out to warm his fingers, turning his face away from West to give him a moment to think. Everything his friend was saying was true. It *would* be hard to see Caroline married to someone else and the fact that her intended husband was one of James's friends would make it even harder. Every social occasion they would be thrown together and he would be reminded of what he could have had. And he was sure it wasn't acceptable to desire your friend's wife in the way he desired Caroline.

'I'll speak to her,' he said, still not knowing what he would say.

'Good.' West stood and joined him in front of the fire. 'Now I'm planning on moving back home later today, I think I've had enough time to contemplate my options.' He held his hand out and waited for James to take it. 'Thank you. You've been a much better friend than I deserve. A lesser man would have left me on Hampstead Heath with a hole in my chest.'

'The room will always be here if you need it,' James said. It was in one of the many properties he owned in London, with the upstairs rented to single gentlemen and the downstairs standing empty for a few months. It wouldn't be difficult to keep it free for his friend for a few more weeks in case he needed a sanctuary.

'Thank you,' West repeated. 'If I can ever repay the favour, I'd like the chance.'

James clapped his friend on the back before leaving, glad that at least one complication in his life was sorting itself out. Without West to worry about he could focus on deciding what to do about Caroline. The Wellingtons' house party would be a good place to start.

Chapter Seventeen

Staring morosely out of the carriage window, Caroline tried to give herself a talking to. Tomorrow evening was the masquerade ball at the Wellingtons'. It was the deadline she had set herself for accepting Lord Hauxton's proposal. In thirty-six hours she would be an engaged woman. That was something to celebrate. If only her rebellious heart could understand that.

'It's beautiful weather for a house party,' Lady Yaxley said, smiling much more cheerfully than should be allowed after so long in a carriage.

She wasn't wrong, it was cold and crisp, with the winter sun shining bright on the frost still clinging to the grass. Caroline wouldn't be surprised if they had snow in the next couple of days and felt herself buoyed by the thought. She loved snow, loved it when the ponds froze over and you could skate and throw snowballs and eventually retreat inside to warm up with a big cup of hot chocolate.

The carriage swayed as they rounded a bend in the drive and through the window Caroline could see the façade of the Wellingtons' country house. It was stark and imposing, much larger than Rosling Manor where she'd grown up, its frontage all grey stone and gargoyles.

Mrs Wellington bustled out as she saw the carriage approach, accompanied by her two daughters, Beatrice and Bridget. Beatrice was a few years younger than Caroline, having made her debut into society two years ago. Bridget was still in the schoolroom, an excitable girl of thirteen who looked eager to be included in the festivities.

'Lady Yaxley, Miss Yaxley, so delighted you could make it,' Mrs Wellington said, embracing Caroline's mother and then squeezing Caroline's hand. 'I hope your journey wasn't too arduous.'

'It was a lovely little respite from the hustle and bustle of the city,' Lady Yaxley said. She and Mrs Wellington had known each other for years, having made their debuts together over two decades ago.

'Come inside, I'll show you to your rooms. We

have tea and cakes being served in a few minutes and then dinner will be at eight with drinks in the drawing room beforehand.'

Beatrice slipped her arm through Caroline's as they walked inside. Although they had never been particularly close, probably due to the age difference, Beatrice was a sweet girl and Caroline always enjoyed spending time with her.

'Tell me not to pry, but everyone has been talking about your proposals.'

Great. The news had even reached as far as Suffolk. Caroline tried not to grimace. Of course she was overreacting—the Wellingtons would have been in London until yesterday and she knew everyone was talking about her in London.

'Have you accepted anyone yet?'

'I'm considering my options,' Caroline said, hoping to remain as vague as possible. Really she didn't have any options. James's proposition had been born from duty, Lord Hauxton's proposal was the only genuine one. She would accept him, of course she would. Tomorrow night.

'It is so thrilling, to have multiple gentlemen propose. And to have them both here for our little party. I couldn't believe it when Mother told me.'

Caroline stopped walking, turning to face Beatrice. 'Both?' She tried to keep the note of panic from her voice.

'Yes, Lord Hauxton confirmed a week ago, but the Duke of Heydon penned Mother a very nice note to say he would love to attend just before we left London.'

'No.'

'Oh, yes. Mother was absolutely ecstatic that two such influential gentlemen will be in attendance. And we have you to thank for it, of course.'

Smiling weakly, she allowed Beatrice to lead her up the stairs to her bedroom, a small but bright room overlooking the gardens to the back of the house. Beatrice seemed in no rush to leave her alone, flopping down on the bed.

'So do you know which one you'll accept?'

Caroline rested her forehead against the window pane, enjoying the coolness of the glass. As usual with any mention of James, her heart was thumping in her chest. She longed to see him again, but also wished he would just stay away. It would be much easier to accept Lord Hauxton if James wasn't there looking on, watching her compromise and accept a man she didn't love as a husband because he could give her the life she wanted.

'I'm sure the rumours have been greatly exaggerated,' Caroline murmured. 'The Duke is a good friend, nothing more.'

'And Lord Hauxton?'

'We have only known each other a few weeks.'

Beatrice looked unconvinced and Caroline wondered how much of the weekend she would spend dodging questions from intrigued guests.

'Well, I think it is fabulous they're both going to be here.' Beatrice gave a little nervous laugh and covered her mouth. 'You don't think they'll come to blows over you?'

Caroline shuddered at the memory of the duel that had almost happened. The worry that James would be hurt still hadn't left her. She knew he had forgiven Lord West, had set about helping him in his distress over his wife, but she didn't think she would forget so easily. Lord West had sent a large bouquet of flowers with a note offering a profuse apology for insulting her. *That* she could forgive, but she would never look at him the same way after his volatility nearly endangered James.

'No, of course not. The Duke and Lord Hauxton are friends, everything will be completely amicable between them.'

Caroline stood in the doorway of the drawing room trying not to let her mouth hang open with disbelief. James and Lord Hauxton were sitting in two comfortable armchairs, both laughing at some shared joke. The men looked completely relaxed, completely at ease and silently Caroline cursed them for not feeling one fraction of the turmoil she did.

As she entered the room properly, all eyes turned to her, then flitted backwards and forward between her and the two men. Both got to their feet languidly, waiting for her to walk over to them before greeting her.

'Miss Yaxley, you are well, I trust?' Lord Hauxton spoke first, bowing in her direction.

James smiled at her, that secret little smile that always made her heart flutter.

'Stop it,' she muttered under her breath, wishing her body wouldn't be so rebellious whenever she was near.

'Very well, thank you, Lord Hauxton.' She turned to James and fixed him with a hard stare. 'I wasn't aware you were invited.'

'I've known the Wellingtons for a long time,' he said serenely, ignoring her stare.

'Strange you've never been to one of their parties before.'

'The busy life of a duke,' he said with an infuriating shrug.

Lord Hauxton pulled over a spare chair and waited for Caroline to sit before he followed suit. If he was anything of a gentleman, James would now make his excuses and leave. He sat.

'I hear Mrs Wellington is putting on games tomorrow morning in the garden.'

'Archery, I hope,' Caroline said, imagining chasing James around the garden with her bow and arrow. There would be a certain satisfaction in seeing him run, although knowing him, he would stand there calmly and wait for her to waver.

'Do you like archery, Miss Yaxley?' Lord Hauxton raised an eyebrow in surprise as if he couldn't imagine her with a bow and quiver full of arrows.

Next to her James laughed. It was a warm laugh, one of remembrance.

'I do, Lord Hauxton. Although I'm not as skilled as I wish I could be.'

'Cara…' James hesitated, catching himself. 'Miss Yaxley once almost shot their butler while practising. Luckily he was a stoical fellow, didn't even blink as the arrow ruffled his jacket.'

'You exaggerate.'

'Fine, perhaps he blinked, but he didn't drop the jug of lemonade he was carrying.'

'Tell me, how long have you two known each other now?' Lord Hauxton's tone was casual, but Caroline could detect a hint of suspicion in his voice.

Caroline felt her mouth go dry and a nervous fluttering in her stomach. Of course he'd noticed the familiarity between them, the shared experiences, the friendship. It was impossible not to, especially as he was friends with James as well as courting her. His tone was mild as he asked the question, but Caroline wondered if there was a hint of suspicion, a question as to how close they were. He'd never pried into the relationship between her and James. It was one thing of many that she was thankful to him for.

'Five years.'

Five years, two months and three days.

'A long time,' James murmured.

Caroline looked down at her hands, seeing

them twisting in the fabric of her skirt, and willed them to be still. She couldn't let Lord Hauxton see how nervous she was in James's company, how much he affected her.

Mrs Wellington bustled into the room and looked around, seemingly pleased that all her guests were assembled in one place.

'Thank you for coming, everyone,' she said, waiting for the conversations around her to die down before continuing. 'I am so pleased you all made the journey to our little house party. Of course the highlight will be the masquerade ball tomorrow evening, but we have lots of other festivities planned as well. This afternoon I propose a little stroll into the village so everyone can stretch their legs after the carriage ride. And tomorrow we will have some games in the garden.'

Caroline forced a smile. The Wellingtons were always overeager to organise everyone, filling every last minute of the day with some sort of group activity. The house parties she liked the most were the ones where there wasn't much structure and everyone could socialise in the way they wanted to. Still, it was a beautifully bright day and she wouldn't mind a little fresh air before dinner.

'We shall be leaving in half an hour. The walk is only twenty minutes each way, but I do advise you wear sturdy footwear—sometimes the paths can get a bit muddy.'

Caroline looked down at her dainty satin shoes and grimaced. She would have to change before they left, preferably into a darker-coloured dress as well as a pair of boots—something that would not show the mud so well.

She stood, eager to have the excuse to leave James and Lord Hauxton. 'Please excuse me, I should change.'

Both gentlemen stood and waited for her to leave before resuming their seats. Caroline was perturbed to see them sitting back down together as she glanced back over her shoulder at the doorway. James was laughing at something Milton was saying and even serious Lord Hauxton had a smile on his face. She would probably prefer it if the two men in her life weren't quite so friendly.

Chapter Eighteen

James whistled as he stood with a shoulder resting against one of the grand stone pillars by the equally grand front door. He was feeling happier than he had done in a while. The sun shining on his face certainly helped his mood, as did the knowledge that any moment Caroline would be walking out of the front door and he would have her all to himself for at least twenty minutes.

'Running a little late?' he asked as she dashed past him, not noticing him until he spoke.

She paused and looked around, frowning when she realised he was the only one there.

'Where is everyone else?'

'Gone. They left ten minutes ago.'

'Everyone?'

'Everyone.'

She glanced around again as if she didn't quite believe him.

'Even Lord Hauxton,' he confirmed.

Caroline scowled at him and he had to suppress a smile. At least she was talking to him and hadn't demanded he leave her alone. Yet.

'Perhaps he's inside...' She turned and looked back over her shoulder, tapping one foot with nervous energy.

'There's no point waiting for him.'

'There's every point.'

'He's gone.'

'You're just saying that. I know he would wait for me.' The silence stretched out between them for thirty seconds before Caroline looked at him suspiciously again. 'Unless you told him otherwise.'

James shrugged. 'I might have told him you'd already left with the first of the group.'

'Might have?'

'I did.'

'Why did you do that?'

'I wanted you to myself for a few minutes.'

When she turned and looked at him there was an expression of exasperation on her face, but he could see the confusion hidden underneath.

'James, do you remember when we spoke last?'

'Half an hour ago.'

'Before that,' she said through gritted teeth.

'Of course.'

'And can you remember what you agreed?'

'To leave you alone for a while.'

She stared at him for a moment without blinking. 'So?'

'I did. For a number of days.'

'Six days,' she murmured.

James stepped closer, catching a hint of her scent, the perfume she wore with lemon and something sweeter he couldn't identify.

'Come on, Cara, we see little enough of one another as it is.'

He wanted to reach out, to wrap a strand of hair around his fingers, to trace a pattern on the back of her neck, to pull her closer until he could feel the heat of her body, but he knew he was on perilous ground and any wrong step could destroy their friendship for ever.

Do it, a little voice inside him urged. If he destroyed their friendship, perhaps there would be space for something new, something better, something he'd been dreaming of for the last few weeks.

Caroline hadn't stepped away, she was standing there as if entranced, looking up at him with her breathing shallow and her eyes wide. If he kissed her, he knew she would react, knew she would melt into him and respond to his caresses.

With a shuddering breath in Caroline took a step back, distancing herself from him, but unable to tear her eyes away.

'We can walk together to the village,' she conceded, but held up a hand to stop him from interrupting. 'But only if you promise to behave yourself.'

'Behave myself?'

She looked him squarely in the eye, her gaze unwavering. 'Behave. Yourself. You know exactly what I mean.'

'I promise to be a gentleman through and through.' Even as he promised he found himself thinking about the last time they'd kissed and wondering if her lips would taste as sweet again.

After a moment he offered her his arm and enjoyed the familiarity of the sensation as she slipped her hand into the crook of his elbow. He'd always enjoyed their strolls together. Even when he was on his travels around Europe he always looked forward to coming home to Caroline, to the afternoons spent walking together in the park talking about everything they could imagine.

'Did I tell you about the time in Italy when I decided to walk to the next village and got so lost in the hills I had to be rescued by an old woman two days later?'

Next to him Caroline smiled and for a moment it felt as though everything were right with the world again.

'You know you haven't. How did you get so lost?'

'I was staying in a little village called San Taomino and I'd got talking to some of the local men in a tavern one evening. We were discussing my travels and they suggested I take a trip to the next village, a beautiful little place in the Tuscan hills. They insisted I could walk the distance in a couple of hours with no problem.' He grimaced, remembering the evening. 'The wine was flowing freely and my companions drew me a map on an old piece of parchment we found in the tavern.'

'You didn't follow it?'

'The next morning I'd sobered up, but I still wanted to make the trip, so I armed myself with my handdrawn map and started out.'

Caroline was laughing, the sound suffusing him with warmth and making him pause and assess the situation. Here he was, strolling along with his best friend on his arm feeling happy. *She* made him happy. She made him laugh and smile and enjoy the little things in life.

What was he doing here? After Lady Yaxley had suggested the trip to Suffolk for the house party he hadn't been able to think of anything else, but not once had he allowed himself to stop and think about what that meant. Surely if he wanted to be with Caroline so much, valued her companionship so dearly, that should tell him something.

Part of him wanted to take her in his arms and kiss her until she agreed to marry him, to make her see that he was serious with his proposal, but still there was a part of him that was hesitant, that wondered if this was truly what he wanted or a reaction to the idea of losing her.

'I was lost after half an hour, couldn't even find my way back to San Taomino.'

'I do wonder how you survive your trips abroad, all the mishaps you've had along the way.'

'The mishaps are the fun part. Take this trip, for example. The old woman who rescued me owned a magnificent vineyard, acres and acres of vines. It was some of the finest wine I've ever tasted, and I wouldn't have even known the vineyard existed if I hadn't set out walking.'

Caroline sighed wistfully as she often did when he regaled her with tales of his travels. He knew she had a burning desire to travel, to see the sights and wonders he described with her own eyes. More than once he'd imagined taking her along with him to marvel at the beauty of Venice, the sights of Rome and relax in the sun of southern Italy.

'I brought a couple of bottles back with me, we should share one of an evening.'

'James…' Caroline said admonishingly.

'I can't suggest sharing a glass of wine with a friend?'

'You know it can't be.'

'Indulge me in the fantasy for a moment. The strike of midnight, two old friends losing track of time over a glass of fine wine and their memories.'

'It sounds wonderful, but it can't be.'

'Perhaps not,' he said softly, taking her hand from where it rested in the crook of his elbow and raising it to his lips, kissing it gently.

Caroline stopped, waiting for him to turn and face her.

'What do you want from me, James?' Her voice was barely more than a whisper.

A friendship, an illicit affair, a marriage. He couldn't answer. He didn't know himself.

'You,' he said after a long moment. 'I want you.'

Her lips parted and she exhaled a rush of air. He could tell she didn't know how to react, didn't know how to respond to this declaration.

'No,' she said slowly, shaking her head, 'you don't.'

'You think you know my mind better than me?'

'Right now? Yes.'

'Don't be absurd, Cara. Feel this.' He grasped her hand and placed it on his chest, feeling the warmth of her fingers even through his jacket. Underneath her hand his heart was pounding faster than usual. '*This* is how you affect me.'

'Desire?' Her voice was tremulous.

'There's nothing wrong with desire.'

'There is. There's everything wrong with it, especially between me and you.'

'No—' he shook his head '—you can't tell me this feels wrong.' He bent down and kissed her, wrapping his arms around her and half-lifting her up to meet him. She might be arguing with him, but her body reacted instinctively to his kiss, moulding into his, hot with desire.

For one wonderful moment it was as though their bodies had merged and then Caroline pulled away, her eyes filled with recriminations.

'You don't get to do that,' she said quietly. He caught her hand, drawing her to him.

'Tell me you don't feel the same way. Tell me you haven't been dreaming of one more kiss. Tell me you haven't been wanting one more touch.' As he spoke he ran his fingers lightly across her shoulders and over the exposed skin of her neck. She shivered at his touch, but didn't make any attempt to step away. 'You want it just as much as I do. You want me to kiss you until you're senseless and then tumble you into a soft bed and make you mine.'

She shook her head, but made no move to step away, instead tilting her neck to give him greater access to the skin underneath her dress.

'Say the words, make me believe them.'

'I can't.' She spoke so quietly he hardly heard her, but as she raised her eyes to meet his he saw an intense desire in them. 'I can't tell you that.'

He kissed her again, pulling her in tight to him, feeling every curve of her body pressed against his. Part of him wanted to pick her up into his arms and run the short distance back to the house, to ignore the inquisitive glances from servants who soon would be gossiping, and carry her up to his bedroom. There they would lock the door and fall into bed and not emerge for at least a day.

James groaned at the thought. It was exactly what he'd been dreaming about the last few weeks and suddenly it seemed within his reach. Quickly, before either of them could catch their breath, he did lift her up into his arms, dropping a kiss on the tip of her nose as he did so.

'What are you doing?'

Before he could answer, before he could even take another step, he heard a shout from behind them, from the direction of the village.

Slowly he turned, Caroline still in his arms, the skirt of her dress falling in layers beneath her and almost sweeping the ground. Striding towards them was a group of four of the guests. Milton was there at the front, followed closely behind by Caroline's mother and then hurrying behind them Beatrice and Mrs Wellington.

'No,' Caroline whispered as she saw the group approaching.

'They haven't seen anything.'

'Of course they have. We're standing here with me in your arms.'

James searched the faces of the approaching group—they looked concerned rather than angry or scandalised and he considered the view he and Caroline presented.

'They think I'm carrying you home,' he muttered.

'You are.'

'But they don't know why.'

Hers eyes widened as if she couldn't quite believe that could be true.

'Play along.'

Just as Milton arrived in front of them James hesitated. Perhaps it would be better if they *did* suspect something.

'Miss Yaxley, are you hurt?' Milton's eyes flicked over her.

'She fell,' James said, a little too abruptly. The concern in Milton's eyes reminded him he wasn't the only man to care for Caroline.

'What happened?' her mother asked as she hurried up.

In his arms Caroline rallied, giving a theatrical little grimace. 'It's embarrassing, really. I overturned my ankle stepping on a stone. Even though I had the Duke's arm I was so unbalanced I fell to the ground. Now when I try to walk on it a pain shoots up my leg.'

'Good job Heydon was here to pick you up,' Milton murmured. James saw the other man eyeing her un-scuffed boots where they were peeking out from under her dress.

'I can probably manage it back to the house,' Caroline said, starting to wriggle in his arms.

'You wouldn't want to do any more damage.' Milton stepped closer, his hand coming up and resting on the tip of her boot. 'Which foot was it?'

She hesitated for only a moment. 'The left.'

'I'm sure Heydon can carry you halfway back and I can manage the rest. It would be prudent not to walk on it at least until you've taken your boot off and inspected the damage.'

'Exactly what I was telling her,' James said. He began walking, marvelling how a woman as slight as Caroline could make his arms feel like lead after even just a few hundred feet.

'Stop wriggling,' he murmured so only she could hear. 'It's like carrying a bag of snakes.'

'It's not exactly comfortable or elegant up here.'

'Stop complaining, I'm your knight, your rescuer, remember.'

She rolled her eyes at him and proceeded to wriggle even more.

'I can take Miss Yaxley whenever you get tired, Heydon,' Milton said, keeping step with him.

James had the irrational urge to dismiss the other man's offer of help. It didn't feel right to hand her over, not when he was the one who'd got them into this predicament.

'She's not *too* heavy.'

Milton suppressed a laugh and Caroline reached up and whacked James on the shoulder.

Up ahead he could see the house and he almost shouted out with relief. He might not want to hand her over, but he would be pleased to deposit her in a comfortable armchair and shake his arms out until the burn in his muscles subsided.

Once they were inside, Mrs Wellington ushered them through to the drawing room and with a groan much louder than he'd meant it to be he lowered Caroline into an armchair.

'Thank you,' she said softly, looking up at him.

For a moment it was as if everyone else had faded into the background. Gone was the anxious bustling of Mrs Wellington and the gruff tones of Milton asking if Caroline was in pain. Only he and Caroline remained, their eyes locked together, their bodies yearning for the closeness they'd just shared.

'Right, we need to have a look at this foot.'

He stepped back as Lady Yaxley took over, organising for a cool cloth to be brought to wrap around the ankle and carefully removing Caroline's boot. Caroline played her part well, stoically biting her lip as the ankle was prodded and poked, whimpering in pain with various movements.

'Just a sprain, my darling,' Lady Yaxley said eventually. 'You'll heal in no time.'

'Luckily it doesn't seemed to have swelled,' Milton observed from his position by the fireplace.

'I'll fetch you a cane, my dear, we have a few from when my mother-in-law lived here with us. It'll help you to get around for the next few days.' Mrs Wellington left to instruct one of the maids to find a cane, her cheeks still flushed from the brisk walk back.

Caroline smiled weakly, sipping the cup of tea that had been placed in her hands a couple of minutes ago.

'Lord Hauxton, perhaps you would be so kind as to help me fetch a couple of pillows from upstairs,' Caroline's mother said, taking his arm and guiding him gently towards the door. 'Caroline looks a little uncomfortable and I think the softness of a pillow will help her more than a firm cushion.'

'Of course.'

For a moment after they left James didn't move, observing Caroline's pained face from his position a few feet away. Even when they were alone her expression didn't change and he realised it was emotional torment that was causing her to frown, not the charade of her twisted ankle.

'They're suspicious.' Caroline watched the door as if expecting someone to leap through it at any second. 'At least Mother and Lord Hauxton are.'

'Perhaps it would be for the best?'

'For the best?' He could hear the suppressed anger in her voice. 'You think ruining me would be for the best?'

Aware he had only a couple of minutes at most

before Milton and Lady Yaxley reappeared, he crouched down next to her, resting his hand so his fingers were brushing hers. At first she wouldn't look at him, instead staring intently at the fire flickering in the grate, but as he moved his fingertips against her he saw her relent and look up at him.

'Our lives are entwined, Cara—would it truly be terrible if everyone were to know that?'

She didn't answer and he had an overwhelming urge to kiss her again, but knew right now he had to hold back. He couldn't coerce her into accepting his marriage proposal and he wouldn't kiss her senseless until someone found them and they were forced to marry to avoid the scandal. He cared far too much for her to do anything like that.

Outside they heard footsteps and James quickly stood, taking a couple of steps so he was back by the fireplace before Lady Yaxley and Milton re-entered the room, carrying an armful of pillows each. To the casual observer it wouldn't look as though he'd moved at all.

'Let's get you comfortable,' Lady Yaxley said, fussing around her daughter, tucking pillows in about her leg to better support her ankle. 'It's a shame you won't be able to dance tonight, but at least there is plenty of good company to keep you merry.'

James waited for another minute before taking his leave, pressing a kiss on to Caroline's hand and wishing her a comfortable few hours. He hoped she might spend them weighing up her options and deciding he was the one she wanted to be with.

Chapter Nineteen

Sitting in the corner of the room, her cane leaning against the side of the chair, Caroline observed the other guests gathered in little groups, talking and laughing. She should feel miserable and excluded, confined to her chair for a non-existent injury, but it was quite liberating just being able to sit and watch without being expected to take part. Everyone thought she should be miserable, her foot paining her and unable to join in the festivities, but instead she felt quite content to be left alone with her thoughts.

She had a lot to think about, not that her mind would let her think of anything except the kiss she and James had shared that morning. The *inevitable* kiss as she thought of it. It had been brewing for a long time, ever since they'd last kissed on the Heath, but now she was left even more confused than before.

James had talked about desire and she knew there was a fierce attraction between them, but he had never talked about love. He cared for her, desired her, but he'd never told her that he loved her.

It shouldn't matter, she'd decided she would marry for reasons other than love at the start of the Season, so it shouldn't matter if James didn't love her, but somehow it did. She loved him so fiercely, so intensely, that she couldn't imagine being with him and him only feeling a mild affection for her. That would be all that was left after the desire wore off.

'You're looking rather serious,' James said as he came and sat down beside her. He'd been socialising all evening, but she had felt the surreptitious glances in her direction and known he was biding his time until he could come and sit with her without drawing too much attention to himself.

'My ankle,' she said with a grimace, 'So painful.'

'You are a talented liar, Cara, it scares me a little how good you are. It makes me wonder what other fibs you've told me over the years.'

If only you knew.

It was imperative James never knew how long she'd loved him for, how their friendship had always been covering her true feelings for the man beside her.

'I think Lord Hauxton suspected something was amiss.'

'Milton's a sharp man.'

'He hasn't said anything, I could just see how he was looking at my ankle and how he watched me earlier as I entered the room, leaning on the cane.'

'I should say I'm sorry for throwing up obstacles to your courtship,' James said, then smiled, 'but if I'm being completely honest, then I'm not sorry at all.' He caught her eye and Caroline found it very hard not to smile along with him. 'What I will apologise for is keeping you from dancing tomorrow at the masquerade ball.'

'I was looking forward to it.'

'Perhaps your foot could make a miraculous recovery.'

'A sprain? Recovered in a day? No one would believe that.'

'No,' he murmured. 'Although it will be a masquerade. We might be able to slip away…'

'Caroline darling, you look a little pale, are

you in pain?' Caroline's mother bustled over and took the seat on her other side. 'Doesn't she look pale, Your Grace?'

James studied her for longer than was absolutely necessary. 'She does. Perhaps you would like me to carry you up to your room?'

Caroline's eyes widened as she remembered how he'd first swept her into his arms earlier that morning, before all the deception about a sprained ankle, when it was just the two of them and their desire for one another.

'I'm perfectly capable of hobbling upstairs myself, thank you very much.'

'You don't want to cause any more damage,' Lady Yaxley said. 'You should consider the Duke's kind offer.'

She stood quickly, only once she was up remembering to grimace in pain and transfer her weight to her right foot. Grabbing hold of the cane, she turned back to her mother and James.

'You're right, I am tired and in pain. I hope you will excuse me.'

She limped off, knowing she had to stop running away from everyone. Soon she would have to face James and Lord Hauxton and make a final decision on her future. A decision that would determine the rest of her life.

Just as she was about to start up the stairs she heard footsteps behind her and saw James ducking out of the drawing room. He strode over to her, pressed something in her hand and then without a word turned and walked away.

Looking down, she saw the small square of paper in her hand. Quickly she closed her fingers back around it and hurried up the stairs.

Only once she was in her room with the door locked behind her, the cane thrown on the bed, did she open the note.

A glass of wine at midnight? J.

A single sentence. A single question, but there was so much layered underneath it. Her first reaction was to screw up the note in frustration and throw it in the bin, but something stopped her just as her fingers began to crumple the paper. It would be reckless to go and, if she were caught, her reputation would be ruined, but that wasn't why she was hesitating. If she went, she knew exactly what she would be walking in to. She doubted she and James would be able to be together somewhere private and not end up in an intimate position.

She wanted that, had dreamed about it for so long, but she knew it was at odds with her other plans for her future. If she went tonight, she would be giving up on her hopes for a marriage, for a family and the future she had imagined. It wouldn't be fair to give herself to James and then agree to marry Lord Hauxton.

Flopping back on the bed, she closed her eyes. Perhaps she should just leave things to fate. If she woke up in time for midnight she would go to James, if she slept through she would marry Lord Hauxton.

Five minutes to midnight. The little clock on the dressing table seem to tick loudly, even though before tonight she hadn't been aware of the sound. Caroline was still undecided, still unsure whether she would stay in her room with her door locked or creep along the corridor to spend one single night with the man she loved.

Standing, she pulled on her dressing gown, tying the belt to make sure she was completely covered, then she sat back on the bed and drummed her fingers against the covers. To go or to stay?

Closing her eyes, she thought of the moment she'd first met James, of the way he'd looked at her and smiled, of every moment since when they'd laughed together, danced together. She'd loved him for five years and here was her chance to have one night of happiness in his arms.

Standing again, she pushed all thoughts of her future away. Tonight she was going to take what she wanted and tell herself the memory of it would be enough.

Caroline paused before opening the door, listening to the silence outside her room. Most of the guests had come up to bed an hour ago, turning in relatively early to save their energies for the masquerade ball tomorrow night. Still, the last thing she wanted was to be creeping along to James's room and to bump into another guest to bear witness to her scandalous behaviour.

Slowly she opened the door and peered out. The corridor was empty and quiet. She had to resist the urge to run down its length instead stepping out slowly. If she walked calmly and were to be seen by anyone else, they would just assume she was up to find a glass of water or something similar.

With her heart pounding in her chest, she made her way out of the east wing and through the main section of the house. The gentlemen had all been placed in the west wing, the ladies in the east. As she reached the stairs in the very centre she paused. After the next step there would be no turning back.

Caroline took a breath and then hurried on, only stopping when she was outside the door she knew was James's. Quietly she knocked, hoping he was standing ready to open the door and usher her in.

'You came,' he said, the surprise evident in his voice as he gently pulled her into the room.

'I came.'

For a moment they just stood there, looking at one another as if they both couldn't quite believe they were here together.

Quietly he shut the door behind her and Caroline moved further into the room. For a moment she kept her back to him, aware that her nerves would be evident in her expression and needing a moment to calm herself before she turned back to face the man she loved.

'Wine?' he offered.

'You actually have wine?'

'Not the bottle from the vineyard near San Taomino, but I did bring a bottle and a couple of glasses upstairs just in case you came.'

Caroline nodded. Wine might help her nerves, quieten down the butterflies in her stomach. As he poured she began pacing around the room, unable to keep still.

'Cara,' James said as he passed her the glass. 'Stop a moment.' He took her hand and held it, watching as she took a sip of the wine. 'Sit and relax.'

Of course she couldn't relax. She was in the bedroom of the man she loved and they both knew what her presence here meant. Soon the wine would be gone and it would just be the two of them and their desires.

Closing her eyes, she sank down on to the edge of his huge bed. It was made of solid oak, the four posts thick and carved, the canopy above finely embroidered. No doubt the Wellingtons' best guest room for the Duke.

She felt the shift of the mattress as James sat down beside her, his leg brushing gently against hers.

'I never dared to believe you would come,' he said with his lips close to her ear.

'I know I shouldn't…' She trailed off as he came in closer and kissed her in the sensitive spot just behind her earlobe.

'Don't say that.' He kissed her again, trailing his lips down her neck. Caroline felt her head drop back instinctively as a warm flush began to spread through her body. 'You have the most perfect neck,' he murmured, his words tickling her skin and making her shiver with anticipation. 'But I've been dreaming about kissing more than your neck.'

Slowly he ran his fingers across her shoulder and down her arm, ending up near her waist. Gently but firmly he pulled on the cord fastening her dressing gown, loosening the thick material and then pushing it from her shoulders. As the gown fell on to the bed behind her Caroline felt a momentary chill from the cool air hitting her body. Her nightdress was thin and, although it covered most of her body, it was only a single layer.

'Better,' James said, eyeing her nightdress, 'but not quite perfect yet.' He loosened the ties that held it together across her chest, allowing the thin cotton to fall apart, then he lowered his lips to the exposed skin at the base of her throat. 'You don't know how many times I've imagined doing this.' His voice was hoarse, filled with desire, and Caroline felt a surge of power. She might have loved him for a long time, but here he was wanting *her*, desiring *her*.

For a moment she allowed herself just to enjoy the sensation of his lips on her skin, to be swept away in the moment. As his mouth trailed lower, pushing against the neckline of her nightdress, she snaked an arm behind him, pulling him in closer, and together they tumbled backwards on the bed. He was still dressed in trousers and shirt, his neck open from where he'd pulled off his cravat. Caroline wanted to feel his skin on hers, his body on hers, and as he continued to kiss her she started to tug his shirt up over his head.

He had to break away as she lifted it off him, but after no more than a second his lips were back on her skin, his hands running over her body.

'I need to see you,' he whispered in her ear, gripping the hem of her nightdress in one hand

and beginning to lift it up, exposing the bare skin underneath.

Caroline held her breath. No man had ever seen her like this before. She knew she wasn't beautiful, but the way James's eyes raked over her, his gaze hot with desire, it made her feel like the most attractive woman on earth.

Slowly James ran a single finger over her skin, starting at her navel and working his way up through the dip between her breasts before settling at the base of her throat. Caroline felt as though her skin were on fire, she wanted more, she wanted everything. As his fingers began their journey back down again she arched her back, pressing herself up, inviting him in.

'You're perfect, Cara,' he murmured as he lowered his head, making her gasp as he caught one of her nipples between his teeth. Little jolts of pleasure shot through her and she felt a low heat begin to burn deep inside. Leisurely he kissed her, then trailed his lips across to her other breast, nipping until she gasped in pleasure again. 'I think that might be my favourite sound ever.' He raised his head and grinned at her. 'I'm going to enjoy hearing it again and again.'

'You sound confident,' she managed to say.

'I feel like I know every inch of you already, Cara. I know where to touch you and where to kiss you and how to make you shout out in pleasure.'

'That sounds almost arrogant.'

'Would you like a demonstration?' He didn't wait for her answer, instead lowering his lips to the spot just beneath her ear and kissing her. 'I know if I kiss you here you close your eyes and drop back your head.' As he kissed her his hands moved across her body, making her arch and writhe underneath him. 'I know you will moan if I touch you here…' His fingers rested on one of her breasts for a second before doing something exquisite to her nipple that made her cry out. 'And I know I can make you scream my name if I touch you here.' Caroline stiffened as his fingers moved down over her abdomen and settled on her most private place. Slowly he started to caress her, responding to the minute thrust of her hips, the little gasps of pleasure. Caroline felt a wonderful pressure building up inside her. She wanted to be lost in this feeling for ever, with nothing more than James's touch making her call out with desire.

Gradually his fingers became faster and just

when Caroline thought she couldn't cope with the pleasure any longer something burst inside of her and she felt a wonderful flood of warmth shoot through her body.

'James,' she cried out, holding him to her, aware only of her heart pounding in her chest and the warmth of his touch between her legs.

He kissed her until she was breathless, his body on top of hers, and as she felt her senses begin to return she knew she wanted more. She wanted this night to never end.

With shaking fingers she began to pull at the fastening of James's trousers, pushing them from his hips and feeling his hardness pressed against her.

'Are you sure?'

She nodded, knowing she would always regret it if they stopped now, always wonder what it would have been like to give herself to him completely. There was a wonderful pressure as he pushed against her and then a feeling of fullness as he slipped inside. He moved slowly at first and Caroline could see by the strain on his face it was taking a monumental effort to hold himself back, but when her hips started to rise to meet his he began moving faster and faster.

Caroline gripped the sheets with her fingers and let herself go, feeling that wonderful pressure build again until the heat flooded through her. At the same time James stiffened and let out a low moan, before collapsing down on top of her.

For a long moment neither of them moved, both too breathless to do anything more than let their bodies recover. After a minute James rolled himself off her, looping an arm around her body and pulling her with him so her head rested on his chest. Gently he stroked her hair back from her face then let his hand drop to her arm where he traced lazy circles on the warm skin.

'Perhaps I should go,' Caroline said when her heart had stopped thumping in her chest and her breathing returned to normal.

'Don't do anything of the sort,' James murmured into her hair as he placed a kiss on the top of her head. He reached down and pulled the bedcovers up over their bodies and Caroline felt a warm contentment. It was a dangerous feeling, one she had no right to feel.

'I can't sleep here.'

'Why not?'

'You know why not.'

James kissed her hair again and pulled her in closer. 'Just stay a little while at least, Cara.'

It was a request she could agree to quite happily. She wanted to stay in his arms for ever, but she knew sooner or later she would have to return to reality. A reality where James didn't love her.

Don't think about that now.

She shut her eyes to try to block out the negative thoughts. This was her one night of pleasure, her one night of happiness with James, she didn't want to ruin it. Tomorrow she would have to face up to her actions, to work out what her future held, but tonight she could just enjoy the sensation of lying in the arms of the man she loved.

A weak, wintery sunlight was beginning to filter through the gaps in the curtains when Caroline opened her eyes. She felt panic seize her, the light meant it was morning already and morning meant she should be back in her own bed. The household might already be awake and that made the likelihood of being caught coming out of James's room much higher.

Turning over in bed, she paused for a moment, taking in every detail of James's face as he slept.

He looked young and carefree, his dark lashes long on his cheeks and his expression peaceful and serene.

'I love you,' she whispered, leaning in and placing a kiss on his forehead. She didn't want to wake him, didn't want to work out what was left between them in the cold light of day. Instead she would slip away and gather her thoughts in private.

Chapter Twenty

It was late when he woke, well after nine o'clock, and he felt better rested and more contented than he had done in a long time. As he rolled over his subconscious expected Caroline's warm body to still be in bed beside him and he felt bereft when he realised she had already left.

With a smile he sat up, indulging in remembering everything that had happened the previous night. He'd been dreaming of Caroline for a while, but last night had proved even his dreams hadn't been able to imagine how amazing they were together.

'Hurry up, married life,' he murmured to himself. Of course they would marry, there was no question of them doing anything else, but instead of feeling trapped and unsure as he had expected to he just felt a wonderful anticipation. He was going to spend his life married to his best friend who also happened to be the woman he could quite happily ravish morning, noon and night.

Rising from the bed, he freshened himself up with the bowl of tepid water one of the servants must have brought up a while earlier. He dressed quickly, eager to find Caroline and somehow whisk her off so they could be alone for a while. His mind turned to all the things they could do while alone, but he knew the first was to decide when to announce their engagement. Caroline would have to let Milton down gently, but after that they would be free to set a date for the wedding.

Four weeks, that was plenty of time for Caroline to prepare for a wedding and would allow the banns to be read. Although four weeks was a long time to wait to tumble Caroline back into his bed. Perhaps it would be better sooner, with a special licence. Two weeks, or maybe one.

As he stepped from his room he caught himself whistling. He wasn't sure he could stop himself being so exuberant but he would have to try for Caroline, it wouldn't do for anyone to work out what had happened last night.

'Good morning,' Lady Yaxley greeted him at the top of the stairs. She was trying very hard to look casual, but he had the impression she had been waiting for him. 'I trust you slept well, Your Grace.'

'One of the best night's sleep I've had in a very long time.' It was the truth—after weeks of waking taut with desire for Caroline, he'd slept peacefully when he knew she was lying there beside him.

He had to remind himself that she could have no idea what had transpired the night before and was waiting for him to discuss something else.

'It was very kind of you to carry Caroline back here yesterday.'

'She was in too much pain to walk.'

'Quite. Her poor ankle. Although this morning she seemed to forget which ankle pained her for a few minutes.'

James stiffened, then suppressed a smile. It didn't matter if Caroline slipped up with the deception, soon their engagement would be announced and one or two little indiscretions smiled on indulgently.

'How unusual,' he murmured.

'She's always recovered from injuries fast, but this seemed nothing short of miraculous.' Lady Yaxley glanced sideways at him. 'Although perhaps I'll hold off informing the church a miracle has occurred.'

'That might be wise. Caroline probably wouldn't like the attention.'

Lady Yaxley stopped and turned to face him, waiting until he did the same before continuing.

'I don't like to see my daughter upset, Your Grace. And she has been particularly flustered these last few weeks. Perhaps it is time to make a decision and stick with it and then we can all get on with dealing with the consequences.'

'I plan on doing exactly that, Lady Yaxley.'

Caroline's mother nodded in satisfaction and then walked away, leaving him to follow her into the dining room.

There were only three other people at the breakfast table, four when Lady Yaxley sat down. Caroline was sitting at one end of the table, deep in conversation with Lord Hauxton. A few seats further down was the elder of the Wellington daughters, sipping a cup of tea and looking as though she were trying her hardest not to eavesdrop on Caroline and Milton.

James hesitated before sitting down. At first he thought Caroline might be letting Lord Hauxton down, informing him that she was going to accept James's offer of marriage instead of his, but as Milton's deep laugh rang out over the breakfast table James paused. Looking up, he saw the other man smiling. He didn't look like a man who'd just been told the woman he'd proposed to was turning him down.

Patience, James cautioned himself. Caroline was probably just taking her time. She'd encouraged Milton for the last couple of weeks, it would be hard for her now to admit their courtship wasn't going to go anywhere.

Standing, he pushed out his chair from the table, crossing over to the sideboard where the breakfast food was laid out ready for the guests to select what they wanted. He passed by Caroline's chair on his way, resisting the urge to lean in and kiss her on the cheek.

'Good morning Milton, Miss Yaxley.' Soon she wouldn't be Miss Yaxley. She would be his Duchess, although always Cara to him.

'Morning.' Milton barely looked up from his toast and Caroline gave him a weak smile over the cup of tea she cradled in her hands. He hadn't been expecting a greeting filled with intimacy and affection, but as she avoided eye contact he felt the first bite of worry in his gut.

'I'm looking forward to the games we have organised in the garden this morning,' Miss Wellington said as James came back with his plate piled high with eggs and toast.

'Mmm,' he agreed, his eyes locked firmly on Caroline. She was definitely avoiding looking at him. In the course of the last minute she'd looked at Milton, the table, her cup of tea and even the ceiling rather than straight ahead where he would be in her line of sight.

'We have pall mall, archery and a treasure hunt set up, although if people would prefer just to enjoy the gardens, of course, there is no requirement to join in,' Miss Wellington said, trying valiantly to engage him in conversation.

'Who doesn't love archery or pall mall?' he managed to reply before his eyes were back on Caroline.

Lady Yaxley took the seat on the other side of Caroline and James was surprised to see she didn't even manage a smile for her mother. Something was seriously wrong. He thought back over the night before—she'd been eager, as overcome with desire as he. He had to concede that it wasn't normal behaviour for a well brought-up young lady to give herself to a man outside marriage, but it didn't matter too much given that they would marry soon.

He frowned. Surely she knew he would marry her. He'd asked her twice already and that was before they'd spent the night in each other's arms.

'Fool,' he muttered to himself.

'Excuse me?' Miss Wellington looked confused.

'Talking to myself,' he said gruffly. He hadn't actually said the words last night, hadn't told Caroline they would marry as soon as possible. Surely she couldn't think he would seduce her and then abandon her, surely she knew him better than that.

Glancing down the table, he couldn't be certain. She looked pale, drawn, worried, not like a young lady who was about to marry her best friend.

He almost stood, placing his hands on the table and half-pushing out his chair before stopping himself. The breakfast table wasn't the place to go to her, to reassure her he wouldn't abandon her now.

'Will you be participating in the games, Miss Yaxley?' He spoke loudly, causing everyone in the dining room to look down the table at him.

Five seconds passed, then ten and for a moment he thought she wasn't going to answer him.

'Probably.' She didn't even look at him as she spoke, her eyes focused on the dregs of her tea. 'Please excuse me, I forgot something from my room.' The teacup rattled as she stood abruptly and James could only stare in surprise as she almost ran from the room, cane tapping on the floor and the theatrical limp looking less and less convincing.

Silence followed and James felt Lady Yaxley's eyes on him, probing and accusing. Milton rose, too, stalking along the length of the table. Before he left the room he paused by James, leaning in close. 'I've no idea what you've done to upset Miss Yaxley, but make it right. She deserves at least that much from you.'

James took a bite of his toast once Milton had left, but it tasted papery on his tongue and even his tea was tepid and unappealing. His plate of breakfast only half-eaten, he stood and excused himself, retreating back upstairs to his room to gather his thoughts before confronting Caroline.

Caroline eyed the selection of weapons in front of her. The bow was traditionally the more lethal, but the mallet used in pall mall could cause substantial damage if wielded correctly. Perhaps she could arm herself with both.

'You're looking at those with a worrying gleam in your eye, darling,' her mother said as she came up beside her.

'Just deciding whether to play pall mall or go for the archery.'

'Good, just remember murder is a capital offence.'

Caroline reached out and took her mother's hand. Lady Yaxley could not know what had transpired the night before, no one but her and James would ever know, but she was sensitive to Caroline's moods and had shown her support ever since she had joined Caroline in the dining room earlier this morning.

'Pall mall might be a bit difficult with your cane,' her mother said.

Damn the cane. Already today she'd forgotten which side she was meant to be limping on at least five times and it was only eleven o'clock in the morning.

'Archery, then.' She selected a bow and a couple of arrows, testing the string for tautness.

'I hope you're not looking for a human target.' His voice was low, almost seductive, and Caroline was immediately transported back to the night before. She could almost feel his lips on her skin, the weight of his body against hers. A warmth began to spread inside her, a carnal reaction that she desperately tried to halt, but couldn't.

'Are you volunteering?'

'I trust you, Cara, but I've also seen you shoot.' His tone was so familiar, his smile so genuine she felt herself swaying towards him. It would be so easy to be swept along, to allow herself to agree to whatever arrangement he would propose.

Marriage. Most likely. He'd already proposed twice and he was a man of honour, he wouldn't leave her vulnerable after last night. It was so appealing, even more so now they'd spent the night together. Now she knew what it would be like to be his wife, at least at first until his desire for her wore off. They would spend long nights wrapped in each other's arms, exploring one another's bodies. At the thought something deep inside her clenched and burned and she almost accepted his silent proposal then and there.

Instead she took a wobbly step away. He would

desire her for a while, but she was astute enough to know that might well wear off. Men often conducted affairs or changed their mistresses—the allure of a woman wasn't enough to hold their interest. What they would have was their friendship, companionship, the compatibility that had bonded them together these last five years.

'Perhaps he could stand with an apple on his head and we could take a shot at him until one of us hits the apple,' Milton said as he approached the table. Lord Hauxton's attitude towards James had cooled over the last twenty-four hours and Caroline had to wonder how much he suspected.

'I haven't seen you shoot for years, Milton, but if school archery lessons were any indication I think I would end up with an arrow in my eye.'

'Or somewhere else,' Lord Hauxton murmured so only she could hear.

'Shall we shoot, Miss Yaxley?'

Caroline hobbled over to the line that had been marked on the grass, setting her cane down when she could pretend to have a stable base. Behind her she felt the presence of Lord Hauxton and James, the two men who were causing her so much heartache.

Trying to clear her mind, she notched the first

arrow, letting out a deep breath as she let the arrow fly. It hit the target, but only just.

Without looking round she notched her second arrow, aimed and fired. This one went completely wide, disappearing into the undergrowth. As she picked up her third and final arrow she felt a movement in the air behind her. Even without turning she knew it was James. There was something in the way her body reacted whenever he was near and now it seemed intensified, as if her subconscious was crying out for her to fall into his arms.

'You're twisting your body as you shoot,' he said into her ear. He was standing close, too close for propriety, and she wouldn't be the only one who'd noticed. Even so she didn't move, her body rooted to the spot, acutely aware of even the most minuscule of his movements.

Making everything a hundred times worse, he laced an arm around her body, pulling her gently until her position was directly at right angles to the target.

'Try like this and keep your hips straight as you fire the arrow.'

Caroline inhaled and raised the bow, but her hands were shaking too much for her to even attempt to aim. She let the bow drop again and took a shuddering step back. Only then did she force herself to look at James. Her heart skipped a beat, its rhythm erratic in her chest as she raked her eyes all the way up from his toes to his face. He was the same James, the same man she'd loved for five years, giving her the same reassuring smile. It was as if nothing had changed.

For him it hasn't.

They might have spent the night together, but for him nothing else had changed radically. He still cared for her as a friend, still desired her as he had for a while, but there was no monumental shift in his feelings.

'Lord Hauxton,' Caroline called, her voice wavering. 'Would you be so kind as to accompany me for a short walk around the garden?'

James nodded as she spoke, as if agreeing she needed to speak to Lord Hauxton.

'Of course, Miss Yaxley. Would you like to lean on my arm?'

Chapter Twenty-One

It was bitterly cold, but the sky was clear and the sun cast a watery light over the frost that lingered on the grass. Caroline pulled the hood of her cloak further forward on her hair, glad of the thick boots and gloves she had put on before venturing out.

'You look troubled, Miss Yaxley,' Lord Hauxton said as they rounded the corner into the neat rose garden. Only the spiky stems of the rose bushes remained, biding their time before they sprung to life again in the spring.

'Caroline. I think by now we know each other well enough for you to use my given name.'

'Caroline.' He smiled at her, although there was a hint of sadness to his expression as if he knew what was to come. 'And I am Thomas, although my family all called me Tom.'

He really was a good man, a kind man. The

sort of man she would have been lucky to marry. There was no doubt in her mind that he would be a good husband, a good father, he was just not the man for her.

'You've been very kind to me these last few weeks,' Caroline said. 'I will always remember that.' She took a deep breath. No one taught you how to turn down a proposal from a gentleman. With Lord Mottringham it had been easier, with the older man already assuming that was what she was going to say. Lord Hauxton, Thomas, would be shocked by her refusal given that up until a couple of days ago she had been convinced she would marry him.

'There is something we must discuss,' she continued, feeling the nerves building inside her. 'I...'

He held up a hand and slowly shook his head with a smile that she was sure was meant to reassure her.

'Come sit.' They made their way over to a wrought-iron bench facing the colourless rose garden. Only once they were sitting did he speak again. 'I do not want you to distress yourself, Caroline. I am well aware of what your answer will have to be.'

'My answer?'

'I know you cannot marry me.'

Caroline studied his face, wondering at how calm he seemed, as if he had known for a long time what she had only concluded last night.

'How did you know?'

'Caroline,' he said indulgently, 'you're in love with Heydon. I've known it ever since we danced together that first night at the Tevershams' ball, but for a while I told myself that it didn't matter.'

She nodded. He was an astute man and it seemed she wasn't as good at hiding her feelings as she had once thought.

'You two should be together. Love is important, perhaps not as important as kindness and compassion in a marriage, but important none the less.'

A cold chill swept through her body and she quickly shook her head. 'We won't be together,' she said quietly. 'That's not why I'm saying no.'

Milton frowned. Leaning in a little to her, he took her hand, but whereas a few days ago it might have been a romantic gesture, now it was one purely of friendship and support.

'You two are meant to be together, even a grumpy old cynic like me can see that.'

'He doesn't love me,' she said quietly.

'Of course he does. You can see it in everything he does.'

'He loves me as a friend, but he believes in true love, in two people being fated to be together, and he doesn't love me in that way.'

Lord Hauxton sat without saying anything for a minute as if trying to digest this piece of news about his friend.

'He's told you that?'

'Not in so many words, but I know. I know him and I know what he believes in.'

'These past couple of weeks he hasn't been able to keep his eyes off you…' Lord Hauxton paused before adding with a smile, 'Or his hands.'

It was a rare man who could speak about this so openly with the woman whom up until very recently he had been courting.

'You saw that?'

'It was hard to miss. Heydon takes every opportunity to touch you, to brush away the hair from your face or run his fingers across your arm. I am a naturally observant man, but I don't think I am the only one who noticed.'

She realised it had been foolish to think the change in their behaviour would have gone unnoticed when the *ton* was intrigued by their relationship.

'I think he has seen me in a different way these last few weeks,' she agreed, 'as a woman and not just as his friend, but not as the woman he's in love with.'

'He's a fool.'

'You're kind to say so, but perhaps I am the fool. For thinking, for hoping, his feelings might change when they haven't wavered in five years.'

'I feel angry on your behalf, Caroline. He doesn't know how lucky he is…' Lord Hauxton paused. 'So you are not going to marry me, but you're not marrying him either?'

Caroline let out a little sigh and sat back against the cold rails of the bench. It was hard to explain her reasoning behind the decision she was making, but it felt like the right one all the same.

'A few weeks ago I decided that I would move on with my life, stop pining after a man who was never going to feel the same about me as I did about him. I decided I wanted a husband, a family, a future that wasn't filled with an empty house and loneliness.' She didn't want to look up, knowing she would see the inevitable pity in his eyes. 'I was resolved, determined, certain

I could put the unrequited love behind me and find someone who wanted to spend their life with me as their wife.'

'And you did, so what changed?'

'It's not fair, not on you or any other man. I love James, I think I will always love James and you deserve more than a woman who is still pining for another man.'

'Have you told him?' Lord Hauxton's words were blunt and to the point, much like the man himself.

'Told him what?'

'That you love him. That you've always loved him, that you spend your days with him always in the forefront of your mind.'

'No.'

'Don't you think you both deserve that honesty?'

Caroline felt a rush of nerves at the idea of admitting to James that their whole relationship had been a lie, that she had felt more for him than friendship all along.

'I know he doesn't feel the same.'

'Give him the chance to hear what you say and see how he reacts. See what he decides to do.'

'I couldn't...'

Lord Hauxton took her hand and waited until she had stopped fidgeting and was looking directly at him.

'You could. In fact, I think you have to. One way or another this is all coming to a conclusion. Your relationship is never going to be the same again. Heydon should know the truth of what you feel and you deserve a frank discussion with the man you love about whether you have a future together.'

Caroline felt another surge of nerves at the idea of telling James the depth of her feelings, but even so she wondered if Lord Hauxton might be right. If she was going to walk away from the man she loved, perhaps it was only fair she tell him how she felt first of all.

'And he might surprise you,' Lord Hauxton said, giving her one last smile. 'Now I am going to make my excuses to the Wellingtons and leave you in peace. I do hope it works out for you, Caroline, and if it doesn't remember you will always have a friend in me.'

'Thank you for being so understanding, most men wouldn't have been.'

He shrugged. 'Emily was the good one in our marriage, the patient one, the kind one. When she died I vowed to try to be more like her in as many ways as possible.'

'You don't talk about her much.'

Lord Hauxton inclined his head. 'People think I should have mourned and moved on in three years, but the truth is…' he spread out his hands '… I doubt I will ever move on, not like people want me to.'

'You will marry again?'

'I will. One day. I'm sure the right match will present itself. Until then I will continue to play the part of the grumpy widower.'

'I'm sorry it hasn't worked out between us,' Caroline said softly.

'Don't be sorry. It wasn't meant to be. Just don't throw away your happiness without knowing for sure exactly what you are doing. And consider whether it really would be awful to live with the man you love even if he doesn't love you in quite the same way.' Lord Hauxton stood, giving her one last friendly smile, then strode away.

Caroline exhaled slowly and sank back into the bench. The metal was cold even through her cloak and dress, but she needed a few minutes before she even tried to move. Lord Hauxton had been more than reasonable. He'd been kind and understanding. She shook her head—she was probably a fool to let him go, but it would have been unfair to him. This way he would mourn his late wife a little longer and then find a young lady who truly wanted to be his wife, someone perfectly matched to him.

'And what about you?' she murmured to herself. Lord Hauxton was right. She needed to sit down with James and tell him how she really felt about him, the whole painful truth. She had to admit how long and how deeply she'd loved him and then she had to ask him how he felt about her. Even just the idea of the conversation was making her heart flutter nervously in her chest, but it was necessary. Only then would she be able to ask the last question, the one that really mattered, the one that would decide her future.

Closing her eyes, she tried to work out what James's answer would be. She would ask him if he still believed in true love, the sort of love that hit you when you first laid eyes on someone else, the love reserved for those fated to be together. She would know by his reaction what he believed. And if he did...well, then she would ask him what would happen if the woman he was meant to be with came along after she and James were married.

‘Courage,’ she muttered to herself. She needed courage to talk to James, but also to make the right decision at the end of it.

Chapter Twenty-Two

James picked up one of the black eye masks laid out on the table at the entrance to the ballroom and secured it at the back of his head. Dozens of masks were laid out, black for the men, beautiful white and gold for the women. All the same, all designed to make everyone anonymous and give the night a magical feel.

He disliked masquerade balls. In his experience everyone still knew who everyone else was, but just used it as an excuse to behave as they wouldn't normally. Tonight would be a little different. There were the dozen or so house guests, but everyone else had been invited from the village and local area, meaning James wouldn't know who many of them were. Not that he had eyes for anyone but Caroline.

She'd been acting strangely all day. First her cool behaviour at breakfast and then when she had disappeared off into the gardens with Milton and never reappeared. He had expected her to let Milton know she wouldn't be accepting his proposal and then to seek him out and they would be able to announce their engagement. Instead Milton had made a hasty exit from the house party, but Caroline had disappeared and no amount of searching on his part had revealed where she was hiding.

'There you are,' he murmured, catching sight of Caroline sitting on a chair at the periphery of the ballroom, mask fixed firmly over her eyes and walking cane tapping on the floor in time to the music. She looked stunning, with her golden hair falling over her shoulders in loose waves, the top half pinned back with sapphire-topped hairpins and the bottom half free to curl down her back. Her dress was a bright pale blue with a silver ribbon and silver embroidery along the hem. It skimmed over her body, hinting at the woman beneath, but not giving much away.

'Cara, you look lovely,' he said as he came and took the seat beside her. She looked at him and immediately he knew she'd been crying. Even though her cheeks were dry and her face immaculate, there was a slight pink tinge to her eyes that he noticed immediately. 'What's happened?'

'Nothing. I…' She trailed off, then looked at him, seeming to need to summon her courage. 'We need to talk.' It sounded ominous and James frowned. Surely nothing could go wrong now. They had overcome their doubts about one another and they certainly knew they were a good fit physically as well as emotionally.

'Tell me what's wrong, Cara.'

'Not here. Not with everyone watching.'

'Where then?'

'The garden. We can get to it from the terrace behind the dining room. I'll go first, you join me in ten minutes.'

'You're worrying me.'

She smiled at him weakly. 'We just need that talk, that's all.'

'Ten minutes,' he agreed, then reluctantly bowed and walked away. Ten minutes was a long time when you felt your future might be hanging in the balance. He strolled about the ballroom, careful not to be dragged into any conversations. He wanted to be able to leave without any fuss, he wasn't about to let himself get distracted by some aimless ballroom chatter.

Resisting the urge to lift his watch out of his pocket every few seconds, he resorted instead to counting in his head, only allowing himself to glance at the time after he had counted to five hundred.

'Close enough,' he murmured, then slipped out of the ballroom, walking purposefully so no one would suspect he was heading to a secret liaison.

As he made his way through the house he tried to think of all the things Caroline could possibly want to say to him, her expression so sombre. Perhaps she had decided to marry Milton after all, or perhaps she had just decided she didn't want to marry *him*.

You haven't asked her. Surely she knew they would get married, she knew what sort of man he was, knew he wouldn't spend a night with her without marrying her after. Still, he *hadn't* proposed again after last night, just assumed they both thought the same thing.

'Poorly done,' he murmured to himself. Although easily fixed. He would ask her again tonight, make sure it was one of the first things he said.

After making sure no one was watching, he

slipped inside the dining room, allowing his eyes a moment to adjust to the darkness, then headed for the doors on to the terrace. He must have been walking quietly as Caroline didn't turn as he approached and he took a minute just to watch her.

Here was the woman he'd spent the most time with ever. From companionable strolls in the park to waltzes in the ballrooms of London. He knew her better than he knew anyone else, she was the one he looked forward to coming home to.

Standing in the moonlight, she looked ethereal, the soft light from the sky reflecting off the blue of her dress and making her shimmer.

'Cara,' he said, watching the fluid movement as she spun to face him, his heart sinking as he saw the tears on her face. 'What's the matter?' Immediately he was by her side, enveloping her in his arms, pulling her close to his body. At first she was unyielding, but after a couple of seconds she relaxed into him, her body slowly losing its rigidity.

For a moment she just let him hold her, then she took a shuddering breath and stepped back.

'I've got something difficult to say to you.'

Caroline watched James's expression, wondering if she would have the strength to tell him the truth. For five years she'd hidden her feelings and in a few seconds everything would be out in the open. It was a daunting thought.

'Just talk to me, Cara, we've never had a problem talking.'

'I will, but will you do something for me first?'

'Anything.'

'Dance with me.' She didn't add *one last time*, but it was what she was thinking.

From their position on the terrace they could hear the music from the ballroom and as James swept her into his arms Caroline felt her body begin to sway to the rhythm. He held her close, much closer than he would be able to if the eyes of the other guests had been watching, but here on the terrace they were completely alone, completely unobserved. Letting her head drop down so it rested on his shoulder, Caroline gave herself over to him, allowing him to guide her every step, every movement.

Even though the dance must have lasted at least a few minutes it felt as though it were over in no time at all and Caroline felt the dread pulling at her as she straightened up and looked him in the eye before nodding silently. It was time.

He was gentle, taking her hand and leading her down off the terrace and into the garden. In the darkness it was difficult to pick out the paths, but James seemed to have better night-time vision than her and he lead her without faltering away from the house and the muted sounds of the ball to a quiet portion of the garden. Even though it was cold, Caroline was glad for the privacy. 'There,' he said when they were ensconced together on the wall of the little pond surrounding the fountain, hidden from view of the house. 'Now just tell me.'

She screwed her eyes tight, feeling the words stick in her throat. 'I love you.'

He regarded her, searching her face, and she felt the full weight of his scrutiny.

'I know,' he said softly.

It wasn't the reply she'd been dreaming of. Even though she knew he didn't love her, not as she wanted him to, a small part of her had still fantasised that he might gather her into his arms and declare an undying love that he hadn't before realised he felt.

Even as her heart was breaking she pushed on. 'I've loved you ever since we first met.'

He was silent, but she could see the admission didn't come as a complete shock to him. Even if he hadn't been totally aware of her feelings for him, he probably had suspected on some level.

'I love you,' she repeated one last time, and although the pain in her chest was becoming almost unbearable with his silence she felt the declaration was cathartic.

'Marry me, Cara,' he said eventually. He was looking at her earnestly, his hand gripping hers. 'We should be together.'

Wordlessly she shook her head, knowing she might regret whatever she did next for the rest of her life.

'We care for one another, we desire one another. Marry me.' Still no mention of love.

'I need to ask you something first and I want you to promise me you'll tell me the truth.'

'I...'

'Just promise me, James.'

He nodded.

'Do you still believe in love? In the sort of love your parents shared? The sort of love that means two people are fated to be together?'

As she spoke he dropped his gaze down to the floor and she knew even without pushing any further she had her answer.

'You promised,' she reminded him.

'It doesn't matter, Cara. I want to marry you.'

'Do you still believe in it?'

'It's irrelevant.'

'Just answer me.'

Finally he looked at her again and nodded once and she could see the desolation blooming in his eyes. He knew where this was going, knew that she was going to make the hardest decision of her life.

'And you don't feel that way about me.'

'Cara, I...'

She waved a hand to stop him, trying to hold back the tears so she could get through the next few minutes.

'You don't need to say anything, James, you don't need to apologise. Just as I can't help loving you, you can't help not loving me.'

'Don't say that.' He looked anguished and she felt her resolve settle.

'If we married, you would always be thinking *what if.* You've held off from marrying, from settling, because of your beliefs, I can't be the one to make you settle now.'

'It wouldn't be settling, Cara. I want to marry you.'

She drew herself up, squared her shoulders and smiled, feeling more tears pour down her cheeks as she did so. 'When I decided to get married I abandoned all hope of marrying for love,' she said quietly. 'I didn't expect it, didn't even entertain the notion. It was to be a business arrangement, a companionship, and I was quite happy with that…' She paused, then added quietly, 'But not with you. I don't want to settle for that with you. It would be too hard, too painful. Knowing every day I would be waking up next to the man I loved who didn't love me back.'

She turned her body towards him, reaching out and running her fingers over his cheek. James was silent and she could tell he was finally accepting her words.

'Don't do this,' he said, his voice hoarse.

'We'll still be friends.' It was a lie, although a hopeful one. She didn't see how they would ever return to their easy companionship after everything that had passed between them.

'I can't lose you.'

Knowing she shouldn't, Caroline brushed her lips against his, feeling the tears wet on her skin as she kissed him. One last kiss before they parted for a final time. With a shuddering breath she stood and began to walk away, hating the small part of herself that was still hoping James would run after her and declare his love.

There was no crunch of gravel, no shout calling her back. Just silence and the coldness of the night. Pulling her cloak around her tighter, she contemplated the house in front of her, but unable to face even the possibility of anyone seeing her instead she turned left and fled into the formal gardens, needing a few minutes alone with her tears.

Caroline looked back out of the window of the carriage and blinked furiously to stop herself from crying again. She knew she would never ever be able to come to one of the Wellingtons' house parties. Even just seeing the façade of the house would drag all the pain right back to the surface.

'Time is a great healer,' her mother said quietly, smiling softly as Caroline nodded her head. 'It may be a cliché, but it is also the truth.'

She hadn't told her mother exactly what had occurred, but Lady Yaxley was astute enough to know something monumental had happened. Caroline had started the weekend at the Wellingtons with two suitors and now she had none.

'We can return to Hampshire if you like, my darling.'

Caroline considered. She loved their family home in Hampshire, the familiar rooms and servants, the large estate you could spend hours wandering around and not see a soul. It was tempting to make that request, to run back to her childhood home and try to rebuild herself there, but she knew it would be selfish. She could quite easily hide away in London—just being in the same city as James didn't mean she had to see him. Her father was due to make the journey to London to attend to his business while Parliament was in session and she knew her mother would be upset to miss him.

'No,' she said eventually, 'London is acceptable.'

Lady Yaxley sat forward in her seat and waited for Caroline to look at her. 'Whenever you need to talk, I'm here.'

'Thank you, Mama.'

She couldn't talk about it, not yet. Perhaps one day it wouldn't feel so raw and terrible, then she would be able to go over where everything had gone wrong. Right now she just wanted the next few weeks to be over. She wanted the time to pass so she did not have to feel quite so wretched.

It'll take years, not weeks.

She grimaced. She knew the little voice in her head was right. She wasn't sure if she would ever go back to being the person she was before she had spent these last few weeks with James. Now she would always have the memories, the echo of the hope she had felt and, of course, the pain.

Closing her eyes, she tried to push away the image of his face, willing herself to think about anything but the man who had broken her heart.

Chapter Twenty-Three

Slamming shut the lid of his suitcase, James looked around the room with a grim satisfaction. With the help of his valet he had managed to pack in less than twenty minutes, a new record even for him. Now all that had to be done was for him to book a passage and he could escape to the Continent and spend a few months in the warmer climes licking his wounds.

Coward. James growled in frustration. It *did* feel as though he were running away and he hated the idea of fleeing from anything, let alone from Caroline. Yet she had been the one to reject him, the one to say she didn't want to marry him.

He closed his eyes and saw her face as she had asked him whether he still believed in true love, saw the last bit of hope shatter in her eyes as he mumbled something incomprehensible. Why couldn't he have just grabbed her by the arms and lied, told her what she wanted to hear?

Not that it would have been a complete lie. He did love her. He loved the way she smiled and the way she laughed. He loved how she looked at him when they were together as though no one else in the world existed. He loved her kindness and her sense of righteousness and how she hated any sort of injustice.

Life without Caroline was going to be painful and dull and he couldn't contemplate staying in England, knowing she was so close and yet unreachable.

'A few months in Italy and things will be better,' he murmured to himself. It was a lie, even he knew that. A few months in Italy wouldn't change the fact that he'd lost his best friend, the one person he could rely on to be there for him no matter what.

With a growl of frustration he flopped down into his armchair. It wasn't as though he could change anything so he just needed to work on accepting it. Caroline was trying her hardest to move on from him and he should do the same.

James closed his eyes and rested his head back, trying to find some modicum of peace. Instead he was plagued by images of Caroline, of her body underneath his, her brilliant blue eyes looking up at him filled with love.

No one else would ever love him like that.

He thought back to the conversation he'd had with Lady Yaxley, where she had stressed to him the different types of love. He'd dismissed it at the time, but some part of that conversation had burrowed its way into his mind and taken root, holding on through everything that had occurred and sprouting up now.

'There are different kinds of love...' That was what Lady Yaxley had said.

His thoughts were interrupted by a sharp rap on the door downstairs, insistent and prolonged. For a moment his spirits soared—it would be Caroline, deciding she had made a mistake, that she couldn't live without him.

He took the stairs three at a time, barrelling into the entrance hall just in time to see his footman admit Milton into the spacious hallway.

'Milton,' he said, trying not to let his disappointment show.

'Heydon. You thought I would be someone else.'

'Come in.'

Milton stepped through into James's study, taking one of the seats by the fire, rubbing his hands to warm them after he'd slipped his thick gloves from his fingers.

James took the seat opposite and waited. Milton looked purposeful and James wasn't in the most sociable of moods so he didn't bother with any small talk.

'I overestimated you,' Milton said without any preamble. 'I thought you were one of the sensible ones, clever even.'

James raised an eyebrow.

'Damn it, Heydon. The woman loves you. And here you are *not* engaged to be married.'

'It was her choice,' James said quietly. He should be angry with Milton for bursting into his house and making accusations.

'And you're too blind to see that you love her, too.'

James blinked, Milton's words like a slap in the face.

'I…' He thought of the surge of happiness he felt whenever they got to spend even just a few minutes in each other's company and the warmth he felt when she laid her hand over his. He thought of the desire that still coursed through his body at the thought of her and the contentment he'd felt lying in bed with Caroline by his side.

'You're so caught up in the idea that love has to be overwhelming and instant and exactly as your parents experienced it that you can't see what is right in front of you.' Milton sounded angry, but James ignored the tone and focused on the words. 'Do you know I pressed Caroline to tell you how she felt? I was sure if she just admitted it to you it would be enough to make you realise you two were meant to be together.'

'You told her to do that?' It didn't make sense. Milton had been courting her himself.

'She's a good woman, Heydon, she deserves to be happy. And whereas she would have been content with me, she could have been blissfully happy with you. I thought she deserved that.'

For a long moment both men were silent, then James scraped a hand through his hair.

'Hell,' he muttered, more to himself than Milton. 'What have I done?'

Of course he loved her. He knew her better than he knew himself, knew every quirk and foible, and he loved every last little bit of her.

'It might not be too late,' Milton said quietly.

'I've broken her heart.' It hurt to remember the shattered look in her eyes when he hadn't been able to tell her he loved her.

'She'll forgive you.'

James wasn't so sure. She'd given him so many opportunities to prove himself, to tell her that he loved her, and over and over again he'd failed. All because he'd been too blind to see that he might not have felt that thunderbolt of love his parents always described, but it was love all the same. A love that had built with time, a love that had started as affection and blossomed into so much more.

'I believe Caroline is attending a fundraiser for The Charitable Foundation for the Orphans of London at Filsbury House,' Milton said with a half-smile. 'If you hurry you'll catch her on the way out.'

James stood, crossing to his friend and pulling him from the chair before embracing him in a hug.

'I won't forget this. You're a good man, Milton.'

'So people keep telling me.'

'Please excuse me. I have a proposal to make.' James strode from the room, stopping only to ask his footman to fetch his coat and gloves and prepare the carriage. Within five minutes he was hurrying towards Filsbury House. Today was the day he would propose to the woman he loved and finally she would say yes.

‘Really we should be doing more for these poor orphans. They have nothing and no one in the whole world and we’re sitting in our grand houses eating expensive food and wearing expensive clothes.’ Lady Whittaker’s voice was high pitched and nasal and Caroline was trying her hardest to block it out.

It was dangerous to let her mind wander at the moment—even a week after the Wellingtons’ house party her emotions were still raw and too close to the surface. Two days ago she’d found herself with tears streaming down her cheeks as she took Bertie for a walk in Hyde Park and yesterday she’d had to excuse herself from a dinner party after failing to focus on any of the small talk around her.

‘The Charitable Foundation for the Orphans of London would be happy to accept donations large and small, but larger would be better.’

Miss Preston slipped into the free seat to Caroline's left, looking pretty in a pale pink dress. For a moment she was silent, seemingly intent on what her mother was saying, but then she moved a fraction closer to Caroline, angling her body so no one else would be able to hear their conversation.

'I hear commiserations are in order. You had the interest of two of the most eligible bachelors of the Season and yet still managed to end up alone.' Miss Preston's eye were sparkling with the intrigue. 'Whatever did you do in Suffolk to drive them away?'

Caroline did her best to ignore the young woman's words, reminding herself that Miss Preston was unpleasant and unkind and had approached her solely with the aim of making her feel bad.

'I do feel sorry for you,' Miss Preston continued with a sympathetic smile that had a mocking quality to it. 'If we're all being honest, everyone knows it was your last chance. Twenty-four and unmarried, that's hardly likely to change now.'

'How are your marriage prospects looking, Miss Preston?' Caroline knew that she shouldn't engage with the spiteful young woman, but was unable to hold herself back. She always had been too impulsive, too quick to let her emotions flare, but Miss Preston had been riling her for weeks now and she just wanted to be left alone.

The smile on the young debutante's face faltered for a moment before she recovered her composure completely. Miss Preston was the daughter of a baron, pretty and well connected and no doubt she had a sizeable dowry, but despite all that she still hadn't been whisked to the altar. Perhaps the eligible gentlemen weren't as shallow or unseeing as Caroline had assumed.

'I hear the Duke has left for Italy again. It's a shame he feels he has to go so far away.'

Italy. Caroline tried not to let the anguish she felt at that particular bit of news show. It shouldn't surprise her, not really. James loved Italy, loved travelling. It would be the logical place for him to go while everything settled and he worked out what he was going to do next.

'He does enjoy travelling,' she said mildly, trying not to picture his face, his smile, the way his eyes crinkled when he saw her for the first time after coming home from a trip away. That would never happen again, things would never be easy between them. If he ever came back.

'But so soon after he returned after his last

trip? The gossips are not being kind about his reasons for fleeing.'

Lady Whittaker had finished her speech and was standing to one side, talking with a couple of wealthy patrons. Now would be the best time to make her escape. She had come with her mother to the fundraiser, but it was only a couple of miles home, she would prefer to walk even in the light drizzle and freezing winds than wait for her mother to be ready to return in the carriage. A snowstorm would be preferable to spending another minute in Miss Preston's company.

'Please excuse me, Miss Preston, I have somewhere else to be.' Before the debutante could say anything else Caroline stood and hurried away, moving as fast as she could without it looking as if she was fleeing.

Outside it was icy, the wind whipping freezing rain that hit her face like hundreds of tiny knives. She almost retreated back inside, but one glance at the crowd of people who'd spent most of the past week giving her pitying looks and whispering about her when they thought she was out of earshot decided her. Rain was better than that, whatever the temperature.

Pulling the hood of her cloak tighter around

her, she dipped head as far as she safely could and still make out the pavement in front of her and then began walking briskly. She could feel every muscle in her body tense up with the cold and began fantasising about the warm bath she would slip into once she was back at home in front of a roaring fire.

In the freezing temperatures it seemed to take a lot longer to cover even a short distance and by the time she had walked a third of the way home she was regretting her decision. The cold was permeating everywhere and even though she was healthy she knew being this chilled wasn't good for her.

'Stupid, rash decision,' she muttered to herself, repeating the words under her breath. If she'd been thinking clearly she would have just taken the carriage and sent it back later for her mother, but in her haste to get away from Miss Preston and the words that struck a little too close to the truth she'd fled without thinking through her actions.

'Get in,' a low voice called, the familiarity almost making her heart stop in her chest.

After taking a moment to summon her courage, she glanced up, seeing James's face looking down at her from the carriage. Effortlessly he hopped down and held the door open for her.

She glanced around, weighing up her options. The rain was getting even heavier and the wind stronger. Really, she would need a very good reason to decline his offer of shelter.

'Get in. You'll catch a chill and be in bed for a week.'

Relenting, she stepped up to the carriage, trying to ignore the spark of energy between them as she took his hand and climbed up into the vehicle. James vaulted up behind her and closed the door before taking his seat and banging on the roof, signalling for the driver to depart.

For a long moment he didn't say anything and Caroline found herself eyeing him nervously. She wasn't sure if he had purposely sought her out or just been passing and seen her struggling on in the wind and rain.

'You're soaked,' he said and absently Caroline put a hand to the top of her cloak, feeling the sodden material. Even in the relative warmth of the carriage she was shivering and as she relaxed a little into the plush material covering the seats, she began to realise how much of her was soaked to the bone. 'Why on earth were you walking in this weather?'

'To escape Miss Preston.' She grimaced.

'Ah. I see.' He smiled at her then and Caroline felt the world shift beneath her. Even after everything they had been through just one smile was enough to rock her world. 'I confess I probably would walk over molten lava to get away from Miss Preston, so I can understand why wind and rain would be a preferable alternative to her company.'

He didn't look any different, still the same face and physique that made her heart clench and her stomach flip over inside.

'She informed me you had fled to Italy.'

'Clearly untrue,' he said, spreading his arms. 'And Miss Preston would be the last person to know of my movements.'

He took her hand, the gesture confident, without any hesitation. Even through her gloves Caroline could feel his warmth and for a moment she let her hand rest in his, before slowly trying to pull away. James gripped her tighter just for a fraction of a second, then released her fingers and waited until she looked up at him.

'I've missed you, Cara.'

It was an admission that cut straight to her heart. She'd missed him every waking moment of every day. She'd spent hours obsessing over what he might be thinking, what he might be doing, even as she told herself she needed to begin to build a wall around her heart and move on.

'It has only been a week,' she said weakly, knowing you could miss a person in just a few hours. A week often felt like eternity.

'Far too long.'

The carriage slowed to a stop and she glanced out the window. The journey hadn't been long enough to cover the distance to her house and she frowned as she realised they were outside James's residence instead.

'What are we doing here?'

'I need to talk to you, Cara, and I need to do it alone, without any interruptions.'

'You know I can't be here.'

'Please, Cara. I'll never ask anything of you again if you wish, just grant me a few minutes.'

Part of her was intrigued, curious to know what had made him seek her out after a week of no contact. The rest of her knew this was a bad idea. She might tell herself she was getting over

James, but the reality was she was still head over heels in love with him and even being in a carriage with him for a few minutes was making her question every decision she'd made.

'Five minutes,' he said, 'and then if you wish to leave I will arrange for the carriage to take you home.'

'Five minutes,' she agreed after a long pause. He grinned, threw open the door and bounded down, reaching back to steady her as she stepped back into the rain.

Inside the house felt wonderfully warm and as she slipped off her sodden cloak, she slowly felt some of the muscles that she'd been holding tense in the cold begin to relax. James led her along to his study, closing the door firmly behind him and directing her towards the fire.

Caroline stood as close as she dared, holding her fingers out to the flames.

'We should get you warm and dry,' James said quietly as he came up behind her. She had a vision of slipping out of her heavy dress and sinking to the floor in front of the fire entwined in James's arms.

'I can change when I get home.' Her voice was stiff, her posture closed and formal. James reached out and ran a finger up her arm and she almost relented there and then.

'I won't be responsible for you catching pneumonia.'

'What do you propose I change into?'

He didn't have an answer for that and at her sharp tone he took a step back and motioned for her to sit in one of the armchairs angled towards the fire.

Chapter Twenty-Four

Looking at her a few feet away, James felt the gulf between them, a gulf that had never existed before. It was entirely of his making and he just hoped he could mend it. As he watched, Caroline wrapped her arms around herself in a protective gesture and then shivered, although whether from the cold or discomfort from the situation she was in, he couldn't tell.

'Cara…' he began, speaking slowly and choosing each word he said next carefully, knowing it would be his only chance. 'Do you think you can ever forgive me?'

Her head snapped up and for an instant her eyes met his before flicking back down to focus on her hands again.

'Perhaps,' she murmured quietly, 'but not yet.'

It was a very Caroline answer, honest even when the reply was detrimental to her cause.

He slipped off the chair and knelt in front of her, taking one cold hand in his. 'I've been a fool, Cara, a complete and utter fool.'

She didn't say anything, although this time her gaze did linger on his face as if searching for his meaning.

'I've been so caught up in the idea of love and fate and experiencing the same things my parents said was key to their happiness that I didn't realise that I was letting my own happiness slip away from me.' He watched as her eyes widened and she shook her head in disbelief.

'Don't say something you don't mean.'

'I mean every single word. I was so obsessed with replicating what my parents had that I didn't realise we could have something better.'

He could see the tension in her body, the way every muscle looked poised to help her flee should the need arise.

'I love you, Cara.'

'No, you don't.'

He smiled, 'I do. I think I've loved you for a long time, but I was too idiotic to see it.'

'You don't. You can't.' She had turned pale and was gripping the arms of the chair as if needing to anchor herself to something solid.

'I can and I do. I love you, Cara. I love your smile and your humour. I love your patience and how much you care about the people you love. I love *you*.'

She was still shaking her head, her brow furrowed with disbelief, and James felt his certainty rock. He didn't doubt his feelings for Caroline, now he'd realised how much he cared for her that would never change, but he began to doubt his certainty that everything was going to fall into place. Perhaps he'd hurt her one too many times, had left his declaration too late.

The idea of losing her for good sent a spike of pain ripping through his chest. He couldn't, he just couldn't.

'Cara, look at me.' He waited for her eyes to stop flitting around the room and rest on his. 'You know me, you know my every expression, my every tone. You know when I'm lying and you know when I'm telling the truth.' He let his words sink in, for her to realise that he was right before continuing. 'I love you and I can't bear to imagine my life without you.'

She searched his face, her breathing becoming more rapid, but James could see this time his words had got through to her.

'But you said…'

'I was a blind fool. Too slow to realise what we could have together.'

'How can your feelings just change like that?'

'They haven't. I've loved you all along, I was just too idiotic to see it.'

'What if…?' She took a deep breath in, then pushed on. 'What if we're together, then someone else comes along, someone you have that instant connection with?'

He reached up and stroke her cheek. 'I love you, Cara, I wouldn't notice anyone else.'

She stood abruptly and for a moment he thought she was going to flee the room, but after a second she just took a step towards the fire, angling her body away from him. He knew she was working through every argument as to why they shouldn't be together in her head, that he just needed to give her time to see they were all nonsense, irrelevant nonsense, but it was so hard not to reach out and pull her to him. James knew he could seduce her, but he wanted her to come to him freely with her decision made by the rational part of her brain.

A minute passed and then another before eventually she turned around.

'Say it again,' she said quietly.

Stepping forward so their bodies were almost touching, he reached around and placed a hand in the small of her back. He took his time, his eyes taking in every detail of her face, his fingers caressing the soft material of her dress.

'I love you,' he said quietly.

There was a pause, only a second or two, then she smiled tentatively. 'I love you, too.'

Caroline closed her eyes as he kissed her, feeling the heat rise up from her core as it always did whenever he was near. The man she loved. The man who loved her. Even as he kissed her she couldn't help smiling. Deep inside she could feel the flutter of nerves in her stomach and she wondered if it would always be like this or if one day they would settle into comfortable familiarity.

He loved her.

Caroline couldn't quite believe it, even though she knew it was the truth. James had been right when he'd said she knew his every expression, knew when he was lying and when he was telling the truth. Every day for the past five years she'd dreamed of this moment and now it was finally here.

James pulled away just a fraction and looked at her, a smile lighting up his face.

'I have a question for you, Cara.'

Nodding, she felt her heart begin to thump even harder in her chest. He'd asked her three times before, but this time she was ready to say yes.

'Will you marry me?'

'Yes.'

He swooped her up into his arms and spun her round, smiling as she laughed with the exhilaration. When he set he back on her feet there was happiness in his eyes and also something else.

'You're not going to want a long engagement, are you?' He leaned in and trailed his lips across her cheek until he caught her earlobe between his teeth.

'Six months?' She tried her hardest to suppress the moan of pleasure that wanted to break free.

'No.' He kissed her neck, pushing the fabric of her dress down to access her collarbone, and left a trail of heat behind him as he moved his lips across her skin.

'Five?'

'No.' Spinning her round, he began tugging at the fastenings of her dress, just loosening them enough to allow him to push the stiff fabric from her shoulders. Underneath she wore a thin chemise, but James deftly slipped that from her top half, letting the material of her dress and chemise pool around her hips. Despite the warmth of the fire Caroline shivered, feeling her skin pucker under his gaze.

'Four?' she offered.

'No.' His lips were back on her skin, kissing and nipping, driving every thought but him from her mind. He caught one nipple between his fingers, the other in his mouth and teased her until breathlessly she whispered, 'Three?'

'No.'

Quickly he went back to work on her dress, loosening it some more until it fell from her hips, then he grasped the hem of her chemise and lifted it up over her head. Now she was clad only in her stockings and boots, but she couldn't feel the cold any more. Her skin felt as though it were on fire, eagerly awaiting his next touch.

She almost cried out as he stepped away, briskly walking over to the door. He turned the key in the lock and then was back at her side in an instant.

'Three is far too long,' he murmured in her

ear and then lifted her up and lowered her into one of the armchairs. 'Perhaps I need to remind you why.'

James knelt down in front of her and ran his fingers along the border of her stockings just where the fabric stopped and the skin began. She gasped as he bent his head and kissed her on the delicate skin of her thighs, feeling the warmth of his breath moving further and further up.

'Two?' she managed to gasp just before his mouth trailed over her most private place and she lost all ability to think. A hot tension began to build deep inside her as his mouth did wonderful things to her and Caroline felt as though she were floating out of the chair. She cried out as the tension burst and the waves of pleasure swelled through her body, her thighs clenching and gripping James in place.

'Two is far too long,' he said as he sat back, watching with a satisfied smile as Caroline nodded. She would agree to anything right now.

He reached out and took her hand, pulling her to her feet, and then tenderly laid her down on the plush rug in front of the fire. She watched as he stripped off his clothes, wondering how she could be so lucky to have this man as her future husband. Within half a minute he had joined her on the rug, his body taut over hers.

She reached out, feeling his hardness, and pulled him in towards her.

He hovered just outside, looking at her with a raised eyebrow.

'One?' she said eventually.

James pressed inside her and Caroline pushed her hips up to meet him. Again and again they came together and Caroline felt the pleasure begin to build, but also a wonderful happiness alongside it. James was going to be her husband and once they were married they would be able to fall into bed together whenever they wanted.

Swept away by the mounting heat inside her, Caroline closed her eyes and let her body soar, crying out as she climaxed and feeling James stiffen inside her.

'One month,' James said as he tucked his body behind hers, laying an arm across her waist. 'One month is acceptable, I suppose.'

Epilogue

Eight months later

Caroline stared up in wonder at the magnificent structure in front of her. She had to lift her parasol a little higher to see the ragged line of stones at the very top.

'How did they build something so impressive all those years ago?' She took a moment to take in the splendor, then looked questioningly at James. 'It puts our modern architecture to shame.'

'I don't know, some of the palaces in Venice are not all that old and they are beautiful in a different way.'

She couldn't argue with that. They'd spent much longer in Venice than they had first planned, enjoying a leisurely life of strolling around the streets and across the bridges, sitting back in the little boats that whizzed along the canals and drinking coffee in the coffee houses that commanded beautiful views of the city. It had been the first proper stop on their honeymoon trip and originally they had planned to spend a week in the city. In the end they'd reluctantly left after three.

On the way to Rome they'd marvelled at the Duomo in Florence and the strange leaning tower in Pisa. They'd enjoyed a leisurely few weeks exploring Tuscany and visiting the vineyards James had told her about almost a year ago. And now they were in Rome, the city Caroline had dreamed of ever since James had started telling her stories of his travels.

'Can we go inside?' she asked, looking round her, amazed at how the modern city had just grown around the ancient Colosseum.

'Of course.'

Hand in hand they walked into the shadow of the monument, James taking Caroline's arm to steady her over the uneven ground. They passed through an outer gate and then the inner gate, and before she could protest, James had led her down a ramp into the tunnels underneath. They weren't underground for long, emerging through a huge archway into the oval ground.

'It's such a shame it wasn't thought worth conserving,' Caroline said as she looked around in awe. The structure was still magnificent and you could imagine how it would have been all those years ago, but in the intervening time the Colosseum had been plundered and left to the elements.

'Perhaps one day.'

They strolled around the base, dodging fallen chunks of stone and gaping holes, looking up at the tiered seating. Caroline could almost see the gladiators and animals that she'd read about in the history books clashing in a bloody spectacle.

They paused in the middle and Caroline took a step closer to James, laughing as her rounded tummy pressed against his. She still wasn't used to her change in shape even as the months of her pregnancy passed and her belly grew a little more.

'Careful with my baby daughter,' he said, placing a hand on her bump.

'Or son.'

'She's a girl. I can just feel it.'

Caroline scoffed, stroking the side of her dress.

They had found out she was pregnant just as they'd arrived in Venice and had needed to make the decision as to whether to cut their honeymoon horribly short or continue in the knowledge that she might well give birth in Italy. James had been ready to whisk her home, but after a few days of persuasion had been able to admit Italian women had been giving birth to babies just as long as English women and they seemed to do it just fine in Italy.

'Thank you,' she said, tilting her head up.

He kissed her, softly brushing his lips against hers.

'What for?'

'For bringing me here. It's always been one of my greatest dreams.'

'Anything for my Duchess.'

'Anything?' She raised both eyebrows in question.

'Why do I get the impression I'm going to live to regret my words?'

'Let's stay in Italy a few months more. Perhaps we could rent a villa on the Amalfi coast, somewhere peaceful and serene to bring our baby into the world.'

James considered, his hand still gently caressing her bump.

'On one condition,' he said eventually.

'What?'

He just smiled at her, stepped closer and kissed her until she felt the wonderfully familiar heat begin to build deep inside her.

'You're insatiable,' she murmured as she pulled him into a sunny nook behind a rock.

'What man wouldn't be when he has the most beautiful wife in the world?'

'I love you.'

'I love you, too, Cara,' he whispered into her skin as his lips kissed her neck.

* * * * *